**Outstanding praise for Michael Hiebert
and *Dream with Little Angels***

"Hiebert has an authentic Southern voice and his protagonist is as engaging as Harper Lee's Scout. A masterful coming-of-age gem."
—Deborah Crombie

"Gorgeous prose and some thoughtful characterizations, with attention given to theme and setting . . . Michael Hiebert's debut delivers . . . a breathless, will-they-get-there-in-time affair, with a heartbreaking resolution. Hiebert's skill at character and storytelling should take him a long way."
—*Mystery Scene*

"A trip to the dark side of a town much like Mayberry, filled with that elusive quality of childhood and the aura of safety that often settles, unjustifiably, over rural small towns in the South."
—Carolyn Haines

"*Dream with Little Angels* has engaging characters, a riveting plot and pacing that flips between languid and runaway train. It's a marvelous portrait of small-town America, and families struggling to come to grips with a trying, terrifying series of ordeals."
—*The Missourian*

"An atmospheric mystery."
—*RT Book Reviews*

"*Dream with Little Angels* is quality storytelling sure to keep readers enthralled."
—*Kane County Chronicles*

Books by Michael Hiebert

DREAM WITH LITTLE ANGELS

CLOSE TO THE BROKEN HEARTED

A THORN AMONG THE LILIES

Published by Kensington Publishing Corporation

A

THORN AMONG
THE LILIES

MICHAEL HIEBERT

KENSINGTON BOOKS
www.kensingtonbooks.com

KENSINGTON BOOKS are published by

Kensington Publishing Corp.
119 West 40th Street
New York, NY 10018

All Kensington titles, imprints, and distributed lines are available at special quantity discounts for bulk purchases for sales promotion, premiums, fund-raising, and educational or institutional use.

Special book excerpts or customized printings can also be created to fit specific needs. For details, write or phone the office of the Kensington Sales Manager: Kensington Publishing Corp., 119 West 40th Street, New York, NY 10018. Attn. Sales Department. Phone: 1-800-221-2647.

Kensington and the K logo Reg. U.S. Pat. & TM Off.

eISBN-13: 978-1-61773-738-1
eISBN-10: 1-61773-738-0
First Kensington Electronic Edition: July 2015

ISBN-13: 978-1-61773-737-4
ISBN-10: 1-61773-737-2
First Kensington Trade Paperback Printing: July 2015

10 9 8 7 6 5 4 3 2 1

Printed in the United States of America

For Yvonne . . .

ACKNOWLEDGMENTS

As usual, props must go out to my absolutely brilliant agent, Adrienne Rosado. Without her, this series would not exist.

I also must thank my editor, John Scognamiglio, and the whole slew of other tremendous people working alongside him at Kensington. It's unbelievable how much support they offer to lowly authors such as me. They almost make me feel like I'm Stephen King. Other than the royalty checks.

Props to my publicity director at Kensington, Vida Engstrand, for constantly going above and beyond the call of duty.

To Yvonne Rupert, my late-night poetry friend whom I've never met and yet probably know better than most people in my life. You are an inspiration, and without you I couldn't possibly write all these books and still teach at Writers Village University Online (www.writersuniversity.com), a very good place to visit if you're interested in learning to write and meeting a lot of friends for support.

To my children, Valentine, Sagan, and Legend. There are days I truly believe I owe my life to you three.

More thanks go out to the Chilliwack Writers Group (And I promise to stop missing meetings, guys. I mean, seriously. My excuses are starting to sound lame even to me.): Garth Pettersen, Mary Keane, Fran Brown, Terri McKee, and Wendy Foster. You all provide excellent feedback.

I'd like to send thanks to Ken Loomes, who continues to read everything I send to him, even the tripe. Ken's yet another friend I've never *actually* met, but hope to one day soon. I especially owe Ken for his help on this book. He really came through for me in the home stretch.

This story came into existence through the help of two friends I met while inside an institution full of beautiful minds. These friends are Shauna Ryall (most of whose ideas will likely be used in the next book, but some appear here) and Hazel Rambaran, who, for such a quiet little religious girl, comes up with some pretty scary ideas involving serial killers.

I have to mention my parents, especially since I occupy their basement. My computers wouldn't last long outside in the rain, so they play a major part in my writing process. Abe and Ann Hiebert, thank you for providing everything that you do, even the occasional supper I have to gag down since y'all are vegetarians.

Also a big thanks to Ginger Moore for coming up with my title. I think it's one of the best in the series so far.

Add to that Pastor Badwell of the Parkway Baptist Church in Alabama for making sure I understand the Baptist faith. You're a busy man, and you're very gracious with your time.

To Mark Leland for all the time he spends answering my endless e-mails full of stupid questions about police procedure and firearms that I either can't find answers to anywhere else or am just too lazy to look for.

To the Mobile Police Department in Alabama and their willingness to answer all my questions about Southern police work. I'm still dumbfounded that most of the sheriff's detectives carry .50 caliber handguns.

I doubt they miss much.

PROLOGUE

Alvin, Alabama—1976

The moon hangs in the sky above Alvin like a sickle surrounded by a field of stars. It's a pretty night, but it's cold, being barely two months since Christmas. Susan Lee Robertson is on her way home from the five-and-dime after buying a quart of milk for her baby, who is at home with her twelve-year-old son. The milk sits on the passenger seat beside her.

Rain had been pouring all day, but it finally let up and a westerly wind quickly blew out all the clouds. But the dampness is still in the air, making the storefronts on either side of her look slick, like oil paintings. She hits a pothole and the car bounces in a splash of rainwater, nearly hydroplaning into the oncoming lane. She's driving east up Main Street when she comes to the intersection of Sweetwater Drive. It's a one-way intersection, with no stop signs for Main Street, so Susan Lee continues through with the streetlights reflecting brightly from the hood of her car.

That may explain why, when it happens, she never sees it coming.

A blue Buick with out-of-state plates screams through the stop sign on Sweetwater Drive from Susan Lee's left. The driver, Anna Marsh, is coming back early from a bachelorette party for one of her friends after having a fight with the maid of honor. The party was at the Rabbit Room, a place normally reserved for male patrons and female strippers who take off their tops for ten-dollar bills. But, somehow, the fourteen girls in the wedding party managed to come up with enough money and a good enough argument to convince the owner of the Rabbit Room, Gus Snow, into letting them have a girls' only night with male strippers. And, of course, cocktails. Lots of cocktails.

Anna Marsh never did well when it came to lots of cocktails.

She doesn't hesitate at the stop sign. Without touching her brakes, she T-bones Susan Lee's silver Honda, hitting it near the rear of the car, causing it to spin, and caving in the driver's side, breaking both of Susan Lee's arms—one when the door collides with it, the other when it's slammed against the console. The top of her spinal column is partially severed on impact. The windshield of the Honda explodes in a shower of glass as Susan Lee Robertson's body (which was not secured by a seatbelt) gets tossed through it in a sideways motion. The glass rains into her eyes, blinding her for life.

She lands headfirst on the asphalt in front of her car after bouncing off the hood and is still lying there unconscious when the authorities show up. "I reckon she's lucky to be alive," one of the EMTs says to another.

"I don't know if you'd call this lucky, Jerrod." They try to ascertain where her head is bleeding from. A pool of blood has formed beneath it, with tiny rivers that run along the road.

Carefully, they lift her onto a gurney and place her in the back of an ambulance. She's taken to Providence Hospital in Mobile, where she'll remain in a coma on life support.

With Susan Lee still alive, Anna Marsh is arrested for first-offense DWI. Her blood alcohol level is measured at just over 0.12. Her license is revoked.

Despite her Buick looking like an accordion, Anna's wounds are superficial. She actually gets out of the car and can walk. She doesn't look any worse than if she'd fallen down a few stairs.

Authorities take a slurred statement from her. Turns out she lives in Clarksdale, Mississippi, and, along with her other thirteen friends, came down to Alvin specifically for the bachelorette party.

Her friends had arranged a limo back to their hotel, but after her fight with the maid of honor, Anna decided to drive herself home.

Probably not the best decision she ever made.

Twelve years later, when doctors take Susan Lee off life support and pronounce her dead, a jury at a circuit court changes Anna Marsh's sentence, giving her five years for reckless vehicular manslaughter, the maximum sentence in Alabama. Her appeal is turned down.

But before that, for twelve years of her life, Susan Lee Robertson lies in that hospital bed unconscious while the world continues to go round without her.

Twelve long years.

For her, it's just a blink.

But for those who love her, it's an eternity. . . .

CHAPTER 1

Almost Thirteen Years Later

It was a clear winter day when the Christmas parade wound its way down Alvin's Main Street. Which, of course, meant it was cold. Dewey said it smelled like snow, but I told him he was crazy. First off, it ain't never snowed in Alvin far as I know, and second, it wasn't *that* cold. I guessed it to be probably in the midforties somewhere. Still, I was glad I had my heavy jacket on. I wasn't used to this sort of weather.

We were all standing together as close as we could, which was extremely strange for my sister, Carry. Normally, Carry liked to be as far away from everyone else as she could get, but I guess huddling to keep warm took precedence over trying to look cool. Other than me, Dewey, and Carry, there was my uncle Henry, who had come down to spend the holidays with us.

Christmas was barely two weeks away, and boy you could sure feel the excitement in the air. I loved Christmas. It was the best day of the year as far as I was rightly concerned. My mother always played Elvis songs at Christmastime and he had this one that was called something like "If Every Day Was Christmas." I found myself thinking that same question all the time. Of course, then it probably wouldn't be so special. Which sounded just like something my mother would say.

More and more, I found myself saying stuff that sounded like it should be coming out of her mouth instead of mine.

Carry was extra lucky. She not only got Christmas to celebrate, but four days later, she got her birthday, too. If she had been born just four days earlier, she'd have the same birthday as baby Jesus. I'm glad she didn't. That would be just too weird.

"Here they come!" Uncle Henry said. "Can you see all right, Abe?" he asked me.

"I certainly can!" I said.

Down the street, the float my mother was on turned the corner and came into view. There was a tall riser up front where Hubert James Robertson, the mayor of Alvin, stood waving to people on both sides of the street. Beside him, on much lower risers, stood my mother on his left and Officer Chris Jackson on his right. Both my mother and Chris worked for the Alvin Police Department. Chris was just a regular officer, but my mother was a detective, which meant she didn't have to drive around in a special car or wear a special uniform. She could go out looking any way she wanted. Although, sometimes, she worked as a normal officer, too. They were the only two police officers in Alvin other than Police Chief Ethan Montgomery, who ran things at the station.

"Where's Chief Montgomery?" I asked, blinking into the sun as I looked up at Uncle Henry. A cold breeze hit my pant legs, sending a chill up my body.

Uncle Henry shielded his eyes with his hand, almost looking like he was saluting someone. "I don't know. You'd reckon he'd be on there, too."

There were all sorts of floats. The one my mother was on didn't seem to "be" anything in particular, but the one coming up behind it was a pirate ship advertising the Alvin First National Bank. It was big and it blocked out most of the stores on the other side of the street. It had a huge Union Jack flag that flapped and snapped in the winter wind.

"Isn't that a weird float for a bank?" I asked.

"What do you mean?" Dewey asked back.

"I mean, didn't pirates *steal* money? It's like they're sayin' they're gonna steal your money."

"You think too much, Abe," Uncle Henry said.

"Maybe they're sayin' that they'll steal money *for* you and put it into your account," Dewey offered.

"Maybe it's *just* a friggin' pirate ship," Carry said.

She could be very unsociable at times.

Someone in a giant kangaroo suit came bounding down the side of the road and stopped right in front of us, waving.

I waved back, but the kangaroo didn't move on. It just kept waving. I felt very awkward and uncomfortable, waving from the sidewalk with the kangaroo two feet from me, waving from the street. Finally, the kangaroo reached up and took off its giant head. It was Police Chief Montgomery. "You guys all havin' fun?"

"Um, yeah. It's dandy," Dewey said.

"It's okay," I said.

"My feet are killin' me," Carry whined. "How much longer is this thing anyway?"

"They're all having a terrific time," Uncle Henry said, swatting the back of Carry's head.

Chief Montgomery leaned in, and whispered to Carry, "At least you don't have to hop around in a stupid kangaroo suit. My legs feel like Jell-O. I can't *wait* until this is over. I reckon there's only three or four more floats until the big guy comes round and finishes it."

"The big guy?" Dewey asked.

"You know," Chief Montgomery said. "Mr. C? Ho ho ho? St. Nick?"

"Santa Claus!" A huge smile beamed from Dewey's face.

Oh my God, he didn't really still believe in Santa, did he? Me and Dewey were practically exactly the same age. Our birthdays were within days of each other, which meant he would be thirteen in March. Someone had to put an end to this.

"Dewey," I said, "you do know there is no real Santa, right?"

I got instant glares from three people. Even Carry joined into the Glare Group.

"What?" I asked. "He's almost thirteen for cryin' out loud. Do you want him to go into the workforce believin' in the tooth fairy?"

"Wait," Dewey said, sounding dejected. "There's no Santa *and* no tooth fairy?"

"Dewey, you have no baby teeth left. Why do you even care 'bout the tooth fairy?"

"She was nice to me. She gave me money."

"He's got a point, ass face," Carry said. Uncle Henry swatted the back of her head again.

"Language," he said. To me, he didn't sound too much like he meant it.

"Are you serious about Santa?" Dewey asked.

I took a deep breath and let it go, looking at all the heads shaking behind Dewey's back. I smiled. It was a terribly faked smile. "No, Dewey, I'm just pullin' your leg. Of course there's a Santa Claus. Who else would be eatin' those carrots and drinkin' that milk you put out?"

His face immediately transformed. The wonder was back. It sort of peeved me off because he was living in a world much more spectacular than the one I was.

"And just so you know," he said, "I *am* aware there is no Easter bunny."

I squinted at him. "Why do you reckon there's no Easter bunny, yet you believe in Santa?"

"Duh. Why the heck would rabbits be givin' out eggs? It makes absolutely no sense."

"He's got a point," Uncle Henry said.

Everyone fell silent and I realized the Existence of Santa Claus and Other Miscellaneous Childhood Lies discussion had come to an end. The silence was finally broken by Uncle Henry asking Carry: "So, what does my little sugar plum want for her birthday this year?"

Carry smiled. "It's super cool."

"What is it?"

"I want you and my mom"—she hesitated and examined me and Dewey—"and I guess you two little rug rats too if you want, to come with me to a psychic while I get my fortune told."

"What a neat idea," Uncle Henry said. "But if you want me there, you're gonna have to do it earlier than your birthday. I'm only stayin' until the mornin' after Christmas and then I have to go."

"Okay, I'll talk to Mom. Maybe we can book an appointment this week. I reckon it'll be so cool."

"Just remember, sugar plum, a lot of those so-called psychics are frauds. They only tell you what you wanna hear. Or they're gypsies. Gypsies give me the willies."

"I'm not gonna *tell* her what I wanna hear. I'm not gonna answer any questions. I wanna see what she can figure out without me sayin' a word."

"Well, that sure should be interestin' to watch."

"Maybe I'll find out that one day I'll be rich," Carry said.

"Or that you'll die an early death in a house fire before you're twenty," Dewey said.

We all looked at him. "What?" he asked.

"Oh, nothin'," I said. "There's just somethin' wrong with you, is all."

CHAPTER 2

Me and Dewey were playing tag in the backyard. Tag was one of those games we didn't play for very long, on account of there being just the two of us and it getting a mite boring. You really need more than two people to play tag properly. Mainly, it was just fun being outside this close to Christmas. Me and my mother had spent the last weekend hanging lights up around the eaves of the house. Now it looked really Christmassy. I just couldn't wait for Christmas to come.

One game we used to play a lot of I would call "balancing rocks on sticks." It consisted of taking a stick and a rock and trying to see how long you could go with the rock on the end of the stick before it fell off. Now this was more of a sport for two people. In fact, you could just as easily do it with one person. It was the perfect multiplayer game.

Truth be told, there just wasn't much to do outside in the afternoon in winter in Alvin. Tag or otherwise. We were too used to the heat to stay outside too long in the cold, and some days it would rain something fierce and it felt like God was throwing ice at you. My backyard wasn't the most fun place on the planet to hang out on those days. Sometimes we'd just run around to stay warm.

Even the trees looked like they hated it outside. We had two cherry trees in the backyard and neither had any leaves left. All the leaves had fallen off and died. I was starting to feel like them leaves, as Dewey touched me, and yelled, "You're It!"

I decided I couldn't be It for one more round. "Let's stop playin'," I said.

"How come, Abe?" Dewey asked.

"Well, for one, I'm outta breath. For two, it's too damn cold out here. I'm dyin', Dewey."

"What's for three?"

"Um . . ." I knew for three had to be the cincher. "For three, I think we can probably go inside and get my mom to make us some hot cocoa."

"That sounds great!"

Dewey never gave up a chance for free food, no matter what it was. It was his weakness, the way Superman couldn't go near kryptonite. Everyone has a weakness I think, and Dewey's was rustling up free food. We could be having the time of our lives and I could stop, and tell him, "Hey, old Newt Parker just called and invited us over for raccoon, wanna go?" And Dewey would be on his bike in a flash, ready to make the trip.

Newt Parker was no longer with the living souls of this world, but when he was here, many folk thought he ate barbecued roadkill. Myself, I have no convictions either way as to whether or not the rumors were true or false. I do know this, though. I had enough belief that the rumors *could* be true that I would never go for a barbecue at Newt Parker's house. Dewey, on the other hand, would go in a flash, if for no other reason than to be able to tell people he ate barbecued road-killed raccoon with Newt Parker. That's just how Dewey was.

So, compared to the dead raccoon, my offer of hot cocoa was a quick way to get me out of the stark cold of the backyard and into the warmth of the house.

We got inside and pulled off our boots. It took Dewey at least twice as long as me to get his off his feet on account of I think he outgrew his last year or something. Do twelve-year-old feet even still grow? I had no idea. Maybe his ma just bought them too small. Dewey's ma wasn't the sharpest crayon in the box. Of course, I never told that to Dewey.

My own mother was in the kitchen on the phone. Carry kneeled on a chair beside her, anxiously watching while my mother made some phone calls. I figured out pretty quick what they were doing— they were trying to book a psychic to see Carry for her birthday present. By the sounds of things, they weren't having much luck.

"No," my mother said, "it needs to be *between* now and Christmas. Sometime this week would be best . . . okay, thank you for your time." She hung up and looked at Carry. "That's eight I've called. They're all not working through the holidays."

Carry frowned. "Stupid psychics. Don't they know that's when they'd get their most business?"

"Maybe it's just as well," my mother said.

"Don't give up now!" Carry said. "There's still some you haven't tried."

"I know, and I will, I just don't want you to get your hopes up too high."

"If they're all psychic and stuff," Dewey said, "why do you have to call them? Shouldn't they just know you're comin'?"

I looked at Dewey. "You're an idiot."

My mother said, "I reckon he has a very good point."

Carry didn't hear the exchange at all. She had her head in the phone book. "Try this one. Madame Crystalle—True Psychic Medium from Persia. One hundred percent satisfaction or your money returned in full."

"Wow," my mother said, "that's going out on a limb. And she's not a gypsy if she's from Persia. I'm a little leery of gypsies. Okay, what's the number?"

Carry told her as my mother dialed. "Hello, I'd like to book an appointment with Madame Crystalle. . . . Oh, that's *you*. Well, hi. My name's Leah and I'm the detective here in Alvin and my daughter, Caroline, would like to see you and get her fortune read for her birthday. . . . It would have to be sometime this week. I know, it's sort of last minute." My mother always told everyone she was the detective here. I think she thought it brought her some kind of respect or something that she wouldn't get otherwise.

She stopped talking, held the phone away, and said to Carry, "She's gone to get her schedule."

Placing the handset back to her mouth, she said, "Yes, I'm still here . . . *tomorrow?* Yes, tomorrow works *fine.* What time? Two o'clock. Perfect. Oh, and is it okay to bring along her family to watch? Okay, that's great. Thank you."

My mother hung up and smiled at Carry. "You're goin' tomorrow at two!"

Carry beamed back. "This is goin' to be so awesome! Thank you, Mother!"

"What if she tells you somethin' bad?" Dewey asked.

"Why are you being so negative?" my mother asked back.

"Because *most* things are bad. Read a newspaper or watch the news. You never see happy stuff."

"I'm sure Carry's stuff will all be nice and happy."

"Yeah, but what if it isn't? What if she says, 'Your mother's gonna get shot next Wednesday while on duty'?"

"Dewey!" my mother snapped. Even I looked at him like this was out of line.

"I'm just sayin' she could, so you should be prepared for somethin' like that."

"I reckon maybe it's time for you to go home," my mother told him.

"Actually," I said, "we was hopin' for some hot cocoa."

My mother took another look at Dewey and exhaled slowly. "All right, but no more talk about 'bad stuff,' you hear?"

"Yes, ma'am," Dewey said.

He fell quiet. I just looked at him, and whispered, "You're an idiot."

CHAPTER 3

The psychic's shop turned out to be a very small building that me and Dewey had ridden by on our bikes many times and had not noticed. The shop couldn't have been more than ten feet tall with a sign in the window that read:

Madame Crystalle
True Psychic Medium
100% satisfaction
Or your money returned in full.

The pink blinds behind the sign were pulled closed, so you couldn't see inside. A large shrub hid most of one side of the building. The rest of the building was painted black, which was obviously the reason me and Dewey never saw it. You don't normally look for small black buildings while out on bike rides.

The only really strange thing on the outside of the place was this statue right beside the door. It stood between the sidewalk and the steps leading up to the door, facing down toward the hustle and bustle of town. It was a frog standing on his hind legs. It stared wall-eyed down Main Street at all the other shops. In its hands it held a top hat, and its mouth was wide open with a bright red tongue. It seemed so out of place it took a minute for my brain to even figure out what I was looking at. Me and Dewey must've missed it because it was set back a bit, and you had to look right at the building to see it.

"Why is there a frog standin' here starin' off down the street?" I asked my mother. "It looks kind of creepy."

"I don't rightly know, Abe, but I think maybe we should all go inside before we freeze to death," my mother said.

"Reminds me of that frog from that cartoon," Dewey said. "The one that will only dance and sing for one guy. Only this one wouldn't fit in a shoebox."

"I agree with Abe for once," Carry said. "It's really creepy. No wonder she was available for a readin'. She probably scares off most customers with this frog."

"Now, don't go writin' her off just because of some crazy statue outside her shop," Uncle Henry said. "Look at her sign. It says, 'True Psychic Medium.' Not only that, she'll refund your money if you ain't satisfied. I'd say that's pretty darn good. I also agree with your mom. We should go inside before we freeze."

"I guess," my sister said.

Uncle Henry looked up at the roof; then his eyes fell to the door. "So what do we do? Just knock?"

"I dunno," my mother said. "Maybe try the door."

Of course, before anyone could say another word, Dewey's hand was on that doorknob. He turned it and the door opened. A bell on the top of the door rang out, announcing our arrival.

We shuffled into a small room that was more like a landing for the top of a narrow stairway. A beaded curtain hung at the entrance to the stairway. The small room we found ourselves in smelled funny, and the walls and ceiling were all colored red, matching near on exactly the tongue of the frog statue outside. The floor was white with repeating red diamonds. Nobody seemed to hear the bell that rang because we stood there, all crammed together on that small landing for a good five minutes and nobody came to see us.

"What's that smell?" I asked.

"Incense," my mother said.

"What's that?"

"It's supposed to have mystical powers, I reckon," Uncle Henry said. He sneezed. "I think I might be allergic to it."

"It has mystical stink," Dewey said.

"What do we do now?" my mother asked.

"Hello?" Uncle Henry called out. "Anybody home?"

From downstairs, behind the beaded curtain, a heavily accented woman's voice called up. "Come downstairs!"

We pushed our way through the curtain. The beads were all glass and very beautiful. Green, red, blue, yellow, with the light reflecting inside of them. They made a loud swishing that sounded almost like water as we went through them. The stairway wound down in two tight circles. I was behind Uncle Henry. It was too narrow to go any way but single file.

About halfway down, Uncle Henry bumped his head. At that exact moment, from the bottom of the stairs, in a much quieter and lower voice than she had used before, we heard the woman say, "Be careful of head. If you are tall, those stairs are like plague."

"You'd think, bein' psychic and all, she'd have told me that *before* I hit my head," Uncle Henry whispered before letting go with a big sneeze.

"I heard that," the woman replied.

When we made it to the bottom, there was another beaded curtain to go through that exactly matched the one at the top. Again, it sounded like a waterfall as we all pushed through it and came to our final destination. I felt my eyes grow as big as paper plates. We had descended into the weirdest room I'd ever seen in my entire life.

Everything was a deep golden yellow. The room was maybe twice the size of the small landing we managed to squeeze onto at the top of the stairs. On one side were rows of shelves holding candles of all different types. Every one was lit, and that was the only light in the room, so it cast an eerie, flickering glow on the yellow walls, yellow curtains (which hung on some walls and were obviously just for show as we were underground), and yellow tablecloth that covered the round table on the other side of the room. The cloth came right down to the floor, which was a deep pile carpet, also in golden yellow.

On the other side of the table sat who I assumed to be Madame Crystalle. I had no idea how she got in to sit on that chair. From where I stood, it looked like she would have to spend the rest of her life seated there, as there was no way in or out.

She wore a leather headband with gemstones set along it, and had long strands of beads in her curly, deep auburn hair. It hung down past her shoulders. Her lips were very red, and her eyes were very blue and they sparkled in the candlelight. I immediately liked her because of her smile. It was one of the warmest, friendliest, and reddest smiles I'd ever seen.

The first thing she did was look straight at Carry. "You must be Caroline," she said, and extended her hand without standing. I didn't think it was possible for her to stand from where she sat.

"I am," Carry said happily.

"I understand it's your birthday," Madame Crystalle said.

"Well, not for another week or so, but we wanted my uncle to come along and he's leavin' the mornin' after Christmas."

"Ah! Early birthday present. So nice!"

"You talk funny," Dewey said.

"Shut up!" I snapped in a whisper to him.

But Madame Crystalle just laughed. "I am from Persia. Everyone talk like this in Persia."

"And I bet she speaks better English than you speak Persian," Carry said to Dewey. Uncle Henry sneezed again.

"I always thought Persians were cats," Dewey said.

Once again, I told Dewey to shut up, but Madame Crystalle laughed very loudly at what he said. "We are people, too. Oh, and also carpet. Or, how you say? Rug. Persian rug."

"How come you ain't got no crystal ball?" Dewey asked.

I wished he'd stop asking questions.

"Oh, crystal balls don't work," Madame Crystalle said. "They're all just hocus-pocus, fluff stuff. You either real medium or you're not. If real, you don't need crystal ball to tell you anything."

"Oh," Dewey said.

"I'm Leah," my mother said, extending her hand with a smile. She did it quickly, before Dewey could say anything else.

Smiling, Madame Crystalle went to shake my mother's hand, but as soon as their hands locked Madame Crystalle's face changed immediately.

"What's goin' on?" Dewey asked.

"Please," Madame Crystalle said. "Sit in chair." Her face was very serious as she gestured to the chair across the table from her.

"No, this is for Caroline," my mother said. "I'm just here to watch."

"There will be no charge. There are things you must know. Sit. Now. Before I lose them."

Reluctantly, my mother sat in the chair. I could tell Carry felt a little put out just by the expression on her face.

"You . . . you work in justice, no?"

"Yes, I told you that on the phone. I'm the detective for the Alvin Police Department." I figured my mother had just caught the psychic in a trap. She was using information she gained ahead of time from the phone call my mother made to set up Carry's appointment.

Madame Crystalle closed her eyes and held both my mother's hands. "I see something almost indescribable. It is someone . . . a sort of, how you say? Maniac. A tailor. Deprives those of their sight. Very dangerous."

"Who are you talkin' 'bout?" my mother asked. I could tell she had grown a bit anxious.

"Just listen, before it goes away," Madame Crystalle said. "I see a body in darkness, waiting. I see writing. Writing on the body."

"What does the writing say?" my mother asked, but Madame Crystalle shushed her.

"I can't see enough to read it, just to know it's there. But remember the number seventy-eight. It is important. Remember the maniac tailor. Knowing this can save many lives over the coming times.

I . . . I see a name on a sign. . . . 'Welcome to . . . to . . . Gray . . .' " She paused again. " 'Gray . . . Gray . . .' " Then she stopped.

She let go of my mother's hands. "Sorry, it's gone."

"What *was* it?" my mother asked, her voice shaky.

"Did it not mean something to you?"

"No, can you give me some more information?"

Madame Crystalle shook her head. "No, I can't tell you what it was I just saw. I don't remember details, the visions come like that. I just knew I had message and it was for you. If not useful now, I am sure you will find useful soon. It was a very powerful message the way it came through."

"That freaked me out a little," I said.

"Me too," Dewey said.

Uncle Henry sneezed.

"You still up to doin' yours?" Uncle Henry asked Carry.

"Yeah," Carry said as though he just asked the stupidest question ever. "Mine better not be in code like Mom's was, though. I want to actually understand it."

"I will try do better for you," Madame Crystalle said. "Please, take seat."

My mother got out of the chair and let Carry take her place. I noticed my mother was shaking, especially her hands. I think she was more freaked out than anyone. It was pretty spooky.

Madame Crystalle took a deck of cards from somewhere beside her and handed them across the table to Carry. She had them with the backs up and the backs were pretty neat. They were black with a silver ring painted on the center. Inside the ring was a red dragon curled up with its wings hanging down over the bottom of the ring. The deck looked thicker than a normal deck of cards.

"Shuffle these," Madame Crystalle said. "Use overhand shuffle, though. I don't want my cards bent."

Carry did as she was told. "When do I stop?" she asked.

"Go for as long as feels good to you. You are imprinting your future onto the cards."

Carry shuffled some more, then came to a stop. She looked like she was about to set down the deck, then she started shuffling again for another minute or so. "I just felt compelled to," she said.

Madame Crystalle smiled. "This is good. It means you go with your instincts."

Finally, Carry actually did stop. "Okay, what do I do now?"

"Hold the deck in your left hand and make three piles of cards on the table from left to right."

Carry did and then Madame Crystalle leaned over and picked up the piles from left to right with *her* left hand. I couldn't figure out what was so important about everything being done using lefts.

She laid out seven cards in all and in the end they formed a T shape. First she laid out five cards in a straight row and then two cards beneath the center card in the row. Some were upside down from me and others weren't. I wondered if that mattered. And boy, if I thought the backs of the cards were neat, the fronts were even better.

Each one was different. The first looked like an old scraggly tree with a green gem tangled in its root. It read "Ace of Pentacles" on the bottom.

The second was the Five of Cups and showed a dwarf drinking something out of a bottle with his back against a tree and five cups in the grass around him. The dwarf looked drunk to me.

The third one was The Lovers and showed two dragons looking like they were about to kiss. That one sort of disturbed me. Dragons don't kiss. They go and burn down castles and collect treasure.

The fourth one was the Four of Cups and showed a lady with very long ponytails standing at a table where four little lizards were playing with four golden cups. Two of the cups were on their side, the other two were standing.

The fifth one (which was the last one along the top row) was the Queen of Wands and showed an older lady with a beautiful dress made from purple and gold silk. She was seated on a tall wooden throne with a blue dragon sleeping at her feet.

The remaining two came down from The Lovers card. The first one was the Knight of Wands, which showed a younger-looking man riding a dragon in the moonlight. This one was pretty awesome. I would love to ride a dragon. Especially at night.

The final card, at the very bottom of the *T,* was the Two of

Cups, and it showed a young man and woman holding hands in a garden with a huge moon over their heads and the face of a dragon inside the moon. It almost looked like they were getting married or something.

"What do they mean?" Carry asked, anxiously, just as Uncle Henry sneezed for what seemed like the hundredth time.

"Well, let's see," Madame Crystalle said. "I see you are smart in school. This is good. I also see you know it. This, not so good. You would have more friendships if you didn't always act so sarcastic."

Carry's face reddened. She hated getting lectured the best of times. Now she was being lectured by a psychic whom she got as a birthday present.

Madame Crystalle noticed Carry's reaction and quickly covered. "It's okay, though, you have good heart. See these cup cards? Cups represent love and compassion. You have many. So your heart is in right place. But . . ."

"But what?" Carry asked.

"You get very lonely at times," Madame Crystalle said.

"No, I don't," Carry said back snarkily.

"You cover it with your sarcasm or your quick wit. But you wish you had more friends. You also long for a boyfriend."

We all sort of giggled at that and Carry's face went completely purple. This was turning out to be the best birthday present ever. I started thinking for my birthday I'd get Carry a psychic reading.

"Well, I have good news for you," Madame Crystalle said. "I see a boy in the immediate future. Someone more than just a friend."

"He won't be nineteen and drivin' a red Pontiac Sunbird, will he?" my mother asked, referring to a boy we once caught with Carry in the backseat of a car. "Actually, he'd be twenty now."

"No, but he will be older than you, Caroline. And he'll probably have dark hair. Brown, black, maybe a dark red. And don't worry about your mother. See this card here?" She tapped the Queen of Wands. "This is your mother and she's sitting right beside one of your cup cards. Which means she will be approving of your love choices from now on. So this new boy for sure your mother will be accepting of him. But, I see at first you won't trust her to be, and you will try to hide your relationship. Rest assured this is unneeded. Your mother will not try and sabotage anything."

There was a little more after that, but that was the main part. That was the part that made Carry happiest (and most embarrassed). I thought it must be weird, living her life now, just waiting for this boy to drop into it who is going to become her new boyfriend.

By the time we left Madame Crystalle, I noticed a change in every one of us. Carry was in deep thought, probably about this new boy. My mother was in deep thought, probably about the stuff she was told that made absolutely no sense to anyone. Uncle Henry had changed because he found out he was allergic to incense. I was quietly cursing myself because I forgot to ask Madame Crystalle about the frog standing outside her shop, and Dewey had changed because he found out that, along with rugs and cats, there were also Persian people.

CHAPTER 4

That night, Leah lay in bed unable to sleep. Her encounter with the psychic kept rolling around in her mind. What happened earlier had affected her more than she had thought. She didn't really believe in psychics or the ability to "see the future" at all; in fact, she normally referred to it as "hocus-pocus gobbledygook." But her ad hoc session with Madame Crystalle had been so intense, Leah couldn't help but be touched by it.

The problem was, the woman didn't make any sense. Leah was a logical person, and there was no logic in what she'd been told. It was just a bunch of sketchy details without any definition. And to top it off, Leah kept going back to the fact that she had *told* Madame Crystalle on the phone she was a detective. That part made it a little too convenient for Leah's liking.

Leah remembered every word the psychic told her. She'd gone over the words at least fifty times in her head, and there was nothing there she could do anything with. None of it made any sense. Some of it was downright ridiculous and funny. A maniac tailor who deprives people of their sight. Now *there's* an image that's really hard to conjure up in your imagination. Something about finding a body in darkness with writing on it. The psychic had been unable to say anything about the writing at all.

Yet, writing on a body found in darkness is pretty specific. They aren't just things you pull out of your sleeves. So this was where Leah was torn into possibly believing the woman and attempting to follow up on the clues. But really, what clues did she have? She didn't even have a name or place for a victim. Or any kind of context to put this into.

It was the last piece of evidence Madame Crystalle had given Leah that made Leah consider trying to follow the sparse path of clues; it was the one thing that was tangible and possible to get something out of. The words on the sign: WELCOME TO GRAY . . .

It was a partial on a road sign. *That* should be traceable.

This road sign was something Leah might be able to find. But so what if she did? She still had no idea what it meant.

Did she even *want* to know what it meant? And sweet Jesus, if Police Chief Ethan Montgomery ever found out she was hunting around on a case with the sparse evidence she had been given from a psychic, he'd have a heyday with it.

It would probably be the day before Leah had to start looking for a new job.

"I guess you ain't goin' to get much sleep tonight," she said to herself, deciding her best course of action at this point was to get up and go fix herself a mug of warm milk.

Sliding her feet into her slippers, she stood from her bed and slowly padded her way down the hardwood floors into the kitchen. Opening the fridge, she pulled out a carton of milk. She closed the fridge door and immediately her pulse went up twenty notches and she nearly jumped right out of her slippers. Hank had moved beside the opened door while she was peering in the fridge.

"God, Hank, you tryin' to give me a coronary?"

"Sorry. I guess I'm a little sneaky in my old age. I just heard you walkin' round and thought I'd come check on you, make certain you were all right."

"Oh," she said, almost in a sigh. "I'm okay. It's just that psychic has me in a bit of a tizzy."

"I can imagine. The woman was pretty intense. *I* was almost left in a tizzy, and it wasn't even me she was talkin' to!"

Leah pulled a pot from one of the cupboards and put it on the stove. She turned on the burner and poured in some milk. "Would you like some warm milk, too?" she asked Hank.

"Hmm. Actually, that sounds like it might just hit the spot. Thank you."

Leah poured more milk into the pot and returned the milk carton to the fridge. Then she came back and started stirring the milk with a spoon as it simmered on the burner. "So," she asked, "seriously. Why *are* you up?"

"Oh, you know me," he said. "I don't sleep at the best of times. And your sofa is comfortable and all, but it ain't no bed in no five-star hotel room." He laughed.

"I'm sorry," Leah said. "I wish we had somewhere else to put you."

Hank raised his hand. "No, no, I'm not really complainin', I'm just bein' funny. I don't mind the sofa at all. So, about that psychic lady—you gonna act on anythin' she said?"

"Well, that's just it. Even if I wanted to do somethin' based on what she told me, she didn't actually *say* anythin' I could possibly use to do anythin'."

"Well, she told you folk are in danger. She told you someone is blindin' them and that he's actin' like some maniac tailor, which could mean lots of disgustin' things when I think it over."

Leah set two mugs on the counter, took the pot of milk off the burner, and carefully tipped it to fill them with the now-warm milk. "Is that what *you* heard?" she asked Hank. "Because that's not what *I* heard. I just heard a bunch of half-baked facts all rolled together." She handed one of the mugs to Hank.

"Thank you," he said. "That's because you chose not to try and form the bits and pieces of information she gave you into somethin' real. You're too analytical. Sometimes you need to fill in the blanks yourself so that you can create—or at least finish—the story. Your story might not always be the right one—fact is, most of the time it probably isn't—but it gives you a place to start. And as you go you can change your story as circumstances change and you gather more facts."

Leah took a sip of her warm milk. It felt good going down her throat. "Ethan would kill me if he knew I was even considerin' doin' this."

"Yeah, well, Ethan owes you a lot. He knows that. Hell, half this town knows that. Take chances, Leah. It's the only way in life to push yourself to your full potential, and if we don't all reach our full potential, what's the point in being here?" He took a sip of his milk. "This is really good milk, by the way."

"It's just milk warmed up in a pot, Hank."

"Still really good."

"Thanks."

A silence followed while Leah thought about what the psychic had told her. "So, say I *do* try and follow this up, Hank. Where the hell do I start? The only thing she gave that's even slightly possible to research is a partial on a road sign."

"Then that's where you start. The road sign. Then at least you'll know what town she's talkin' 'bout."

Every bone in Leah's body was telling her not to do this, telling her that following the scattered advice given to her from a Main Street psychic was a dumb idea. And yet, she knew, deep down in the pit of her gut, that was exactly what she was going to do. So she may as well stop fighting it and just give in and get it over with.

"What made you so smart, anyway?" she asked Hank.

"Watchin' you grow up," he replied.

"We both know what I'm gonna do," she said.

"Yep, you've decided already," Hank said.

Leah sighed. "I guess I have. Sometimes I hate my gut instincts."

"Your gut instincts are what make you good at your job."

Turned out, this time, she didn't have to listen to any instincts.

CHAPTER 5

The body was discovered washed up on the shore of Willet Lake in the northwestern part of Alvin at approximately 6:55 A.M. Tuesday, just as the sun was rising. Leah had calls from the station being forwarded to her house, and she took the initial report from a witness named Luanne Cooper. Luanne was a photographer who just happened to be up early in Willet Park. She was taking pictures of winter birds and anything else she could find worthy of picture taking. Willet was a pretty little park, and its lake probably the prettiest in all of Alvin. With everything near on frozen and crystalized, it looked even prettier than usual.

When Leah asked why Luanne was in the park so early, she replied, "I don't want pictures of people, I want pictures of nature. And by eight, even in the winter, people are out doin' stuff. Walkin' their dogs, walkin' their spouses, just goin' for walks. Gettin' in the way of all my good shots."

Leah asked her to remain at the site but not to touch anything. "If any other member of the public shows up before I do, please make sure they stay well away from the crime scene. The last thing we need is someone corruptin' any evidence we might have."

Luanne agreed to keep an eye on things.

Leah called Chris, waking him up from what must've been a

helluva good dream to make him so cranky. "Why the hell you callin' me at not even yet seven?" he asked.

"We got ourselves a body. Washed up in Willet Lake. Get yourself in uniform and meet me there. Sooner is better."

"All right. I'm up. I'm comin'. I don't suppose there's any chance of there bein' any coffee when I arrive?"

"Just get there," Leah said, and hung up the phone.

It took her under twenty minutes to get dressed and make the drive to the park. It took Chris an extra ten or so before he arrived. By the time Leah got there, she could see what Luanne meant about the public starting to come into the park. They'd already begun encircling the crime scene, although Luanne had done a good job keeping them away from anything important.

The body was a woman who had washed up beneath one of the two wharfs that stretched out into the lake. She was lying facedown on her stomach with her arms outstretched, one in the sand on the beach, the other waving in the water. She wore a white collared shirt that floated ghostly. Her blond hair was long and full and matted with algae. From where Leah stood, it looked like the dead woman was wearing a long skirt. Leah couldn't see her feet in the murky water's depths, but she imagined that an outfit like this would probably go with heels, and that heels or any other kind of slip-on shoe would've likely fallen off into the lake.

Leah immediately cordoned off the surrounding landscape with police tape, giving the crime scene a very wide berth. She wanted to keep the public as far away as possible. It was now going on eight and already over a dozen or so had collected to see what all the fuss was about.

Luanne Cooper, a short, slender woman with cropped, spiky, deep red hair and bright green eyes, stood to one side with a Canon camera slung over one shoulder and a camera bag over the other. She had red lipstick that reminded Leah of Christmas. Her ears were full of hoops (four in each); the last two on both ears had crosses hanging from them. The camera had a pricey telephoto lens attached to it. At least from what Leah knew about cameras, she guessed it to be pricey.

Leah tried to pin an age on Luanne, but it was tough. Likely, she was in her late twenties or possibly early thirties.

Chris brought the CSI kit and Polaroid camera from the trunk of his squad car and took pictures of the body from every angle. Then he scraped the fingernails and toenails, and bagged each in separate evidence bags.

Then, while Chris interviewed Luanne, Leah tried to discern different shoe prints in the muddy clay and sand around the wharf. It was hard to make out anything clearly because the location was well trodden. There were, however, four different shoe prints that looked like they'd pressed into the ground fairly recently. Leah made a cast of those, even though there was really no reason to believe that this was the place the body was thrown into the lake. It could've easily floated to this location on its own.

Leah took a look at Luanne Cooper's feet. She was wearing brown boots with a slight heel. "Can you carefully walk down here, along the side of the wharf where there are no footprints?" Leah asked her when Chris had finished taking her statement.

Luanne gave her a look that sort of questioned why she was being asked this, but she did it anyway.

Sure enough, the imprint her shoe made matched one of the fresh ones Leah had just taken a cast of. "I thought you told Officer Jackson you only came to the edge of the grass?" Leah asked.

"I did."

"Then why does your shoe print exactly match these ones down here?" Leah asked. "You came down here, Luanne."

Luanne's face reddened. "Okay, maybe I took a closer look. But I didn't *touch* anything."

Leah eyed her suspiciously but decided to take the woman at her word. She led her outside the police tape and asked her to stay back while they finished examining the scene.

Having taken Luanne's statement and gotten all the DNA data he could, Chris said to Leah, "We gotta turn the body over so I can photograph her from the front."

Officer Chris Jackson was a tall black man who had at least three inches on Leah. He started with the Alvin Police Department a dozen or so years back, and when he did there had been an uproar on account of his skin color. Since then, he had proved himself and become somewhat of an icon in the community.

Leah helped turn the body over and almost instantaneously she and Chris gasped. What they saw made Leah's stomach clench. The woman's eyes had been stitched shut with thick black thread. Chris's eyes met Leah's, but neither said a word. Most of the view of the body was blocked from onlookers by the wharf. Leah was thankful for this. Keeping things contained made her job a lot easier.

Like a maniac tailor . . .

"Look at the buttons on her shirt," Leah said.

The man's white shirt was buttoned up wrong. The bottom button was in the second to last hole, like it had been buttoned up in a hurry or by someone who simply didn't care. The water made the shirt almost translucent and Chris noticed something else.

"There's something written on her chest."

"I'll cut the buttons off so we don't destroy any possible prints."

"Before you do, let me take some pictures."

Just like before, Chris took pictures of the body from all different angles.

"Okay, go ahead," he said.

Leah took the scissors from the CSI kit. Carefully, not letting her fingers touch the buttons, she cut around them, removing them from the shirt. They were dropped into an evidence bag and tagged. Chris opened the shirt enough to read the words running across the dead girl's bosom in waterproof Magic Marker. It said:

Justice Is Blind
in the Eyes of the Lord

"What the hell does *that* mean?" Chris asked.

"What the hell does *any* of this mean?" Leah asked back.

Writing on the body . . .

That part of it was exactly as the psychic said it would be.

Astonishment took her breath away for a moment. It was impossible and yet . . .

She was brought back to the present by the clicking sound of Chris taking more pictures.

Leah noticed a bulge in the single front pocket of the victim's shirt. Using the tongs from the CSI kit, she extracted a cross, roughly hewn from what appeared to be hickory. "Looks like she came bearin' gifts," Chris said.

Dropping the cross into an evidence bag and tagging it, Leah and Chris pulled the body completely out of the water. Leah had been right; if the body had had shoes on when it entered the lake, they were long gone now.

Leah looked at all the evidence they had collected. Ultimately, it would be sent down to the forensics lab in Mobile, where the experts would look at it and send back their reports. Alvin simply wasn't big enough to have its own crime lab. At least not yet. The population was growing, though. In the last year, it had seen its population jump near on a thousand people to its current number of approximately 5,300. Good thing there wasn't anything for miles around it. It had room to grow.

Leah looked at the body from the other side and immediately saw the cause of death. "Well, she didn't die from drownin'," she said.

Chris came around. "Entry wound that small couldn't be more than a .22, especially considerin' there's no exit wound."

"Which means we're gonna have to wait on the medical examiner before we get that round back. See any brass anywhere?"

Chris examined the immediate area. "No brass. No blood splatter. I don't think she was killed here. 'Course he could've been smart enough to bring her into the lake a ways before making the shot and take the bullet casing with him."

"Let's assume that's just too much work for our guy. Then you reckon she was killed somewhere else and dumped here, or just killed somewhere else on the lake and she floated here?"

Chris shrugged. "No way of knowin'." He was trying for finger-prints on the buttons and the cross.

"Get anythin'?" Leah asked.

"Nothin'. He must've worn gloves."

"Try the eyelids." Taking prints off of skin was tough, but not impossible. And even if you got them, trying to match them was tough, but again, not impossible. "Really?" Chris asked.

"It's worth a try."

Chris tried each eye and looked up at Leah. "Nothin'."

"It was still worth a try." Leah noticed the number of spectators was growing at an amazing rate. "We need to get this body out of here. Wait, what's that around her mouth?"

Chris took a sample of it and bagged it. "It looks like glue residue, probably from duct tape. Whoever did this didn't want anyone to hear her screamin'." He scraped some off and put it in an evidence bag, where it joined the other bags.

Leah went up to the edge of the road and examined the tire tracks. Four of them looked recent. She made casts of those four.

The medical examiner from Satsuma pulled up to the edge of the lake. "Look at that," Chris said. "The Death Mobile arrives right on time!" Leah had called Norman Crabtree, the closest medical examiner to Alvin, just after calling Chris this morning. Norman walked down to the shore and took a quick look at what he was dealing with. "Those eyes are somethin' else," he said.

"You can say that again," Chris said.

"I ain't seen nothin' like it. And I been doin' this a long time."

The body was toe tagged and put in the back of the Death Mobile. An expression Leah hated more and more every time Chris used it.

The winter sun was just starting to fill the easterly sky and casting everything in an array of pinks and yellows. All Leah could think of was how much of a stark contrast that sky was compared to the eyes of the victim she had just seen loaded into the back of the Death Mobile and driven away, the sunlight winking off its back bumper and the smell of fresh winter flowers filling the air.

CHAPTER 6

Within four hours after Luanne Cooper found the body, word of the story had swept through the city, putting everyone into a state of high alert. That's one thing about living in a small town, it didn't take much to unbalance the nature of things. Leah started taking phone calls back to back from concerned citizens all wanting to know that their safety wasn't in jeopardy.

She didn't blame them. She'd tried to keep the gawkers as far away from the victim as she could, but when they turned that body over, people got a look at those eyes—and those eyes would give anyone nightmares.

The police even ran an official photograph in the *Alvin Examiner* (formerly called the *Alvin Alerter*) and on the eight o'clock news that showed the eyes. Leah figured they had to. If she was going to find this woman's killer, she was going to have to canvass with a photo, and she only had the one. There would be no way of doing it without showing the sewn-up eyes.

What the police didn't release was the writing across the woman's chest or the whittled cross Leah had found in her pocket. Police often leave things out of press releases. It's a way to differentiate the fake weirdos wanting to take credit for something they didn't do from the real weirdos who actually committed the crime.

The story hit the front page of the *Examiner,* which ran a special afternoon edition, and, of course, it was the top story in the news. Both complemented each other with the information they gave.

Both stories (the one on the television and the one in the paper) covered the same basic information. They said a body was found washed up on Willet Lake in Willet Park and that foul play was suspected. (What gave them *that* idea? You'd think that part would be pretty obvious. The woman didn't sew her *own* eyes closed.)

Leah and Chris both knew the article would likely be syndicated but prayed it wouldn't get much farther than the outskirts of Alvin. This was ridiculous. They knew the reaction to the image of the dead girl lying there with her eyes all stitched up was going to echo through the population, but neither was prepared for just how much panic it would stir up.

Ethan Montgomery called Leah into his office.

"Tell me somethin'," Ethan said, after closing the door and taking his seat.

"What's that?"

"What in the name of everythin' holy made you decide to run that picture?"

"The press wanted a photo."

"Then you say we don't have one."

"Ethan, I'm going to have to show it around if I want to find anythin' out 'bout the woman. We would just be delayin' the inevitable."

"But you'd also be avoidin' a landslide. It wouldn't all come at once like this. I've fielded at least seventy calls today, mainly just calmin' folk down."

Leah looked at the floor. "I know. Me too."

"From now on, do me a favor?" Chief Montgomery said. "Bounce any great ideas like this off of me before runnin' with 'em? Don't just confer with Chris?"

Leah met his gaze. "I can do that."

"Okay. Now go put your phone back on the hook and keep calmin' people down. We don't need a town full of hysteria."

"Okay."

Leah exited his office, flopped into her chair, and, with a slow count to three, put the receiver back on its cradle. She jumped when the phone rang a second later.

It was going to be a long day.

It didn't take long for Leah to establish a name for the victim. Curiously, it didn't come from any of the news reports but an unrelated missing person's report a few hours later the same day the body was discovered. It came from the victim's sister, Mary Lynn Carpenter, who hadn't heard from her sister Mercy Jo in a week and was worried something had happened to her. She hadn't even seen her sister's picture on the TV or anything. Once she started talking, Leah pretty quickly put two and two together.

Mary Lynn told the police the woman they had found was named Mercy Jo and that she used to live in Auburn, Alabama, with her before leaving and moving to Alvin.

"I think you need to drive down to Satsuma," Leah said.

Once they got a name for the victim, the police did their own background checks and, indeed, they concurred with what Mercy Jo's sister had told them. Mercy Jo had been a longtime resident of Alvin, moving down to the small town four years ago from where she used to live in Auburn with her sister. The police released this information and went on to say that they had nobody in custody and were actively looking for anyone who might have any evidence about the crime to come forward with details.

This is how they were able to supply the newspaper with a name to go along with the picture Ethan Montgomery said they should never have run. They soon had a picture without the eye stitches from Mary Lynn Carpenter, but it didn't reflect how Mercy Jo looked today. It was over four years old, and her body had changed dramatically. Alcohol and drugs will do that to you. And through all this, Leah's phone never stopped ringing.

Is it safe for me to go to the park with my baby?

You will find the man who did this, won't you?

I'm the one you're lookin' for. I killed her and stitched up her eyes. And I'll do it again. (This was a case where the held-back information was vital. All Leah had to ask was, "What was in her pocket?" and the man on the other end hung up. The world was full of crackpots.)

Leah was getting so fed up with calls, she left the receiver off the phone for an hour, just for a brief respite.

"She usually calls me every Thursday," Mary Lynn said once she met Leah at the medical examiner's office in Satsuma. Mary Lynn was a slender brunette with high cheekbones and looked like she'd be more at home in high heels and a designer handbag than in the old jeans and sneakers she was wearing. "But when I didn't hear from her, I just figured she was, you know, busy. But then, when I still hadn't heard from her after the weekend, I started to get worried." Mary Lynn attended a university in Auburn, studying business. When she started describing her sister, Leah's heart sunk. Leah knew why Mary Lynn hadn't gotten the call.

Mary Lynn had come down to ID the body. Luckily, Norman hadn't started the autopsy yet. But still, Leah had no idea how to prepare Mary Lynn for the shock of seeing her sister's eyes sewn shut.

"There's somethin' I need to tell you before we walk into the refrigerator room," Leah said.

"Let me guess," Mary Lynn said. "Lots of track marks? I've just been waiting for her to kill herself. She's been heavy into drugs. From what I've heard, despite what she claimed, she was gettin' worse, not better."

"Actually, I don't think we found *any* track marks. I'll have to ask Norm to be certain. But no . . . it's worse. It's somethin' the killer did. With her eyes—"

"What? What could—"

"He sewed them up."

Mary Ann's hand came to her mouth. "Who would—I . . ."

"It's okay. We can do this another time."

"I just can't imagine. Was she . . . was Mercy *alive* when he did it?"

Leah shook her head, even though it was a lie. Norman Crabtree had already told her he was quite sure the sutures were in place days before the victim was killed. But Mary Lynn didn't need to know this about her sister's last days. "No, she wouldn't have felt a thing. Are you sure you're up to this? We can wait until tomorrow?"

Actually, by tomorrow, Mercy Jo's body would be split down the center and cracked wide open. They couldn't *really* wait until tomorrow.

Leah saw Mary Lynn swallow. "N-no, no, I'm okay," she said, almost to herself. "I'm okay. Really. I'm ready for this."

They walked into the refrigerator room, where Norm was busy washing up. Mercy Jo was lying on a table, ready to be cut open.

"Oh my God," Mary Lynn said, the words catching in her throat. Leah saw tears standing in her eyes. "She's . . . she's really gone. And the eyes. They're . . ." She didn't have to finish the sentence. Leah could do it for her. *Hideous.* Nobody deserved to die this way.

"Okay, come on, let's go," Leah said, putting her arm around her.

"No," Mary Jane said, holding back Leah's lead, "let me look just a minute longer at my Mercy." She glanced up to Norman. "You found *no* track marks on her arms?"

He shook his head. "None."

"She told me she was goin' to try and get clean. I didn't . . . I didn't believe her." She was sobbing now. Leah pulled her into a hug. "She had nobody down here," Mary Lynn continued. "I could've . . ."

"There's nothin' you could've done," Leah said.

"Yes, I could've been here, I could've . . ."

"Come on, let's go."

Leah led her outside, hating this part of her job.

"Can I ask you a few questions 'bout your sister before you go, Miss Carpenter?"

"Sure," she said, her voice still shaky.

"Did she have any enemies you know of? Any boyfriends who might feel slighted by her? Anyone who might want—"

"No," Mary Lynn said, cutting her off. "Nobody like that. She was even a good drunk. She liked to make people happy." She started crying. "Why would someone do this to her?"

Leah gave her a hug. "I don't know, hon, but I plan to find out." They broke their embrace. And Leah lifted her chin until their eyes met. "Can I just ask you a few more questions? You up for it?"

Mary Jane nodded.

Leah wasn't able to get much more useful information out of the woman. Maybe it would take some time.

"Now, if you think of anythin', *anythin'* that might be even slightly applicable to this, please give me a call, okay?" Leah pulled one of her cards from her pocket and handed it to the woman.

Mary Lynn took the card, nodding. Her cheeks were tearstained. Leah had a pretty good idea that the woman's ride home was going to be a cry-fest. With a very heavy heart, Leah walked Mary Lynn to her car and watched her get on her way, heading back to Auburn and her studies, one sister less than she had yesterday.

Mercy Jo Carpenter had lived in an illegal basement suite in Cloverdale—one of the low-cost housing districts in Alvin. Mary Lynn was able to provide an address. Later, Leah went and interviewed the people Mercy Jo rented from, Roger and Sarah Quinn. They lived above her, and after convincing them she wasn't about to fine them for anything, the only real information they could provide was that Mercy Jo had a fairly healthy drinking problem. Seems like everyone knew that.

"She was also often a week late with her rent payment," the husband, Roger, had told Leah.

"That was on account of her spending all her money on booze," the wife chimed in.

So maybe she had cleaned up the drugs. Or maybe she had just changed to a different crutch. Whichever it was didn't really matter now.

Sarah Quinn let Leah into Mercy Jo's apartment. Mercy Jo was anything but neat and tidy. The place looked like a hurricane had run through it. There were empty cartons of beer everywhere. Empty vodka bottles were lined up against one wall. Leah wondered why she hadn't returned all her empty bottles. She'd have been rich.

Where there weren't bottles, there were the remnants of take-out food. Chinese cartons, pizza boxes, you name it. "Do you guys have a cockroach problem or anythin' like that?"

"No, thank the Lord," Sarah said. "This is actually the first time I've been in here for 'bout six months. I can't believe how much worse it is. I'm surprised we don't have no bug infestation or, even worse, rats."

"Once our investigation is complete, I'd get this cleaned up as soon as you can," Leah said.

That all happened yesterday, and today, Chris and Leah drove into Satsuma once again to visit the medical examiner, Norman Crabtree, this time to get his full report on Mercy Jo.

They met with Norman in the refrigerated section of the autopsy room. Leah was thankful there was no stiff on the table. The room had a strong disinfectant smell and was very cold (forty degrees, to be exact, Norman had told her on a previous visit). The floor was tiled and the room just reminded her of death. She saw the selection of tools and saws he used, and shivered. She could never be a medical examiner.

Norman told them the body couldn't have been dead more than thirty-six hours before they found it. Forty-eight at most. There was very little decomposition, and floating in that lake, the body would decompose fairly quickly.

Postmortem blood alcohol levels are fairly unreliable, but the victim's measured .40, which is near fatal, especially in someone weighing in at 135 pounds. Some research indicates that death can raise the blood alcohol level. Norman also found traces of Rohypnol, a drug better known on the street as "roofies."

"Rohypnol was developed in 1963 by a team led by Leo Sternbach at Hoffmann-La Roche," Norman explained. "Its use was initially intended to be a short-term treatment for chronic or severe insomniacs who were not responsive to other hypnotics. It is considered to be one of the most effective benzodiazepine hypnotics on a per-dose basis."

Leah thought this over. Norman practically read her mind.

"Someone wanted this woman knocked out or possibly killed

by drugs and alcohol," he said. "He must've kept her on a continual diet of alcohol and roofies."

Strangely, and to Leah's surprise, the medical examiner found no evidence of any sexual contact. Leah had expected the quickly done-up shirt pointed toward this being a crime of passion, but now it appeared that it was a crime of waterproof marker, simply baring her chest so the killer could write his obscure message.

But whom was the message for?

Chris was right. The bullet the medical examiner dug out of Mercy Jo's brain was indeed a .22 caliber round. He sent it to the Satsuma ballistics lab to have it checked out. "Twenty-two calibers are suicide rounds," he explained to Leah, "simply *because* there's no exit wound. The bullet does more damage than, say, a full-metal jacket would because it bounces around the brain hitting all different parts of it. A full-metal jacket can make a clean shot and just take out a piece of the brain, leaving enough intact to keep the victim alive."

"So you're sayin' our killer knows what he's doin'?" Leah asked.

"Would appear so."

"Find anythin' else?" Chris asked.

"Yes, ligature marks on the ankles and wrists. Wherever she was kept before she was killed, she was tied up and tied up tightly. Appears to be either thick rope or leather bands—hard to tell which. Did you find any fibers at the scene?"

"No," Leah said. "If there were any, they were washed away into the lake. Can you reckon how long she was tied up for before bein' killed?"

"The ligature marks are deep. She struggled a lot. Given that when you found her she was zonked out on alcohol and roofies, I'd say the killer was bringing her in and out of consciousness with drugs and alcohol for a while. A few days at least. More likely six or seven. I'm puttin' my money on a week."

"Why keep her alive for a week if it's not sexual?" Chris asked.

"Maybe because it *is* sexual," Leah said.

"What do you mean?"

"Maybe for *him* it is sexual. Maybe he gets off on watching her struggle. Like David Berkowitz, you know, the Son of Sam? He'd go back to his murder scenes and masturbate. For him it was purely sexual, but not *with* the victims. Maybe our killer is the same. Maybe he gets off while he watches them struggle."

Chris's eyes grew for a minute. "You're a little scary sometimes. Things you know."

"Yeah, two days ago I saw a girl with her eyes sewn shut. So did you. The whole world's a little scary."

"What about the thread in the eyelids?" Chris asked Norman.

"Size forty all-purpose black cotton thread. Size forty is thicker than standard cotton thread, which is a size fifty. The stitch pattern used was a French knot followed by loop stitches and ending with another French knot. Obviously done by someone who knows something about stitching."

Leah thought about this a minute.

A maniac tailor . . . Very dangerous . . .

This was a little too close to the psychic's prediction for comfort. An uneasy feeling filled Leah's stomach. And the number seventy-eight being important. Could this psychic actually have *predicted* this homicide? Leah shook her head clear. That was ludicrous. Besides, she said a body in darkness. This one was outside under a wharf. And then there was the sign: Welcome to Gray . . . *something.* That made no sense. They were in Alvin, not Grayland or anything like that.

"If this thread isn't a standard size," Leah asked, "do you have to go somewhere special to buy it?"

"Unfortunately, no. Any sewing supply store should sell it."

"So there's no way to trace it? Find out what brand it is, track where it came from? Who distributed it?"

"I highly doubt it."

She looked at Chris. "I guess that answers all our questions," Chris said.

"Well," Leah said, "not all our questions. Just the ones you can answer. I still have one big one that needs answerin' and I'm gonna make sure it gets answered."

"How're you gonna do that?" Norman asked.

"By huntin' down the bastard who did this."

CHAPTER 7

Carry felt the Christmas rush slipping away beneath her as she walked down Hunter Road toward Main Street. A cold breeze was on her face, and she felt her cheeks stinging, likely turning pink. The rest of her body was quite warm. She was wearing her winter jacket, a pair of knitted gloves, and a scarf that a friend knitted for her in the seventh grade. The scarf was purple with yellow lines running through it.

She couldn't wait until Christmas break. She loathed school. The only part of school she even half liked was the socializing aspect, but even that had lost her interest lately. The weird part was that she actually was fairly popular, only there were more and more kids at school, and so her percentage of popularity always seemed to be going down. Because of the new car assembly plant they built on the outskirts of town, Alvin's population kept growing. She had definitely lost ground from last year and the year before to this year. It just felt as though the older she got, the more everyone went in different directions. School was now just full of cliques, and it was too much of a bother for Carry to try and keep up with which ones were cool and which ones smelled like a cat fart.

She was sure if she *tried* to make new friends, she wouldn't have any problems. After all, she was witty and charming and had beautiful golden curls. Okay, that last one might have been a bit over the top, but she wasn't half bad to look at. Now, of course, she was thinking about what the psychic said—that she was going to meet a boy soon who would become more than a friend. She doubted that was going to happen in the next two weeks, but this possibility was the only thing Carry had to look forward to other than a great Christmas, a lonely New Year's, and then the horrific going back to school that followed all that.

The idea of a new boyfriend thrilled her. Especially if it could be someone both she and her mother liked. As hard as she could, she tried to picture in her mind how he might look. Maybe he'd be tall and muscular with black hair. She'd always liked boys with black hair. And blue eyes.

Muscles would be a definite bonus.

She realized she should've added "daydreamer" to the list of attributes she had given to herself, because she had been so busy thinking about this boy that she ran right into someone coming up the sidewalk carrying a bunch of pizza boxes.

He was a redheaded guy maybe a couple of inches taller than Carry and had on a jacket that said RAVEN LEE'S PIZZERIA. Under his open jacket, he was nicely dressed, with a gray button-down shirt and black trousers. He wore boots that looked recently shined. His clothes didn't look nearly as warm as Carry's.

"Whoa!" he yelled. He must've had at least eight large pizza boxes stacked in his hand. He tried to keep them from falling, but the two top ones slid off and landed on the sidewalk. One landed upside down and opened. The other just opened and the pizza looked a bit squashed.

"I'm so sorry," Carry said.

"At least I saved six," the boy said, smiling. Carry couldn't pin an age on him. He looked maybe sixteen.

"The other two are still . . . edible . . ." Carry said. "Just a little . . . squashed."

"Yeah," the boy said, scratching the back of his head while balancing the other six boxes on one hand. " 'Fraid we can't deliver 'em that way, though."

"I really *am* sorry."

"Oh, don't be. It was at least half my fault. I took too many at once. I couldn't really see where I was goin'."

"Want me to help you clean these off the sidewalk?" Four crows landed in a bare maple tree about ten feet away. Carry was pretty sure *they* wanted to help clean the pizza off the sidewalk more than she did.

"Actually," said the boy, "have you had lunch?"

"No, why? I was just goin' down to Main Street to see what I could find to eat. I was gettin' antsy and bored sittin' at home."

"Well, like you said, these ones on the ground are still edible, they just don't look pretty. How 'bout you share an ugly pizza lunch with me?"

Carry gave him a big smile. "I'd love to!"

"My name's Jonathon," the boy said. "Jonathon Mitchell."

"I'm Caroline, but most folk just call me Carry. Carry Teal."

"Nice to meet you, Carry." They shook hands over the squashed pizzas.

They both sat on the sidewalk on either side of the pizza disaster and ate pizza. One was ham and pineapple (which just happened to be Carry's favorite), and the other was pepperoni.

They sat there for almost half an hour and Carry began wondering about the other six pizzas. "Ain't the people you was deliverin' these other pizzas to gonna be pissed off that you're not only thirty minutes late, but their pizzas are cold?"

"It *is* cold out here, ain't it?"

"It is. I bet those pizzas are frigid by now." One of the crows from the maple hopped down to the sidewalk and gave the pizzas a sideways glance. He took three hops toward the open box. Carry and Jonathon just watched him. Carry wondered if Jonathon was going to let him take a piece if he got close enough.

"Oh, well. I hate this job anyway. I have a second job that's a lot better. So I'm kinda hopin' I get fired."

Every time a car went by, Carry had to increase the volume of her voice and then lower it again when the car was gone. It was quite annoying.

"Where's your second job?"

"I work at Shearer's cotton farm. They pay real well. The only problem is, the work is sporadic and I have to do it round goin' to school."

"Where do you go to school? I don't remember seein' you at Satsuma High or on the bus headin' there or nothin'."

"That's where I go. I'm in the eleventh grade. Don't take the bus, though. I got my own car. Shit box car."

"So you're—" Carry looked up. "Sixteen?"

"Seventeen," Jonathon said, ignoring her embarrassment at displaying her lack of math skills. "You gonna eat any more of this pizza?"

"No, I'm stuffed. It was *really* good, though."

"No, it wasn't. Our pizza tastes like the inside of a donkey. It was terrible."

Carry laughed. "You're a funny guy."

"Am I? Funny enough to give your phone number to?"

The crow hopped closer. He was only about three feet away. "You gonna let him have a piece if he gets close enough to take one?"

"I dunno," Jonathon replied. "I haven't decided yet. Besides, I am far more interested in the answer to my last question."

Carry laughed. The inside of her head was a swirl of colors. Could this be the boy Madame Crystalle told her about? "Sure, I'll give you my number," she said. "Do you have some paper and a pen?"

"Of course. I deliver pizzas. Gotta have paper and a pen." He pulled out a little pad and a fountain-tipped pen from his front pocket.

"That looks like a nice pen," Carry said.

"It is. I like to write everythin' I write in calligraphy."

"Why?" A cold breeze picked up and blew down Hunter Road. Carry barely noticed.

"Because I can. Why develop a skill and then not use it? It would be useless. Usin' your skills gives you power. Even if the skill is somethin' dumb like bein' able to write in calligraphy."

Carry thought this over. "I like that. It makes sense on some really weird level."

"A lot of stuff I'll tell you is like that. It won't make sense until you rearrange the world to fit it. Then it will be perfectly at home."

Carry told him her number, looking at his red hair glistening in the cold afternoon sun as he wrote it on his pad. He was a strange boy, this Jonathon Mitchell. She'd never met anyone exactly like him. But one thing was clear—she thought she really liked him.

"What's the best time to call?" he asked.

"Any time before ten o'clock."

"What about your supper, when is that?"

"My mother is the town detective. We usually make our own supper and just eat it in front of the television, so you wouldn't be interruptin' anythin'."

"We? Who's we?"

"Me and my little brother, Abe. He's the reason you can't call past ten. He goes to bed at ten. He's okay, although sometimes he acts like an ass face."

Jonathon laughed. "I have a little sister. I think you just gave me the perfect name for her. Until now, I'd been callin' her Frustration Girl, but ass face gets so much more across with just two little words."

"Yeah, I like it. I'll give you permission to use it. Not like it's copyrighted or anythin'." She laughed.

Jonathon pushed the box containing the leftover four pieces of pizza toward the crow. It got scared and flew back into the maple, but within five minutes all four of them were down in the box basking in the delight of Raven Lee's pizza.

"I always knew crows had no taste," Jonathon said. "Anyway, I really gotta get these pizzas delivered. It certainly was an incredible pleasure to meet you, Carry."

"Same for me. Call me soon. *Please.* I always feel like a princess locked up in some tower unable to get away. We can go out and do stuff. Even before Christmas break if you want. I would love to do *anything* between now and after New Year's."

"Sounds like you just *love* Satsuma High."

"It's not any particular school I hate, it's *all* schools. And it's not that I do badly at it, my marks are usually quite good. I just hate goin' to school."

"I think I understand. Anyway, see you later, Destroyer of Food."

"See *you* later," Carry said, "Deliverer of the Ice Pizza."

Jonathon stood and Carry followed suit. Then he said, "Do you mind if I hug you?"

She felt her face flush. "No, not at all. I'd like that, in fact."

He gave her a nice, tender hug that lasted at least ten seconds. Carry felt her insides melt in his arms. When he broke free of their embrace, he picked up the remaining six pizza boxes and said good-bye with a smile before he continued up Hunter Road, whistling as he went.

Carry watched him until he disappeared over the hill, disbelieving what had just happened. Madame Crystalle's premonition had come true. She'd met a boy. And he may not have black hair and muscles—he had blue eyes and was extremely funny and cute. And in the end, extremely funny and cute wins out over muscles any day.

She was a little leery about introducing him to her mother after what happened last time her mother met a boy she was seeing. Madame Crystalle may have said her mother would be okay with it, but when your last experience ended with your mother pointing a loaded firearm at your boyfriend's private parts and threatening to blow his balls off, you tend to become a little skeptical.

But Carry didn't care. She still had a stomach full of air balloons from Jonathon's hug. She felt herself falling into a big hole, like the one Alice did in *Through the Looking-Glass*. Only, Carry wasn't sure she'd ever want to get out again.

CHAPTER 8

Leah stood in her kitchen trying to think about what to make for supper. She was home unusually early, so she wanted to take advantage of it. Uncle Hank had gone to Satsuma for the day to do a little shopping, and the kids were out, so it was just her and her thoughts—always a bad combination.

She still couldn't get her last view of Mercy Jo out of her mind. Leah hated autopsy rooms, and she felt like she was really starting to let Mercy Jo down with the investigation. Leah was running out of leads, and she was running out of them fast.

Putting on some coffee, she sat down at the kitchen table and thought about all the things they *didn't* know about this case. Questions like, *Why did the killer keep her alive for a week with her eyes sewn shut, basically torturing her before finally killing her?* Was this symbolic in some way?

Why was she left with a sculpted cross in her pocket? Again, was this a symbol of some sort? Or a gift? Or did it hold some bigger meaning?

What is so important about the words drawn across her chest? This one really bothered Leah. She felt certain they were there for one reason and one reason only: to taunt the police. And that meant this was someone who should be on the radar. In a small town, you don't run into people this devious very often. She should've known by now *just from the phrase* where it came from.

Why was there no sex involved? Why keep the woman alive if you aren't having sex with her? What makes the killer decide it's time to actually kill her?

She let her mind wander over the clues Madame Crystalle gave her as though they were a checklist, and came to one that hadn't really been any help as of yet.

The number seventy-eight is important. . . .

That was a weird one. It seemed like such a random number. What could seventy-eight point to? It wasn't a caliber size for a bullet; at least, nothing standard. It wasn't even right to be something like a social security number or a bank account number—it was too short.

Could it be somebody's age? Maybe a street address? In Alvin there were probably many seventy-eights on different streets. That certainly would narrow things down, but still leave a large handful of suspects.

It could be a speed measurement of a vehicle.

It could be someone's age.

It was one thing: frustrating as all hell.

Leah continued wracking her brain. Like most of Madame Crystalle's clues, out of context, this one was pretty much meaningless. There were just too many possibilities.

"You look a little lost in thought," Uncle Henry said as Leah was pouring her coffee. His voice made her jump.

He laughed. "Sorry, wasn't tryin' to scare you." He was carrying a big brown bag full of stuff he bought while in town.

"How has your day been?" Leah asked him.

"By the looks of things, better than yours," he said. "What's up?"

She poured Uncle Henry a coffee of his own and handed it to him before taking hers to the kitchen table and sitting down. "Oh, it's this case, Hank. It seems like the whole thing is one step forward, two steps back. Every time I think I'm getting on top of it, things suddenly get slippery as a fish and I lose it again."

"Keep asking questions," he said.

"That's all I *have* is questions."

"That's all you *need.* You're a goddamn good detective. Asking questions is your job. The universe's job is providing you with answers to them."

Leah thought about this and took a deep, heavy breath that turned into a sigh. "You believe that?"

"I do."

"Okay, thanks for the pep talk. Believe it or not, I think you gave me my second wind. I needed that."

"Much obliged, my friend. Much obliged."

CHAPTER 9

Lately, me and Dewey had discovered the world of Dungeons & Dragons, quite possibly the best invention known to man. It actually came out in 1977, but we only found out about it when the local comic shop started carrying it. Now they hold tournaments there and everything.

The game is different from a normal game in that there isn't any board. You play the game in your head using your imagination. One person is designated as the dungeon master and he runs the game while the other players explore dungeons and fight monsters and collect treasure. I was always the dungeon master when we played. That meant I ran the game while Dewey played it.

The players take on different personas and have different strengths and weaknesses in different categories, like Strength, Wisdom, Dexterity, things like that. It's not as complicated as it sounds. You keep track of everything on a Character Record Sheet. Dewey always played the same character: an elven fighter named Malchunar. I had no idea where the name came from.

"I reckon this would be a lot better if we had figurines," Dewey said.

Some people play with small metallic figurines that you can

paint. The comic shop also had painting contests. Some of their figurines were incredibly detailed with their painting.

"Dewey, I had to save up two months' worth of my allowance to buy this set. Be happy with it. The next thing I'm gettin' is the *Dungeon Masters Guide* and the *Player's Handbook.*"

"What 'bout the *Monster Manual.*"

"Oh, I forgot 'bout that. I'll need that, too."

"This game's gonna cost you a small fortune," Dewey observed.

"This is why I think you should buy some of the stuff."

"With what? I don't even *get* an allowance. Besides, ain't all those books for *advanced* D and D?"

"Yeah, but I reckon we're ready to move up."

"I further reckon this game would be tons more fun with more players. Even just one or two."

"I agree. I wonder what Bo Burkett's doin'?"

Dewey laughed.

"What?"

"Bo Burkett?"

"What's wrong with him?"

"Bo Burkett couldn't find no cheese in the middle of a dairy farm. He'd never understand this game."

"The game isn't that hard."

"Would be for Bo Burkett."

"I don't think Bo Burkett is dumb. His marks seem okay in school. He's in some of my classes," I said.

"Maybe you couldn't find no cheese in the middle of a dairy farm neither, then."

"Where did you get that expression? I'm not even a hundred percent sure they'd have cheese at a dairy farm."

"Well, you and Bo Burkett should play together, then. I'll play somethin' else."

"You're weird. Anyway, where were we? I think next time we play I'm going to have some NPCs go out with you." An NPC is a nonplaying character controlled by the dungeon master.

Carry walked into the room. "What are you two turds doin' now?" She picked up one of the dragon dice off the table. It was the ten-sided one. "Hey, what's this? It looks kinda neat." D&D comes with a bunch of different dice, all strange and exciting. There's a four-sided (which looks like a pyramid), a six-sided (which was a normal die), an eight-sided, a ten-sided, and a twenty-sided.

We were currently in the middle of a game. Dewey was in the dark recesses of a dungeon where torches lined the walls, stuck in a very short and narrow passage. He had just come up to a door on the western side of the hallway. The torches threw weird shadows in their flickering light.

"Hmm," he said. "I'm betting the door's a trap."

I asked Carry for the ten-sided die she'd grabbed. "Can you please just let us play?" I begged.

"What? I finally show an interest in somethin' you're doin' and you want me to just leave you alone?"

"You'd never understand this game," Dewey said.

"Like, whatever," Carry said back. "If y'all can play, I am sure a cat could play it." She gave me back the die and continued on into the living room and turned on the television.

I rolled the ten-sided die.

"Why'd you just roll that die?" Dewey asked.

"It's a secret." I actually rolled it to see if any wandering monsters would be coming down the hallway toward him if he didn't open the damn door. Wandering monsters are monsters that aren't already set in the game. They just appear at random, by specific dice rolls.

"Hmm," he said again. "I still can't decide on this door. The last time I opened a door and you rolled a die right before, there were four basilisks behind it waiting to eat me. This time my strength is 'bout half as much as it was then. Four basilisks would *kill* me."

I rolled an eight-sided die. *Bingo.*

"Quit rollin' that damn die!" Dewey snapped.

"You hear a rumble from down the hall."

"Which way?"

"You can't tell yet. Too many echoes off the stone walls and floor."

Dewey sighed. "Okay, I open the damn door."

"Just as you do, a gelatinous cube comes into view. It's coming down the hallway from the direction you was headed."

"Okay, I get into the room and close the door." Gelatinous cubes are like the garbage collectors of dungeons. They are like Jell-O and they take up the entire hall as they squish their way through caverns, picking up whatever they can. They aren't very pleasant.

"All right, you successfully outwitted the cube, which since they have no brains isn't such a feat. You are in a very old bedroom. There is dust covering everything and it smells very old. The room is about twelve feet across and maybe ten deep. It is dark because the only light is through some slits in the ceiling letting the sun leak down inside. There is a bed, a chest of drawers, and a very old and ornate chest at the end of the bed. The chest has a padlock on it as big as your fist."

"Oooh," Dewey said. "We like chests. I strike it with my sword."

I rolled a ten-sided die. "The padlock doesn't open, but you make a tremendous clang."

Dewey looked at me. "How sturdy is that door coming into this room? Is it locked?"

"You left it unlocked," I said, and rolled an eight-sided die.

Chapter 10

The forensics reports from Mobile and the ballistics report from Satsuma came into the Alvin Police Station at near on exactly the same time. Leah sat at her desk and decided to pull the information from Mobile out first. It was in a large manila envelope and contained only a thin, two-page document that she laid in front of her on the table.

Outside, an Eastern meadowlark flew by just as a few drops of rain began hitting the street.

The first thing Leah read about was the nail shavings. No blood was found beneath them, and there was no external DNA. Mercy Jo Carpenter gave every indication that she went willingly or was highly inebriated. Leah guessed it was the second. Of course, there was always the possibility that this was done by someone Mercy Jo knew.

What *was* found under the nails was a high concentration of cedar shavings and some small particles of dirt and soil. Going by the nutrient and contaminated content, composition, trace elements, and acidity of the soil, it matched the same sort of soil you'd find in the northern parts of Alvin. It definitely didn't come from Willet Lake.

With a heavy sigh, Leah turned to the next page of the document.

The shoe casts she had made came back with three different types of running shoes and one type of loafer. She hadn't bothered to send the cast she made of Luanne Cooper's shoe prints.

The sneakers were a man's size-eight Reeboks, a woman's size-seven Nikes, a man's size-seven Nikes, and the loafers a man's size-ten Hush Puppies. Leah gave another big sigh. These weren't going to be much use in catching the killer. That pretty much covered everyone in Alvin, and there was nothing stopping a killer from wearing a shoe too big for him.

The last thing she looked at was the information garnered from the casts made by the tire tracks they found in the mud up by the side of the road. They were almost all from trucks. Chevys and Fords mainly. Anywhere from a 1981 to a 1986. There was one set that could be from a Toyota, but the lab was unsure because they were an off-brand that would fit any vehicle.

Near on everyone in Alvin drove trucks. These could belong to anyone. Nothing in this report was really going to help narrow things down to find the killer.

Leah ground her teeth. It was a habit she had and something she did when she was frustrated. Setting the information from Mobile aside, she opened up the ballistics report from Satsuma.

The slug was a .22 short caliber, and ballistics' best guess was that it was shot from a rather ancient handgun. One of the original Beretta Model 950 Jetfires, a model that has been manufactured by the gun company since the early 1950s.

The report explained that the Beretta Jetfire is a simple blowback pistol with a single-action trigger mechanism and tip-up barrel. The frame is made out of aluminum alloy; the slide and barrel are carbon steel. Early models did not have a safety lever, employing a half-cock notch on the hammer instead.

The .22 caliber magazine has an eight-round capacity; nine if the first round is chambered. Because the pistol lacks a shell extractor, it relies instead on blowback pressure to clear shell casings. Misfires are easily removed manually by tipping up the barrel and prying them out.

The weapon was intended to be simple and reliable and fit in a pocket. It's a semiautomatic pistol, building on a long line of small compact pistols manufactured by Beretta for self-defense.

"Not for shooting directly into the temple of women bound up with their eyes stitched up," Leah mused aloud.

The report went on to say that the .22 short calibers it takes are not very powerful, but when well-placed can be lethal. The accuracy of the pistol is adequate enough, but only for short ranges.

Leah couldn't figure out why the killer would use such a gun when there were so many other more obvious choices around. Did he have sentimental ties to it? Had he used it before? Was this not his first murder?

If this wasn't his first murder, she might be able to track down others. But not using the same MO. At least not in Alvin. She'd remember another victim with those eyes. As it was, she'd be finding herself remembering these ones for the rest of her life.

"Judging from the slug we found in the victim's skull, our shooter is using original bullets, or at least very old ones. I'd date the one I found back to the early fifties, possibly as late as the midsixties," Norman, the medical examiner, said to Leah.

Leah couldn't help her mind from going back to what the psychic said.

A maniac tailor . . . Someone dangerous . . . Welcome to Gray . . . something. Again, it certainly wasn't Welcome to Alvin.

Like everything else, forensics was unable to detect any latent fingerprints on the slug or anywhere on the body. The crime lab in Mobile came up with the same big ball of nothing. This killer was pretty organized. So organized, it was starting to piss Leah off.

And outside, the rain continued to fall.

CHAPTER 11

Leah decided to check the one place she figured she might find people who knew Mercy Jo: the Six-Gun Saloon on the western outskirts of Alvin. It was just over the city limits and sort of corralled the city's slum area, with Oakdale Road taking up the other side on an angle.

The rain had picked up as Leah walked into the establishment that, as the name gave away, was a country bar. At least that was the idea. The floor was covered in peanuts and peanut shells. The bar was circular and in the center of the room. A dance floor wrapped around one side with booths along the edge of the place. Tables filled the other side. By the looks of things, the bar did a pretty good business. Chairs at the bar itself were mostly filled with women, most alone, some with guys who looked like they were on the prowl.

Leah pushed her way through to the barmaid, who wore a tag that said MARGARET. "Hi, Margaret," Leah said, raising her voice above "Crazy" by Patsy Cline. "My name is Leah Teal. I'm the police detective here in Alvin."

Margaret stopped wiping a glass and gave Leah the once-over. Margaret was a large black woman who wore a dress that had the look of her being poured into a glass and she'd forgotten to say when. She had very large breasts, black hair to her shoulders, and enough makeup for three people. Her fingernails were very long and very pink. So were her lips. Pink, that is. Not so much long.

"What can you possibly want with me?" she asked.

"Found a body washed up on Willett Lake. Have a hunch she might have been a regular here. Wonderin' if you could tell me anythin' 'bout her."

"And what makes you think she'd be a regular here?"

Some guy down the bar was getting restless to buy his new "girlfriend" a drink and started whistling for Margaret's attention. Margaret turned, and said, "If I was you, I would make that my last whistle or the next time you do it, you'll be doin' it outta your ass."

The guy quit whistling.

Margaret set down the glass she'd wiped clean, picked up another, and began wiping some more.

"Well," Leah said, "from what we can tell, she was a loner and a heavy drinker, and there aren't too many places in Alvin that—"

"You're sayin' she was probably a prostitute and not too many places in Alvin cater to hookers. That's okay, Miss Leah, just lay out your cards. We're all grown-ups here."

"*Detective* Teal, if you don't mind. And I wasn't meanin' no disrespect, Margaret."

"I know you wasn't. I'm just a busy lady without time to dick around and make things all clean and sterile. Who we talkin' 'bout?"

"Mercy Jo Carpenter."

Margaret stopped wiping the glass and thought this over. "Mercy Jo," she said to herself a few times. "Sounds vaguely familiar. If she was a workin' girl or a stripper, she probably went by a stage name. You don't happen to have that, do you? Or a photo?"

Leah sighed. She had a photo, but it was four years old. Other than that, she had a newer one, but it wasn't one she wanted to show unless she *had* to. "Can you ask anyone else if they might know of her?"

"Only other person other than me that's in here nearly every moment we're open is Gus Coleman, old man behind me."

Leah looked. The man must've been eighty. He wore a fedora on his head and a cardigan sweater. "Oh, Gus," Margaret called out without turning.

"Yes, my love?" he called back.

"Remember anybody comin' in or workin' here goin' by the name of Mercy Jo . . . what was her name, hon?"

"Carpenter," Leah said.

"Carpenter?" she called out more loudly to Gus.

"Sort of rings a bell, but I can't really place it. Why? Who's askin'?"

"I'm friggin' askin'. Go back to your beer."

After a long pause, Leah decided to go with the newer picture. It was so much different from the older one. "I do have a photograph, but I have to warn you, it could be a mite shocking to you. Remember, we found her dead."

"I've seen dead bodies, love. When you live a life like me, you've pretty much seen it all. Don't worry, I'm a big girl."

"I'm not so certain you'll have seen this. The killer . . . he . . . he sewed her eyes closed."

Margaret winced. "You mean with needle and thread?"

Leah nodded.

"Now you *have* to show me. That's just gross."

Leah pulled out the photo and showed it to Margaret, who took one look at the eyes, and said, "You're right. *Nothing* prepares you for *that*. I think I'm gonna puke." She still hadn't looked away, though.

"Do you recognize her otherwise?"

"Autumn Rain," she said, her hand visibly shaking. "She used to strip at the Rabbit Room, takin' off her top while guys stuffed ten-dollar bills in her bikini bottoms. Lately she'd been hangin' out here. Tell you one thing—the woman could drink. I'd seen her drink three quarters of a bottle of tequila one night just to avoid goin' home with the guy payin' for her drinks. She wound up leavin' him passed out in the booth."

"Did she use drugs?"

Margaret shrugged. "None of my business. But most of the girls in here full-time don't. Usually if you're into drugs, you have trashy hotel rooms you live in and just buy your booze and take it home with you. Sometimes you find a john on the way, sometimes you don't. If you don't, you party until the money runs out; then you walk Oakdale until you hook your next fish."

Leah wrote all this down in her pad. "You gonna be okay? From the photo, I mean."

"As okay as anyone could be after seein' that. Do you know who did it?"

"That's what I'm tryin' to find out. So, Mercy Jo was a hooker?"

"To be completely honest? Can't be sure, but I have seen her leave with men from time to time. Just because she strips, doesn't make her necessarily play. But sometimes she'd leave and come back alone only to go for round two. She was either a hooker or just really friendly. A lot of the girls are just nice to guys and the guys are nice to them in return, buyin' them things. They don't consider themselves as hookers."

"It makes no difference to this case; the only thing I'm interested in is finding the son of a bitch who did this to her."

"Well, I hope you do. If there's anythin' I can do to help, please let me know." The guy down at the bar whistled at her again. She turned to him, making a fist. "You don't wanna get me mad. Not only will you be tossed out, you'll be tossed out with no teeth." He stopped whistling.

"You've been more than helpful," Leah said. "Do you have a phone number I can reach you at?"

"Your best bet is right here." She handed Leah a business card for the bar. It said MARGARET PERKINS, OWNER. "I'm pretty near the only one ever working bar. Occasionally my brother, Tom, subs in for me, but that's quite unusual."

"Thank you. I'll probably end up callin' you with questions before this case is over."

"Please do." Another whistle came her way. "And please get outta here before I beat the shit out of that guy and you arrest me for it."

CHAPTER 12

Me and Dewey took a break from all our D&D playing and sat in the backyard for a picnic lunch my mother put together for us before leaving for work this morning. It consisted of peanut butter and jelly sandwiches, pears, cheese and crackers, a slice of pecan pie, and a box of orange juice. As far as picnic lunches went, this one was pretty good.

"You know," Dewey said, and as soon as he said it I winced. Any sentence coming out of Dewey's mouth that starts with "You know . . ." generally has a ridiculous ending. Just like all the other times, this time didn't let me down either.

"You know," he said, "I reckon I could be a pretty good psychic. At least as good as that Madame Crystalle. I reckon she's a phony."

"And what are you basing this bit of wisdom on?" I asked.

"Just what she said. First off, everythin' she told your ma. Anyone can come up with that kind of stuff. Stuff like: I see a crazy T-shirt designer. He blinds with his designs. The number six hundred is important. Twenty-five people might die in two days if you don't do somethin' with the number six hundred. Or is it the number six? I can't really tell. It might even be an upside-down nine.

"Wait, I see a name. It's Fart. No, it just looks like Fart. No, it just smells like Fart." He started laughing. I couldn't help myself. I started laughing, too.

"Now it's racin' away," he continued. "No, I'm racin' away backward down a road and passin' by a road sign with two flags. One says left, one says right. The road sign says Welcome to Al Pa . . . Pa . . . Pa . . . Al Pacino." He laughed so hard orange juice came out of his nose.

"Okay," I said. "I get your point. Still, my mom has been usin' the information Madame Crystalle gave her to solve a crime."

"It's just a fluke."

"What do you mean?"

"She just happened to find a crime that fit the vague descriptions that Madame Crystalle gave her. I mean, come on, Abe. Think 'bout Carry's fortune. She reckoned Carry was smart in school. Have you ever *seen* one of her report cards?"

"Can't say that I have."

"Well, she certainly ain't smart *out* of school. I can't imagine the situation changing once she gets behind a desk. And, okay, so she called Carry sarcastic, but *everyone* knows Carry's sarcastic, so that really wouldn't have been hard to figure out ahead of time. She also said Carry had wit. What kind of a joke is that? Carry is a *dim*wit, I'll give her *that* along with the sarcasm. Carry's sarcastic like most people walk on two legs. I liked that she said Carry didn't have many friendships, but the problem is that Carry *is* popular, so that's just another one she got wrong."

"You're starting to sway me in your direction," I said. And he was. Everything she'd said about Carry, now that Dewey was retelling it, really wasn't so accurate after all.

"And she said Carry had a good heart," he laughed. "What kind of person with a good heart makes her brother paint her toenails once a week all through summer break just because he asked her to help make some wooden swords?"

"You got a point there," I said, feeling my face redden in embarrassment. I still wanted to kill Carry for that one.

"What else did she say?" Dewey asked me.

"That Carry gets lonely."

He laughed again. "She's got thirteen channels' worth of friends constantly visiting her in the living room when she's not out shoppin' with her real ones. She doesn't get lonely. She gets annoying. That was the word that Madame Crystalle would have seen if she was a *real* psychic."

"Yeah, even Carry told her she didn't get lonely and Madame Crystalle argued with her, telling her she covered it with sarcasm," I said.

"And then came the big one—the proof that Madame Crystalle doesn't have any 'super psychic powers' or anythin' like that. When she said she saw a boy for Carry in the immediate future. Well, far as I'm concerned, the immediate future has come and gone, and I ain't seen one single boy show up at the door for Carry."

I thought this over. "You're right. Madame Crystalle *is* a fraud. We have to tell my mom!"

"Sure. She'll figure it out eventually on her own, though," Dewey said. "My point is that I think *I* could be a better psychic than Madame Crystalle and make some good money doing it. They called *eight* psychics before they found one that wasn't completely booked the entire two weeks before Christmas."

"You don't know the first thing 'bout telling the future."

"I can learn. I'm gonna get me some tarot cards."

"With what?" I asked. "You ain't got no money."

"Do too. I got twenty dollars from my granny for my birthday last year. I figure with Christmas right around the corner, I'll get twenty more, so now it's like free money. The twenty I got from Gran should be enough for a deck of cards and a book on how to do it. Feel like ridin' your bike to the Brookside Mall?"

"I guess," I said. "It's kind of entertainin' watchin' you waste your money on stupid purchases."

"Just you wait. Pretty soon I'll be rich and people will be bookin' appointments for me to tell 'em what's gonna happen to 'em and what lucky numbers they gotta watch out for and what kind of maniacs might blind 'em."

Turned out the Barton's Books in the Brookside Mall sold only one type of tarot card and it wasn't the ones with the super-cool dragons on them like Madame Crystalle had. These were called Rider-Waite cards and had images of people. They were oversized and barely fit in Dewey's palm. Even though they weren't as neat as the other ones, Dewey bought them anyway, along with a book on how to read them. The book was called *Mystical Tarot.*

Dewey couldn't wait to get home and start studying how to use them to tell the future. "I'm gonna be so rich," he kept saying.

"You're gonna be so bored," I kept replying, but he ignored me.

"You're just jealous cuz you never thought of this idea first."

"Yeah," I said. "That's it."

CHAPTER 13

I am pretty used to answering the phone at my house on account of nine times out of ten? It's for me. And nine times out of nine, it's Dewey calling to see what I'm up to or to ask me some weird question about nuclear physics or something that he really has no interest or understanding of, but only wants to sound smart.

So when the phone rang this afternoon, I got up from where I was sitting on the floor by Carry's feet—she was taking up the entire sofa and we were watching *The Partridge Family,* a show *she* picked—and ran to answer it.

I was quite surprised by the response on the other end after I said hello.

"Is Carry home?"

It was a boy's voice. He sounded a bit nervous. Boys never called our house for Carry, so I wasn't about to let this one go by unnoticed. It was just too bad my mother hadn't been home; then I could've really worked her over with it. "Oh, Carry!" I called out to the living room. "Phone's for you! It's a booooy."

She was at that phone faster than any deer you've ever seen in any forest. I couldn't believe the speed with which she leaped off that sofa. She was just a blur.

"Hello?" she asked anxiously.

"Oh, hi, Jonathon. Nice to see you—er, *hear*—you again. Can you hang on for one sec?"

She covered up the receiver on the phone, and said to me, "Can you get out of this room and give me some privacy, ass face? Or I swear to God, I'll kill you when this call is over."

I had never seen Carry so serious in my entire life. I decided to heed her warning. Carry could have a rough side, and I'd rather not be attacked by a fifteen-year-old tiger high-school student when her call was over. Some things just weren't worth the pain they caused. This one was close, but still, in the end, I decided to leave her alone.

She was talking pretty loud, though. I could tell she was excited. So I turned the TV down about halfway and heard most of Carry's side of the conversation anyway. "Sure, I'd love to go for a walk," she said. "No, I can leave right now. My mom won't care." And then, "Yeah, we can meet where we had the pizza catastrophe."

What the heck was a "pizza catastrophe"? I wondered.

"Okay, see you in about twenty minutes," she said, and hung up the phone.

"Who's Jonathon?" I asked while Carry put on her boots.

"None of your business, ass face."

"Where did you meet him?"

She lifted her eyes to me. "Again, none of your business."

"How old is he? Mom's gonna ask me and I'm gonna say he sounded about twenty-two because I reckon that's how old he sounded on the phone."

She exhaled deeply. "He's seventeen. You better not say anythin' to Mom 'bout this."

"She's gonna ask where you are."

"I'm gonna leave her a note sayin' I went for a walk with a friend. Which is the God's honest truth."

She struggled into her winter coat. "What's a 'pizza catastrophe'?" I asked.

"Did you eavesdrop on my *entire* conversation? You really *are* an ass face."

She tore a piece of paper out of her pad of artwork paper that was still sitting in the kitchen by the phone and quickly wrote our mother a letter:

> *Dear Mother,*
> *I went for a walk with a friend. Shouldn't be any later than five or six.*
> *Carry*

"Make sure Mom sees that, okay? And no adding any embellishments to it, or I will seriously kill you."

"Okay," I said. I thought it sounded like a good trade: my life for not embellishing.

Then she left out the back door, practically skipping as she went.

The first thing I did was call Dewey. "Guess what?" I said.

"What?"

"Madame Crystalle's not a fraud."

"What do you mean?"

"A boy just called here for Carry. She's gone to meet him for a walk," I said.

"No way."

"Way."

"Holy cow. This changes everything."

Now he had me worried. "What does it change, Dewey?"

"It means I can develop *real* psychic powers."

"No, it don't. You ain't Persian."

"I don't think you have to be."

"Well, you ain't smart neither."

"We'll see. I gotta go. Been studyin' my cards like crazy."

He hung up and all I could think was that I just hoped this boyfriend turned out better than the last time Carry got herself one.

Jonathon was waiting on the exact spot they had their squashed pizza lunch when Carry made it down Hunter Road to meet him. She had spotted his red hair from nearly a block away. "Sorry I'm late," she said. "I had to threaten my little brother with his life because he's such a tool."

"What do you mean?" Jonathon said, laughing.

"He threatened to tell my mother he didn't know how old you were but when he answered the phone you sounded twenty-two."

"That's hilarious. He sounds like a pretty smart kid." Jonathon was wearing a brown bomber jacket. And he had on denim jeans that were nice and tight, along with a pair of Converses that looked like they'd gone through enough hikes in their life that it was time to put them down and out of their miseries.

"That's smart to you?" Carry asked. "That's the dumbest thing in the world. He'd have to get all his teeth replaced after I hit him with the baseball bat." Carry noticed most of the pizza mess was gone, but there was still a faded stain there. It looked sort of like the blood splatter and other evidence still present from a murder scene after it had been cleaned up. "So what do you wanna do?"

"I thought we were gonna go for a walk," Jonathon said. He looked like he was dressed very warmly this time, with his jacket and all. The jacket made him look especially scrumptious, Carry thought.

"Okay, where to?" she asked.

"I was thinking there's some nice trails down around Bullfrog Creek, or we could go up to Cloverdale."

"Bullfrog Creek sounds nice. As long as we stay away from Skeeter Swamp."

"Why's that?"

"Do you remember the murdered fourteen-year-old girl last year who turned up beneath a willow beside that swamp?"

"The Cornstalk Killer stuff?"

"Yeah, well, my mom worked the case. I still get nightmares from it."

"Oh. Are you sure Bullfrog Creek's okay, then? It's awfully close to Skeeter Swamp."

"Oh, it should be fine. As long as I don't see that willow tree that body was left left under."

"Okay."

They began walking down Hunter Road and not five minutes had gone by before Jonathon reached down and took Carry's hand, interlacing his fingers with hers. She felt her heart start to pound against her ribs. "I wonder what my mom would say if she knew I was going for a walk in the woods with a strange boy I don't really know. She *is* a police officer, you know."

"Probably somethin' like, I hope he's not a serial killer," Jonathon said. But the way he said it put Carry slightly on edge. There was no laughter behind it. It was almost like he wasn't kidding.

CHAPTER 14

Leah returned to the crime scene, not really expecting to find anything new—it was just something in her gut that pulled her that way. It was late afternoon and the park was pretty empty. She walked along the wharf they had found Mercy Jo's body beneath and talked to herself as she did. She realized quickly what she was really trying to do was put herself in Mercy's shoes or even the murderer's. Try and figure out how it felt to be either of them. It was much easier pretending to be Mercy Jo than it was pretending to be the killer. Even adding in that Mercy went through such an ordeal, the thought of being a cold-blooded killer just made her shiver.

The police tape still cordoned off the site and she was forced to step under it in order to get in close to where the body had been. Her feet were in standard-issue police boots, but the rest of her clothes were civilian.

Despite knowing all the forensic evidence had already been nabbed, she was careful with the scene anyway. Some habits die hard.

First, she sat herself down in the sand and clay beside the wharf where the body was discovered in the shadow of the wooden pilings and slats. "So how did it go down? What did I, Mercy Jo, do differently that night than on *most* nights? What made him pick me?"

Leah stood and climbed out from under the wharf and walked

along the top. The sun gently touched the water of the lake, dancing gently on its pallid surface in emerald greens and sapphire blues. The trees lining the park's edge (most of them evergreens) looked beautiful this time of year, but Leah couldn't shake the shiver she had running through her.

"So I got out of bed late and decided to head to the place where everybody knows my name. Fair enough. Life throws me curve balls that are actually lemons, so I make martinis out of them. Only on this night I maybe make a few more than usual. Makes me an easy target.

"Guy walks into the Six-Gun Saloon and spots me, obviously alone. Maybe I'm a bit melancholy, a little maudlin. Guy muscles up to where I'm sitting and throws me some pathetic line like, 'Hey beautiful, what's a nice broad like you doin' sittin' in a place like this all by yourself? Let me buy you a drink.' And of course, I do, because that's what I've always done.

"Only this drink is different. It looks like the rest of the ones I've had all night; it even tastes the same as the ones I've been drinking all night. But he's crushed some drugs into it to make sure I'll be completely out of it in the next twenty minutes.

"Twenty minutes later, he's helping me outside and into his car, telling anyone who happens to glance our way that I'm a featherweight drunk and he shoulda stopped me at three."

Leah stopped and watched the sun sparkle in the water. The reflection off the lake was nothing short of breathtaking and the word filled her mind: breathtaking. Breath taking. That's what this man did to Mercy. He took her final breaths away.

"By now, I'm so out of it, I can't even fight him off. I don't even *know to* fight him off. So I get into his car and he drives me . . . where? To his house? No, that would be too chancy. He drives me somewhere else. Somewhere secluded, but not too far away. Some little hidey-hole away from home he's gonna stash me away somewhere around Alvin."

Leah walked farther down the deck. "I occasionally come to my senses for brief moments, and in those moments, I'm scared. What does he want, sex? I get to wherever it is he's taking me and decide to give him whatever he wants so I can just leave and go home. But he doesn't want sex, and he certainly doesn't want me going home."

Behind Leah, there's some screams. Startled, she turned to see a group of kids playing Frisbee in the afternoon's crystal sunlight. She continued her train of thoughts pretending she really was in Mercy's shoes that night.

"Instead, he ties my wrists and ankles very tightly and puts me somewhere in his home away from home. Likely, he leaves me left lying on my back with my wrists tied behind me. Then he brings out the unimaginable: the sewing kit. And, even though I may be drugged and drunk, it doesn't stop the pain as he carefully stitches both of my eyes closed. In fact, my screaming becomes too much for him and he slaps a piece of duct tape over my mouth to keep me quiet."

Leah was growing more and more impatient with the clues she had to this case. They didn't add up. She sat down on the end of the wharf cross-legged and looked back toward the park where mothers were nursing babies, children were being pushed on swings, and the Frisbee game was still in full play. "It doesn't make any sense," she said. "Why doesn't he want to have sex with me?"

The writing on the body, according to the medical examiner, likely came postmortem. But he didn't just let Mercy Jo die. He kept her alive for six or seven days on a constant diet of alcohol and roofies.

Why?

None of this case made any sense.

"Okay, now let's run it again from his point of view."

"I walk into the bar that night and see Mercy Jo all by herself and think, 'She should be pretty easy pickin's.' Only, I've been snubbed before, so when I ask her if she wants a drink and she says yes, on my way back from the bar I make sure this one works by crushing a roofie in it. I had the roofie in my hand all ready to go."

Mercy Jo seems to like me. She doesn't put up any sort of fight. Nobody reports anything out of the ordinary or even remembers her leaving, even though she would've been completely out of it.

Or would she? Perhaps she left under her own volition before the alcohol and drugs hit. Perhaps she knew me. That would make sense. Then the drugs kicked in along the way to my hidey-hole.

After that, for you, it was all a blur.

CHAPTER 15

Carry and Jonathon continued their walk down Hunter Road until they came to the end of it. Then they followed the dirt trails leading into the woods that surrounded Bullfrog Creek. Most of these were walking trails, not nearly wide enough for a vehicle to drive down.

The rain from the night before had given the forest that dewy wet smell that almost made it feel like spring, if it weren't for the naked branches on everything but the evergreens.

Since thinking about what her mother's reaction would be to her walking in the woods with a strange boy, Carry began to question her own intuition. Had she made a terrible mistake agreeing to go on this walk? She really didn't know anything about Jonathon Mitchell other than that he worked at Raven Lee's Pizzeria. That is, *if* he still had a job there after missing two pizzas during his delivery and being a half hour late with the others.

"So what happened yesterday after I left? Did you get in major shit about the pizzas being a half hour late and cold and not havin' the missin' two you left with?"

"Of course," he smiled. "But my grandpa owns Raven Lee's, his name actually *is* Raven Lee Emerson, so he wasn't so rough on me, especially when I told him I had a very good reason for being late."

"And what reason did you tell him?" Carry asked.

"That I met the most fantastic girl who was nothin' like anyone else I'd ever run into in my life. My grandfather is a complete romantic. He believes in eternal and everlasting love. Him and my grandmother were together fifty-five years before she died last year of cancer. I thought for a while her death was going to take him with her. He became so sad. But he's sort of bounced back again now."

"Wow. That's a long time to be together," Carry said.

"My family comes from a history of romantics. We all should've been born in the early eighteen hundreds; we would've definitely fit in better. Nobody is romantic anymore. I think that's a shame, don't you?"

Carry had just been walking, listening to the cadence of his voice, and not really listening to the words. She'd been smelling the forest. Occasionally, she'd glance over at Jonathon's red hair, which looked very curious as they walked through the shadows of the trees. The sunlight would hit the top of Jonathon's head, almost making it look engulfed in flames, and then it would be bathed in darkness a few seconds later.

It took her a minute of silence before she realized he had asked her a question. Then she quickly tried to think back to what it was. She couldn't remember. "I'm sorry, I missed your question," she said.

He laughed. "You're *already* ignorin' me and you don't even hardly *know* me yet. I asked you if you think the fall of romanticism is a shame? Because nobody is a true romantic anymore."

"Definitely. I love romance." The butterflies from the other day were back and they'd brought helium-filled balloons with them. It felt like they were fluttering in Carry's stomach and unleashing the helium, making her start to become buoyant, and soon she would just rise up into the sky and probably get trapped in one of the bare branches above their heads.

The bare branches came to an end about a half block later and they found themselves under a veil of evergreen boughs. Douglas fir and pine—those were the only two Carry knew for sure. A hard wind wound up and hit Carry and Jonathon in the back.

Carry shuddered. "It's getting cold."

"Want my coat?" Jonathon asked.

"No, then you would freeze to death."

"Better me than you." He stopped walking, took off his coat, and handed it to Carry, who hesitantly put it on.

"Thanks," she said.

"Sure." Once again, his hand found hers as they headed farther into the woods. "You okay now?"

"Yes, I'm fine. But you look cold."

"You look beautiful."

Carry felt her face flush.

"How 'bout we walk well around Skeeter Swamp and head to Painted Lake? It's beautiful over there," Jonathon said.

"Okay." At this point Carry would get into a rocket and follow him to the moon and back.

The walk to Painted Lake took almost an hour, but time stopped meaning anything to Carry. She just kept looking at Jonathon, wondering how she got so lucky to actually "run into" such a fabulous guy.

Once they made it to the lake, they walked around it a bit until Carry said she better get going home because God only knew what her little brother actually told her mother about where she was going.

"When will I see you again?" Jonathon asked.

"When do you want to see me again?"

"The moment you walk away from me."

Oh, this guy definitely knew how to say the right things. "How 'bout we go to a movie. There's that new comedy coming out. You know . . . I can't remember the name."

"*Beetlejuice?*"

"Yeah, that's it. We could go on Tuesday or Wednesday. It would at least give me something to look forward to."

They walked out of the woods by Painted Lake and found themselves at the Anikawa River. It was low and hardly moving. This was unusual. Normally the Anikawa is a dangerous river.

"There's a place to cross over here," Jonathon said, and guided Carry to a footbridge that looked like it was made by fourth-grade students.

"Are you sure it's safe?" Carry asked.

"I use it all the time. It's safe."

"I dunno."

"You have trust issues, don't you?"

Carry thought this over. "If I do, I've never noticed before and definitely nobody's ever pointed them out to me."

"Well, we all have *some* sort of trust issues. It's what keeps us alive. Your instincts are pretty good at tellin' you when to trust and when not to, but some people have trust instincts that are a bit wonky. I think yours are a bit wonky."

"I'd have to check with my mother. She likes the family to go carolin'."

"What?" Jonathon said. "What does that have to do with your trust issues?"

She laughed. "Sorry, I'm still back at the movie. Probably Monday would be better."

"Ah, so we could celebrate the day after Christmas. I like that, too."

"It gives me at least *some*thing to look forward to between Christmas and going back to school."

"I noticed you changed the subject about your wonky trust issues," Jonathon said.

"Oh, was it that obvious? I was hoping to slip it past you."

"Why are you so messed up?" Jonathon asked.

"With what? How am I messed up?"

"With your trust issues," Jonathon said.

"I'm not. I have normal trust issues like everyone else," Carry said.

"You won't trust me," Jonathon said. "Why not?"

"Okay," Carry said. "Maybe they're a little messed up. After all, my mother's a cop. It makes you a little strange."

"Well, it's time to take your strangeness away."

"And how do you propose we do that?" Carry asked.

"By startin' to trust people you feel are trustable. People like *me,* for instance. Now, walk across the bridge." He was standing two thirds of the way over already.

Carry decided to do as he said. She started walking across, took two steps, and made the mistake of looking down. "I'm scared," she said.

"Oh, man, just be happy this isn't the spring or summer when the Anikawa looks like one of the entrances to hell. Come on, you're a third of the way across already. You can do it."

She took two more steps and was halfway across. Then two more. Then two more and she'd made it. Jonathon quickly grabbed her and pulled her into a hug. "See? I *told* you you could do it. You have to face your fears; otherwise, they have too much power over you. Speaking of which, you're going to have to face your fear of the cold because I need my coat back."

She slipped out of the brown bomber jacket and handed it to him. "Thanks for freezing to death and letting me use it."

"No, you don't understand. I had an ulterior motive."

"What's that?"

He held the jacket to his face and sniffed it. "Now it smells like you." Then he put it on.

"Do I get another hug?" he asked.

"For certain," Carry said.

This one lasted at least a minute. Any coldness Carry felt was quickly disappearing. No, that was one hug that would go with her all the way home.

She looked into his deep blue eyes. A warmth filled her from head to toe. She liked Jonathon Mitchell.

A lot.

CHAPTER 16

Leah was already at her desk when Chris came in with a newspaper tucked under his arm. Leah liked to get in early so she could get home early. That was the plan, anyway. Usually it never worked. She wound up getting in early and working late.

"Ever read the *Birmingham Times*?" Chris asked her as he poured himself a coffee from the freshly brewed pot on the small table beside the water cooler.

"If I had time to read newspapers from every city in Alabama, I wouldn't have no time for police work," Leah replied.

"Well, I don't usually either, but I got a call last night after you left. Guy named Douglas Stein told me I should check out the front page of the *Birmingham Times* issue from September twenty-fourth."

"Who the hell is Douglas Stein?"

"He was one of the looky-loos at our crime scene. Apparently, he got a better sight of the body than most others. Anyway, I went to the library and found the issue. They carry all the major newspapers going back near on three months before they microfish 'em."

Leah took a sip of her own coffee and smiled. "I think you mean micro*film* or micro*fiche.*"

"Whatever."

"So, what's on the front page?"

"You're gonna get excited."

"Just show me, goddamnit."

Chris flipped the paper open in front of her and he was right; excitement, along with repulsion, whipped through her body. "It's . . . it's our body." She looked up at Chris expectantly.

"No, it's *a* body. But not ours. A different one."

On the cover was a close-up of a woman's face and shoulders, the shot going down just below the neckline. Her eyes had been sewn up exactly like Mercy Jo Carpenter's had been, and at the bottom you could just see the top of a message that was written across her chest. She had blond hair, full and long enough that it went down out of the shot. At first glance she looked almost identical to Mercy Jo.

Leah read the article. When she was done, she said, "There was no mention of finding a cross anywhere on the body like we had, but the authorities may have held that back. They hadn't held back the eye stitches, though."

"Like us, they probably weren't able to," Chris said. "Apparently the body was found by a bunch of schoolkids. If they got to it first, the authorities may as well come up with the fact 'bout the stitchin' 'cause everyone would've known 'bout it sooner or later. Besides, they'd need a picture to canvass with like we did."

At the time of the article, the woman was unidentified, making her a Jane Doe. She showed up in a small town about fourteen miles northwest of Birmingham called Graysville.

Welcome to Gray . . .

It was too much of a coincidence. This had to be what the psychic had meant. Leah's skin tingled.

Graysville had a population that didn't even make a dent in the size of Alvin's. They found the body in an abandoned coal mine that hadn't been used since the 1960s. During the 1950s and 1960s, Graysville's coal mines and steel mills attracted families from all over Alabama.

"Chris?" Leah asked.

"Yeah."

"What interstate is Graysville on?"

"Uh, let me check." He typed on his computer for a minute, and said, "Highway Seventy-eight."

Leah sighed. "There goes another one of that psychic's clues." She lifted the paper and scanned the article once more. The statement was issued by Daniel Truitt, the homicide detective from the Birmingham Police Department who was working the case.

Leah doubted he was still working it. Two and a half months was a long time to go without solving something. It had probably grown cold, maybe even slotted cold. Leah decided to call Detective Truitt up and ask. She didn't expect to get much cooperation, though. Detectives were renowned for not enjoying other detectives asking about their cases.

"I'm looking to talk to Detective Dan Truitt," Leah said when a woman from the Birmingham Police Department took the call.

"One minute."

Leah knew she was checking the board. Looking to see if he was on duty or off duty or in or out. "I'm afraid he's away for a while," she came back with.

Away for *a while?* How long is *a while?*

"Can you get him to call me when he returns? My name is Leah Teal and I am the detective from down here in Alvin."

"Alvin. Is that in Alabama?"

"Yes, it is." Sometimes Leah forgot how small Alvin really was.

"What's your number, Detective Teal?"

Leah gave her the numbers for both her office and her home.

"And what's this concerning?"

"It's . . . it's in regard to one of his cases. I may have a lead for him." Leah thought this was the safest way to handle this question, and probably the most probable way of getting a response. "Please get him to call me back as soon as possible."

CHAPTER 17

Leah had just gotten in the door from work when Detective Dan Truitt from the Birmingham Police Station returned her call. As usual, Abe grabbed the phone before anyone else could, and then yelled (mostly into the receiver), "Mom! It's for you!"

"Thanks," Leah said, taking the phone from him.

"Detective Truitt here," said the voice on the other end. "You say you've got a lead on one of my cases?"

"Thought you were away for a while," Leah said.

"Not for people with leads."

"Ah."

"Which case we talkin' 'bout?" Truitt asked. "No, wait . . . Bradley Thomas."

"What?"

"I'm guessin' which case you're gonna tell me you have something on."

"No, not Bradley Thomas. This is from September, it's—"

"Terry McDonald."

"No, Detective Truitt," Leah said, losing patience. "If you'd just let me get to the point. It's about the Jane Doe you found in the abandoned mine."

"Oh, that one." His voice lost all its excitement. "I didn't find it. A bunch of sixth graders on a field trip found it, and boy how I wish it had been me instead. That one still gives me nightmares and it's been what? Two months?"

"Two and a half."

"Two and a half. Wow, how time flies when you're tryin' to get those stitches out of your mind. What sort of lead do you have for me, Detective . . . ?" He trailed off, obviously forgetting her name.

"Teal. I'm from the Alvin Police Department."

"Alvin. That in Alabama?"

Leah rolled her eyes. "Yes, not far from Satsuma."

"Okay, I think I know where. I drive down to Mobile a lot. Probably pass right by you."

"Yep, you probably do." Leah was getting frustrated that they still hadn't started discussing Mercy Jo Carpenter.

"So, how can you help me, Detective Teal?"

"We found a body in one of our lakes pretty much matching the body of your Jane Doe you discovered in the abandoned mine."

"In what way?"

"In every way," Leah said. "I only saw the front page of your September twenty-fourth issue of the *Times* today, but it's uncanny how similar the bodies were. Right down to the stitching of the eyes. Even the patterns matched. I'm willing to bet the thread type is even the same."

"Yeah? How much?"

"How much what?"

"How much are you willing to bet?"

"It was a figure of speech, Detective Truitt."

"Oh. Well, tell me some things about your Jane Doe that you can't tell from our picture."

"First off," Leah said, wishing she had made herself a cup of coffee before taking this call, "ours isn't a Jane Doe. Her name is Mercy Jo Carpenter. We found her washed up in Willet Lake, but the medical examiner figures she was killed somewhere else and dumped in the lake afterward. The body was probably found within twenty-four hours of being killed."

"Our medical examiner said the same thing about our Jane Doe," Detective Truitt said. "What else?"

"Was she fully clothed?"

"I guess," Truitt said. "She was wearing a red top that looked more like a bra with a leather jacket halfway zipped up and ripped blue jeans. She had on Reeboks that looked like they'd seen better days. Judging by her clothes and makeup, I guessed she worked for a living."

"Worked?"

"The streets. Graysville may be small, but being a hooker is the one job that will bring in cash anywhere. Was yours a prostitute?"

"Hard to know. She was dressed more business casual in a man's shirt and a skirt that came down to her midthighs. Was there any sign the killer sexually assaulted yours?" Leah asked.

"None. That was one of our biggest surprises," Truitt said.

"Ours too. Especially since her shirt wasn't done up properly. Tell me, did you find a cross on her anywhere? In a pocket? Around her neck? Tucked into a sock, maybe?"

"Now, how did you know that? We kept that out of the papers. It was in the left pocket of her leather jacket."

"Yep, ours was in the top shirt pocket."

"So, you thinkin' we got ourselves a serial, and the cross is his signature?"

"It's startin' to feel that way to me," Leah said. "I assume for you the case has gone cold."

Detective Truitt's entire demeanor completely changed and Leah immediately regretted saying what she just said.

"No goddamn way the case has gone cold," Truitt said. "Just because it's taken a while to solve, I plan on solvin' it. Don't think you're gonna ride in here on your white horse and scoop up all the glory."

"Sorry," Leah said, backing down, "that came out wrong. I meant, I'm assumin' you ran out of leads? Otherwise, you'd be the one callin' me 'bout the serial killer connection, rather than me callin' you?"

"We still have some leads," said Truitt. Leah could tell that was a lie.

Leah looked out at the backyard where two cardinals ducked in and out of the bare branches of her cherry trees, following each other in flight. "I think we should share what we got," she said. "Besides, I think there's a good chance the killer lives in Alvin."

"Why's that?"

"The soil content under her nails. It is quite unique and matches the soil and clay found in the northern valley just outside the limits of our town. I'm assumin' y'all tried to match soil samples and whatnot and didn't get any hits?"

There was a long pause. A yellow butterfly with black spots fluttered outside the kitchen window. "You're right," he finally said, "we didn't."

"I think the first body got dumped outside of Birmingham because the killer was scared if we'd found it too close to home we'd close in on him. Now that he's killed twice, though, his confidence is increasing. He's becoming cocky. What did he write on the chest?"

"Your victim had that, too?"

"Yep, waterproof Magic Marker. It said, 'Justice Is Blind in the Eyes of the Lord.' I'm assumin' yours said the same?"

"Actually, no. Our Jane Doe said, 'A Thorn Among the Lilies.'"

"Ah, a biblical quote. Old Testament. Kinda."

"Yeah, we found it. Song of Solomon 2:2, only inverted from the original text. The *King James Version* has it as: 'As the lily among thorns, so is my love among the daughters.'"

"Interestin'," Leah said. "Wonder why the change? He's obviously tryin' to tell us somethin'."

"You think it's a message to *us?* As in the *police,* us?"

"I most certainly do. Who else would he be sendin' it to? He's taunting us. Or he wants to get caught. But he's too organized to want to be caught. I think our suspect has a chip on his shoulder when it comes to cops."

"Hmmm. Okay, how 'bout this? How 'bout we work this case together? I share my evidence with you, and you give me copies of everythin' you have?"

Leah quickly thought over the offer. It wouldn't hurt anything. She'd get flak from Ethan about it, but nothing she couldn't handle. "Okay, I can do that," she said. "When can we meet in person?"

"Well, you're actually in luck. I have to be in Mobile tomorrow at three. I can stop in for lunch on my way, and we can go over things then. Sound good?"

"Sounds great. That will give me time to convince my superior I'm doin' the right thing," Leah said.

"I have a trick for that," Truitt told her.

"What's that?"

"Just don't tell 'em."

"Yeah, but you ain't in an office with only two other people. Tough to keep secrets."

"Alvin. You *sure* it's in Alabama?"

"I'll draw you a map and fax it to you," Leah said with a sigh.

"Sounds good. See you tomorrow. Oh, wait. One last thing. Where do you want to meet?"

"Um, how about at the station?"

"Sounds exquisitely borin'. I'll be there for lunch, remember?"

"Oh, okay. And technically tomorrow's my day off, so—"

"Perfect! I suggest we go out for Texas barbecue somewhere. I'm sure you have a place in that town that serves up Texas barbecue, don't you?"

"Yes, we do. It's on Main Street, and it's called Vera's Old West Bar & Grill. It's at about the fifteen hundred block somewhere."

"I'll find it," he said. "I have a nose for grilled steak. So if I leave here at say, ten o'clock I should be there by just after twelve."

"You can't possibly make it from Birmingham to Alvin in two hours," Leah said.

"I'll be using the siren. That's what it's for. And speed zones aren't for officers of the law, for us they're just suggestions. You did say you were close to Satsuma, right?"

"Right."

"See you around twelve-fifteen, maybe twelve-thirty."

Wondering what she'd gotten herself into, Leah hung up the receiver and took another look at the picture in her lap. It was uncanny how similar the two victims looked. And the eyes. They were so . . . she couldn't even think of the word.

So *desperate.*

CHAPTER 18

I waited a while after my mother got off the phone before approaching her with my question. I had just gotten home from playing at Dewey's for a change (a suggestion from my mother), when I came in to find her sitting in the kitchen, going over some files. I needed to ask her the question that had been running through my head while I overheard her talking with that detective from Birmingham. "Mom, can I ask you somethin'?"

She looked up. "Certainly." She motioned to the chair beside her. "Why don't you have a seat?"

I pulled out the chair and climbed on top. I started to think about how to start my conversation, but I couldn't come up with anything good.

"So," she said, "tell me what's on your mind."

"Well, I was wonderin' . . . Mom, what's a serial killer?"

She hesitated and I saw her swallow. "Now, who told you about serial killers?"

"Nobody, that's why I'm askin'."

"Well, someone must've mentioned them for you to even know the term."

"I overheard you talkin' to that officer from Birmingham on

the telephone earlier on. And you was talkin' 'bout a serial killer and I ain't never heard of one, so I thought I'd ask."

My mother took a deep breath and let it out slowly. The setting sun shining through the kitchen window went behind a cloud, making everything slightly darker. The world felt a bit gray for an instant.

"Well," my mother said, "serial killers are murderers who kill more than one person. Actually, technically, I think it has to be three or more, but that doesn't matter. One, two, three, ten, it's all horrible. Their victims are generally people they don't know, but the killers usually follow some sort of pattern."

"What do you mean they follow a pattern?"

"Well, one might only kill college girls with black hair and wearing dresses who he manages to encounter alone on the street. Things like that."

I thought this over. "The other night when you were talkin' to Officer Jackson, you mentioned 'rituals.' What are rituals?"

My mother let out another very audible sigh. "Are you sure you're ready for a conversation like this?"

I nodded. "Yes, I'm old for my age. You always tell me that, remember?"

"Okay, well, some serial killers will always murder their victims all the same way. Say they use a gun and shoot them. They might shoot them all in the heart. That becomes their tag or their trademark."

"But they can be more complicated in the way they kill them, right?"

"*Much* more complicated. And much more horrible. And I'm afraid if I went any further with this conversation you would be havin' nightmares."

"What sort of pattern does the case you're workin' now have?"

I could tell my mother was considering whether or not to answer this question. Finally, she gave me an answer, but I was pretty sure she left a lot out. "Well, without goin' into the gruesome details, this killer knows how to sew, and either drives or has access to a Chevy or Ford pickup truck."

"How do you know all that?"

"This is what I do, honey. I'm paid to figure things out."

"So do you think serial killers are people who, when they're not out killin', still follow patterns in their lives?"

She thought about this, staring up at the ceiling. "That's a very good question, Abe. One I hadn't thought of before. Let me consider it a while and I'll get back to you."

I smiled. I was always happy when I managed to come up with good questions. I was even happier when I happened to come up with good answers, but that happened less often.

"So, Mom?"

"Yeah?"

"There's a serial killer livin' in Alvin?"

"Oh, we don't know that for sure, honey. Right now we're just speculatin'."

"What do you base your speculatin' on?"

"The fact that we've discovered two murders, both with the same distinguishin' features that contain elements that point to them happenin' here. Serial killers are habitual. They usually can't control themselves. I am talking to a detective from Birmingham 'bout it tomorrow. I'll know more then."

"These distinguishin' features. Is that part of their pattern?"

She smiled. "I suppose it is, yes."

The first thing I did with my new information about serial killers was go over to Dewey's and fill him in. I figured, if there's a serial killer in Alvin, and all serial killers follow patterns, me and him should be able to figure out who it is just by watching people. We were good at watching people, and finding the ones who followed patterns every day should be easy.

"So," Dewey said when I finished explaining, "anyone we see who, say, does their dishes every morning after breakfast, then goes for a jog, then has lunch, then watches TV every day before supper is probably out killin' folk at regular intervals?"

"I don't reckon *every*one who follows patterns kill folk, but I think it's an indication that they might," I said.

"So you reckon we should ride around town and start documentin' who's doin' the same thing every day at the same time?"

"Exactly," I said. "Those are the unstable people we have to be

careful of. Once we've got a list of maybe twenty potential suspects, I can present it to my mom. I'm sure she'll be super happy
when I do."

"You know, my ma follows a pattern pretty much," Dewey
said. "She even has certain days she does laundry and certain days
and times she vacuums. Think she might be out slaughtering folk?"

"She very well could be, Dewey. This whole serial killer thing is
so new to me that I don't know who we can trust, if anyone. I'd
suggest you start documentin' her behavior, just in case."

"I'll definitely do that. What 'bout your mom?"

"What 'bout her?"

"Does she follow patterns? Should we be documentin' her?"

"Dewey," I said, "she's the one tryin' to *catch* the serial killer.
She ain't the killer."

"But how do we know? She might have the best disguise of
anyone."

I thought this over. "Actually, she doesn't really follow any
patterns. All her days are different on account of all the different
crimes she's constantly tryin' to solve."

"Oh."

"All right, I suggest we head out tomorrow after school on our
bikes and start documenting what we see. Main Street will be a
good place to start. In the meantime, make sure you keep tabs on
your ma. I don't want to see her get shot or anythin' in some kind
of police standoff."

"No, that wouldn't be very good. I also wouldn't wanna find
out she'd been killin' people. Would make her seem not as nice a
ma as she does now."

"Yeah, I s'pose that's true. Anyway, I'll see you tomorrow."

And with that, I rode back home, my brain quickly switching
through all the people I knew in town. Most of them *did* follow
some sort of pattern every day. I knew this already without having
to go document it. Especially the ranchers. Their days rarely
changed. And the more I thought about that, the more convinced I
became that one of the ranchers was most likely the serial killer. But
then there was Mr. Wyatt Edward Farrow, who I know I wrongly
accused once, but this time was different. He completely lived his

life by a pattern: going into his shop at the same time every evening, leaving it the same time every morning, sleepin' during the day, grocery shopping Saturday mornings. Problem was, if I accused Mr. Wyatt Edward Farrow again, my mother would not only not take me seriously; she'd likely get really angry about it.

No, I was sort of stuck when it came to him. I decided not to put him on our list, but to keep a close eye on him just the same. Besides, odds were it was a rancher. There were more of them than just the one Mr. Wyatt Edward Farrow, and they ran through just as many patterns in their life as he did.

Me and Dewey needed a way to prove who it was. But how?

CHAPTER 19

Leah sat in Ethan Montgomery's office cradling a steaming cup of coffee and waiting for Ethan to get off the phone. He'd waved her in when she knocked on the door, and she closed it shut behind her. Montgomery's office was plush, with a lot of wood. It had a big window looking out front with wooden blinds he kept open. Beyond that window was a fig tree that was currently being checked out by a hummingbird.

The room also had windows looking into the main room with wooden blinds he usually kept shut. Even the door had a window on it with blinds. Those were shut, too.

His desk was a hulk of a thing, taking up probably a quarter of the room. Leah often wondered how the movers ever got it in here. Ethan continued chatting while sipping his coffee. He leaned back and his chair groaned and creaked, something it had been doing for as long as Leah could remember. She wished to hell he'd either buy a new one or oil this one.

An avid sports fan, Ethan had a television hanging from the top corner of the room opposite his desk. Below it was a side-loading VHS VCR. The other side of the room was taken up by bookcases stuffed with law books.

Leah liked the smell in this room. It had that musty old smell of wood and books that reminded her of how her father's study used to smell before he got cancer.

The ceiling was tiled, and in the center was a big wooden fan that turned so slowly Leah doubted it accomplished much of anything, summer or winter. In fact, it was always on, summer and winter, just slowly turning away the years.

Finally hanging up the phone, Ethan took a big swallow of his coffee. "So," he said. "I hear you reckon we have ourselves a serial killer livin' right here in Alvin."

"Well," she said, "what we have are two victims with the same MO with similar nail scrapings matching the soil in parts north of Alvin along with a high concentration of cedar shavings on our victim. The first victim showed up in Graysville, just outside of Birmingham, but she had scrapings they couldn't pin down. I reckon they're goin' to end up bein' the same as our victim's. I am meeting with their detective later today. The soil samples they found match nothing up there. As you know, the second vic washed up here on Willet Lake."

She looked at him for a reaction but saw none. "Don't worry," he said. "I'm following you. So far, this isn't rocket science."

"Well," she said. "My guess is that after the first murder, our suspect got scared and tried to cover himself by gettin' the body as far away from Alvin as he could. But when he didn't get caught, he started gettin' cocky."

"So now he's just leavin' 'em in his backyard?"

"*Our* backyard. And it's just a theory."

"Why do you say our backyard?"

"Because in both cases there was writing on the chest of each victim that I believe was put there to taunt law enforcement."

"What did they say?" Ethan asked, suddenly a little more interested.

The body we found, as you likely already saw in the report, had 'Justice Is Blind in the Eyes of the Lord' written across her chest. The body they found in Graysville said, 'A Thorn Among the Lilies,' which is a sort of mixed-up version of the Song of Solomon 2:2, which *actually* reads, 'As the lily among thorns, so is my love among the daughters.'"

"Creepy. So you're thinkin' whoever did this just got out of the joint and missed his mother's funeral? Actually, the last quote points to a sister. Maybe there's a woman still in prison who's about to miss her mother's funeral and the brother's a little pissed 'bout it."

"Hadn't thought of that, thanks." Leah copied down what he'd said and put it in her book.

"And what else do we have to go on, I mean, besides the eyes?"

Ah, so Ethan had seen everything so far. Leah hadn't been sure how much of the loop he'd actually been in. Judging by his questions, it was really hard to tell. "Well, I've told Detective Dan Truitt, the homicide detective from Birmingham, that I'd work with him on this case. We're gonna trade evidence this afternoon. But so far, we've got the stitched eyes, the nail scrapings, some shoe castings, tire castings, and the phrases written across the chest of both bodies."

"That's it? Nothing else?"

"No, there's more," Leah said.

"There always is."

Outside a dog started barking. Leah turned to look at a man walking his bull terrier, which didn't look like he wanted to be walked anywhere at all. He seemed to be fighting it every inch of the way. When she turned back to Ethan, Ethan's eyes were up on the television, as though he wished there was something playing on it. Anything but this conversation they were having.

Leah wasn't about to let him get away too easily. She still had lots to say.

"Both victims were found with roughly chiseled wooden crosses in their pockets," she continued. "They also had ligature marks on their wrists and ankles. Their final deaths came from a .22 caliber shot to the right temple. I haven't got the report from Detective Truitt yet, but it looks like our round came from a Beretta Model 950 Jetfire."

Ethan sat back and his chair complained. "Sounds like you've made this your personal project. *Find the Serial Killer.*"

"I'm doin' my duty."

"The crosses might just be a signature."

"What do you mean?"

"The killer might just leave them there as his marking, so you know it was him. He'd know the cross would be something that wouldn't be leaked to the press. It's his calling card."

"Or he could be a religious wing nut. We've had our share of those throughout the years," Leah said.

Ethan took a big breath, picked up some papers on his desk that seemed completely unrelated, flipped through a few, then glanced back to Leah. "You do realize you're a significant pain in the ass."

"I've heard that before."

"Well, it's fine and dandy that you're investigatin' these murders, 'cept for one little problem."

"What's that?"

"I know your habits. Don't start goin' out and questionin' everyone who's ever used a sewin' machine or driven a truck."

"Well, what other options do I have? I mean, obviously I'm not questionin' everyone who sews, but I have to question anyone who fits." Leah took a sip from her coffee mug.

"All right. Whatever you do, though, try desperately not to get the Feds involved. That's rule one. They'll just take over, and the last thing this town needs is that. What you want to do is pretend *you're* a Fed and profile the subject like they would do. Don't aspire to be an FBI agent, just become one. Number one rule: You're no longer looking for a suspect. You're looking for an unknown subject, or unsub as they say at Quantico." He chuckled to himself.

The ceiling fan in Ethan's office continued to turn slowly above their heads. For once, the television hanging in the corner was turned off.

"How do I 'profile' someone? I thought that was spooky FBI stuff you had to go to Quantico for years to learn," Leah said.

Ethan picked up the paper from his desk again, pretending to read it. "Nah," he said, "you can do it. It all just comes out of those feelings you carry around in your gut. And *you* more than anyone have those gut feelings. So you really already know how to do it."

"No, Ethan, I don't know nothin'. Why don't you explain it to me?"

He paused, drumming his fingers on the top of his desk. Leah suspected he was trying to decide how much time he wanted to spend with her this morning. "Well," he finally said, "tell me about your victims. First, why do you think they were both killed by the same person?"

"There's just too many things in common with their deaths for them not to have been."

"Like?" Another loud chair squeak as Ethan sat back again.

"Like what I've already told you. Everything. The sewing of the eyes, the message across the chest, the chiseled wooden cross in the pocket. Oh, and they were both kept alive for up to a week before the suspect—sorry, unsub—killed them."

"How were they killed, again?"

".22 caliber round to the side of the head."

"Which side?"

"Both on their right temple."

"What if there were two?"

"Two what?"

"Unsubs. You're making too many leaps of faith. What if it's a woman? What if it's a man and a woman? Or two men or two women workin' together. One down here, the other in Birmingham? Or what if it's a copycat?"

"There wasn't enough info in either our press release or Birmingham's to have such a detailed copycat."

"What if it's a cop?"

Leah paused and her breath caught. She never would have suspected a cop serial killer. "You mean a cop doin' both killings, or a cop coming to Alvin to copycat the first killin' knowing exactly what went down?"

Ethan shrugged. "Either. My point is, don't jump to conclusions until you have the evidence to back it up. Right now you have nail shavings possibly putting both victims at the same place and that place *could* be in the forests of northern Alvin. There's not much up there. Can't imagine spending seven days alone or with a hostage all bound up with her mouth duct-taped shut."

Suddenly Leah felt nauseated. She had a sudden urge to vomit. There were just too many potential suspects. "This is a big case," she said. "Bigger than I thought."

"It happens," Ethan said, nodding. "And your first suspect killed his victim sometime around September twenty-fourth, according to the *Birmingham Times.*"

So, Ethan knew a *lot* more about this situation than he was really letting on. Leah found that very interesting. "Right. I am meeting with Detective Truitt this afternoon and we will find out exactly when the victim was discovered."

"Pretty much two and a half months apart. That means if we *are* dealing with a serial killer, you probably have three weeks to a month to figure out who it is before he gets to number three."

"Now how did you figure that out?"

"Because I've read about serial cases. Killing is about power and about thrill, and the more the suspect kills the more power and thrill he feels. He can't help himself. He's like a drug addict. He will kill more and more often to keep the feeling goin'."

"Our girl had a lot of booze in her and had been drugged with roofies. Folks that knew her referred to her as a 'loner.' Maybe this guy targets girls in bars who are by themselves. Drinkers. Heavy drinkers. Easy prey. Especially if he can drug them before taking them."

"Okay, you're usin' your detective gut. Good. Keep going."

Leah took a big breath. "They were both killed the same way. With their wrists bound and tied lying somewhere in sawdust. It could be a barn, a farmhouse, anythin' like that."

"What makes you think they were lyin' down?"

"I don't know, I just . . . there's no indication of them bein' tied *to* anythin'. I suppose they could've been propped up, or tied to a chair. Then the killer unties them before bringing their dead bodies out to be dumped. Having them seated would make it easier to stitch the eyes."

"I think they were tied to chairs," Ethan said. "Otherwise, they would wiggle like fish during the sewing, making it almost impossible. That is, unless they were unconscious, but I think our killer is the kind of guy who would want them conscious through the process."

"They'd be screaming, but we found residue of glue around Mercy Jo's mouth that matches the glue used on duct tape. So that took care of any sound she made. It's interesting that he took the duct tape off before dumping the body." Leah finished her coffee. Above her, the wooden fan continued to slowly turn.

"Yes, I saw the duct tape in the report. Hence my earlier comment." Ethan came forward, his big arms landing on his desktop. "So your guess is he drives them to the dump site after killing them."

"If I had to guess, then yes. That's what I think."

"Why stitch their eyes closed?" Ethan asked.

"No idea. 'Justice Is Blind,' it said on the chest of our vic. I believe that alludes to him blinding her. But in the first killing there's no reference to blinding. To be perfectly honest, I don't know, Ethan. I've thought that one over and nothin' 'bout it makes any sense."

"Think 'bout it some more right now."

She gave him an answer right away, the one she'd been playing with for some time. "I think they are blinded so they won't see the rest of it."

"The rest of what?" Ethan asked.

"Their deaths bein' played out."

Ethan nodded. "That might make sense. Why would the killer not want them to see the rest of it, though?"

Again, Leah had this one pegged. It was the only thing she'd come up with since trying to solve these murders. "To save them havin' to go through the trauma of witnessin' what he was 'bout to do. So they don't see the shot comin'."

Ethan leaned even farther across his desk, as though trying to get as close to Leah as possible. "So you're sayin' this person who stitches their eyes shut, then after keeping them alive in agony for six or seven days before shootin' them in the head, is full of compassion?"

Leah sighed. "I told you I wasn't good at this." She went for another sip of coffee, then remembered she'd finished it.

Something came to Leah then. "Um, what if the killer was a war veteran with PTSD. He had been somewhere like Iraq where he'd come across a wounded enemy soldier and decided to spare him his life, so he left him there alive. Only, the vet didn't know the enemy had a gun, and when the right moment came, the Iraqi managed to shoot the vet's buddy in the head, killin' him?" She paused for a second. "These murders might be him relivin' that feelin' of helplessness. Maybe him gettin' payback."

"Wow. That was good. You're a natural. Yes, it could very well be somethin' like that. In fact, I'd definitely say this comes from some trauma the killer went through in the past."

Above them, the fan turned slowly around and around.

"I think that's 'bout all we have to go on for now. Let's continue this discussion once you've got a chance to go over the evidence this Detective Truitt is bringin' you this afternoon."

"So you don't mind me bringin' him into the case?"

"I mind the fact that you didn't come to me and ask first, but it's a little late for that. But no, my only concern is gettin' this guy off the streets."

"Thanks, Ethan." Leah got out of her chair and started for the door.

"Oh, and, Leah?"

She turned. "What?"

Two things. "First, we keep referring to the suspect as 'him' because most serial killers are men, but don't trap yourself into thinking it can't possibly be a woman. And second, the suspect you're looking for is left-handed."

Leah paused, scrunching up her face in bewilderment. "Now how the hell do you know that?"

"If he had the victim tied to a chair and shot her in the right temple, odds are he wanted to see her die. He wouldn't do it from behind. If he was right-handed, he'd have shot her in the left temple, but he didn't. He shot her in the right. So more than likely, you're looking for a lefty."

CHAPTER 20

Detective Truitt beat Leah to the restaurant. As soon as she entered Vera's she knew which one was him. One look at the long brown trench coat, mussed-up near-on white hair, and button-down shirt and tan trousers and there could be no doubt: He was a detective. She was willin' to bet dollars to donuts he had a shoulder holster on under that coat. He just looked like the kind of guy who'd use a shoulder holster. Probably had a second gun in an ankle holster, too.

He stood from the table as she approached. She was carrying a file folder containing copies of all the evidence found so far on the Mercy Jo Carpenter case.

"Detective Teal?" he asked, holding out his hand. "I'm Dan Truitt."

They shook hands. "Nice to meet you, Detective Truitt," Leah said. Dan Truitt had a nice chin and chiseled good looks. A little like Harrison Ford, with that halfway grin, in some ways.

"Please call me Dan or Danny or even Danny Boy. Anythin' but Detective Truitt."

"Um, okay . . . Dan."

He smiled a big, white, toothy grin. "See? Isn't that a lot better."

"Then you may as well call me Leah."

"Look at that," Dan said. "We're already on a first-name basis. Pretty soon you'll be pregnant."

Leah blinked. What the hell did he—

"Relax," he said. "That was a joke, Leah. I'm a funny guy. Get used to laughin' instead of lookin' like someone just sideswiped you on the interstate. Laughing's good for you."

If only he knew 'bout Billy, Leah thought. *Wonder if he'd still have said that bit 'bout bein' sideswiped then? Someone like him, he just mighta.*

A waitress came up to their table. She spoke with a bubblegum voice and looked about sixteen. "Hi. My name is Candy and I'll be your server today. Would you like to start with some drinks?"

"This place licensed?" Dan asked.

"Yep!"

"Then we'll have two cranberry apple martinis, please. No olives."

Leah leaned forward, and whispered to Dan, "I can't drink. I've gotta drive home."

He batted her words away. "So do I. How big's this town, anyway? You can't possibly live more than a twenty-minute walk from anywhere. Besides, I'll give you a ride. And it's not like you're gonna get smashed. Hey, I even have to drive another three hours to get home. Two if I keep the siren goin'."

There was no way Leah was ever getting into a car with this man. "I'm surprised you haven't been fired years ago."

Dan grew serious. "Hey." He pointed at her. "I'll have you know, I'm good at my job. Very good, in fact. I bet I beat out your lead detective just like that." He snapped his fingers.

"*I'm* our lead detective."

"Oh, sorry."

"I'm our *only* detective. Our town's only got fifty-three hundred people in it. Not a lot of detectin' goin' on."

Dan leaned back and put his arms up on either side of his seat of the booth they were in. "So . . . you wanted to know somethin' about my Jane Doe."

"Yes." She picked up the file from the booth seat beside her and set it on the table. "I've brought you a copy of all of the evidence we've gathered so far on our Mercy Jo Carpenter case."

Dan reached down beside him and brought up a thicker file folder and a videotape in a white case.

"What's on the video?" Leah asked.

"It's a shot of the crime scene, taken by one of the gawkers standing around. It's not great, but it's something. It was taken fairly early, before anything was disturbed. Thought it might be of use."

"Okay, thanks."

The waitress brought back the martinis and set them before Leah and Dan. They were red on the bottom and clear on the top. Leah had never had a martini before in her life. "Are you ready to order?" the waitress asked.

"I'm sorry," Leah said, "but we haven't had a chance to even check—"

"How's your New York steak?" Dan asked, interrupting Leah.

"Very good. Hot off the barbecue, any way you like it."

"And your ribs?"

"The best in town."

"Okay, we'll both have a T-bone and ribs. Leah, how do you like your steak?"

Sort of dumbstruck, Leah answered, "Medium well?"

"And I'll have mine medium rare. Thanks."

The waitress took the menus and left the table.

"Why did you just order for me?" Leah asked Dan.

"To speed up the process so we could get back to this case. You have caught my interest, oh, grasshopper."

"What if I hadn't liked steak and ribs?"

"Then you would've never agreed to meet me here. Now, can you please tell me about this murder victim of yours?"

"Not much more to tell other than what I told you on the phone. We found her washed up on the shore backside up. She was under one of the wharfs at Willet Lake."

"Where's Willet Lake?"

"It's a small lake just a few miles northwest of here."

"In Alvin?"

"Yep, anyway, when we turned her over, I found the cross in her pocket. Here's a picture of the cross." She passed a blown-up black-and-white photo across the table.

"Pretty much matches the one we got off our Jane Doe," Truitt said.

"And, of course, we discovered the writing across her chest."

"This is where, to me, it gets interestin'," Truitt said. "The differences in the messages. Yours said . . . what?"

Leah passed over another image. "Justice Is Blind in the Eyes of the Lord."

"And ours said, 'A Thorn Among the Lilies,' which comes from the Bible."

"Well," Leah said, "like I told you on the phone, it *sort* of does. It's been reversed from what appears in my *King James Version* of the good book. The real text I found in the Old Testament in Song of Solomon 2:2 read: 'As the lily among thorns, so is my love among the daughters.'

"To put it in context, I included here the passages surrounding it."

She pulled another sheet from her file folder and began reading from Song of Solomon:

2:1 I am the rose of Sharon, and the lily of the valleys.

2:2 As the lily among thorns, so is my love among the daughters.

2:3 As the apple tree among the trees of the wood, so is my beloved among the sons. I sat down under his shadow with great delight, and his fruit was sweet to my taste.

2:4 He brought me to the banqueting house, and his banner over me was love.

2:5 Stay me with flagons, comfort me with apples: for I am sick of love.

"And what do you make of all that?" Dan asked.

"I reckon this is more than enough to see what the killer had meant by the expression. He was the opposite of what was in the verse. He was the thorn in the valley. The one not to be trusted. The one son not to put your faith in. I believe the message is to *us*. It's a taunt."

"You really think that?"

"I do. I assume final death for your Jane Doe came from a .22 caliber round fired into her right temple?" Leah asked.

"Yes, same with your Mercy Jo?"

"Yeah, my chief of police figures the killer must be left-handed because he went for the right temple while he likely had her bound and tied, probably to a chair. Figured he would've wanted to watch her die."

"Interestin' conclusion."

"Did your guys find glue around the mouth where she had been duct-taped?"

"Yeah, but there was no tape anymore. The killer had removed it before dumping the body in the mine. Yours too?"

"Ours too. Sounds like the same MO exactly. We need to get ballistics to check both our rounds out and see if they match. I assume yours are in the crime lab in Birmingham?"

He nodded.

"Mine are in Mobile. Here's the report from ballistics." She began reaching into the file.

Dan Truitt put his hand on her arm. "Don't worry 'bout showin' all that to me now. I can go through it myself later. Right now it will just flood my head with useless numbers. Same goes with footprint casts and tire-track casts. Let's get the experts to look at 'em and cross reference 'em and get back to us and tell us what matches and what don't."

"Okay . . ." Leah said, passing him the file folder. He put all the pages she had given him back into it. He passed her his folder and the videotape.

"For now," he said, "let's just relax, have a few drinks, and enjoy our steaks. Too much police work makes Dan a dull boy. He goes a bit crazy." He looked around the room and spotted the waitress. Tapping his glass, he ordered another drink. "Two, please," he shouted out.

Leah thought that he must've had too much police work a while ago. This guy was just a few apples short of a full cart.

CHAPTER 21

Turned out nobody follows patterns like ranchers. After church, despite the downpour of rain, me and Dewey started our mission with Isaac Swenson, the owner of Southpoint Ranch way up in the northern part of Alvin. You have to ride your bike up Fairview Drive, which splits off into Bogpine Way, which you want to avoid at all costs because it leads to the bog, which is full of stench and toads. It's probably not so bad during the winter.

But we stayed left, which meant we had to continue uphill near on a mile and a half before we came to Swenson's ranch.

We picked Isaac Swenson to start with on account of I overheard my mother telling Officer Chris that a pickup truck was used during the serial killer's murders. Unfortunately, everyone in town drove pickups. However, there were two people who seemed particularly suspicious to me. They were Jacob Tyne, the owner of the Red Lightning Cattle Farm, and Bubba Swenson, Isaac Swenson's son. I picked Isaac Swenson over Jacob Tyne on account of Jacob Tyne also owning Superfeed and K's Bait & Tackle. It seemed to me like having so many things on the go would lead to less patterns in your life and probably a lot less time to go out killing people.

We started watching Isaac Swenson on Tuesday after school

and planned to do so for two days. We had lots of people we wanted to watch, and so we didn't have a whole bunch of time to spend on each one of them. Sure enough, on the first day, Isaac Swenson started a routine he followed near on exact to the T on the next day. Everything from feeding the hogs at the same time, to wiping down the horses, to feeding the chickens. His wife even called him in for dinner at the same time both days, almost right down to the minute. I was sure glad my Uncle Henry had given me my very own watch a year ago. More and more it was coming in very handy in my life.

CHAPTER 22

Wednesday, Leah woke to a cold, wet rain. The forecast called for it to get even worse and possibly turn into thundershowers. It wasn't the best day to have to walk twenty minutes to pick up your car from where she'd left it the night before after having too many martinis to drive it home.

But Leah managed to make it, despite the weather.

And after finding her car where she'd left it in front of Vera's, Leah went back home and watched the videotape Dan Truitt had given her the night before. Thank God she hadn't tried to drive home. Her head felt like a construction site. She'd lost count of how many cranberry apple martinis the two of them had drunk, but it was more than Leah needed, that's for sure. Everything was a blur of martini as the video went into the slot and she pressed the PLAY button on the machine.

Truitt was right, the video was amateurish, the camera unstable. Also, because it was taken inside a mine, the picture was rather dark. But there was no escaping the body lying on its back, looking like a life-sized rag doll with its eyes sewn up with thick black cotton thread and its arms outstretched. Leah felt her heart go out to this woman who, like Mercy Jo Carpenter, looked to be in her late twenties, lying there dead for all the world to see.

The camera zoomed in on the face as well as it could do given the fact that the photographer was obviously being held back by police tape cordoning off the area. Then the cameraman did a slow sweep of the officers tending to the crime. There were six. Leah couldn't help but be envious of a town with enough of a police force to send six officers to a crime scene. As the picture continued to pan, the shot slowly coming out of the cave entrance, she saw Detective Truitt, with his notebook in hand, talking to someone. Probably that was the witness who called the scene in, Leah suspected.

Then the camera did a slow sweep of the gawkers gathered trying to get a glimpse of a real dead body. There must have been thirty or forty of them. They were all clumped together, pushing their way toward the incident, held back by a fragile line of yellow tape.

Then something in the video caused a surge in Leah's stomach. She wasn't sure what it was, but there was something she had seen that caused her to react. Did it have something to do with Truitt? Or the officers tending to the crime scene? She didn't know. She just knew that something was wrong, and it tugged at the back of her brain like a small dog gnawing on a piece of bone.

She even forgot her hangover for a moment.

The video came to an end and Leah immediately rewound it and played it again. And again she felt that same feeling. It was almost a déjà vu feeling, only not quite. She didn't know what to make of it.

She watched the video four more times until finally pulling herself away, deciding that whatever it was would come to her in time. She went back to the rest of the evidence Truitt had given her, going over it meticulously, making sure there was nothing she'd missed during their conversation at the restaurant.

CHAPTER 23

"If you're right," Detective Dan Truitt said, "and your killer lives in Alvin, then there's a good possibility my Jane Doe is from Alvin. Do you mind circulating her picture in the more . . . how do I put this . . . *seedier* parts of town and see if anyone knows who she was?"

Dan had called shortly after Leah got into the station. Chris had brought in donuts. She was on her first bite. She had just finished pouring herself a cup of coffee and was watching the rain pound the street outside, wondering when they were going to hear their first clap of thunder, when the phone rang. Somehow Leah beat Chris to it. It was Dan.

"Not at all. I think that's a great idea," Leah said, trying not to sound like she had a full mouth.

"Why do you sound like you have a pillow over your head?"

"Sorry," she said, swallowing, "I was eating a donut."

"I know it's going to be tough to get an ID with the eyes stitched. Some folk ain't gonna wanna even look at the picture, but see what you can do, okay?"

"I will. And, Dan . . ."

"Yeah?"

There was a pocket of silence while she collected her thoughts.

"That video you gave me . . ."

"Yeah, sorry it couldn't be better. It was taken by a kid. I think he was sixteen or something."

"No, no. It's not that, it's just . . . something about it."

"What?"

"Well, I don't rightly know. Somethin' doesn't sit right with me."

"Hmm. How good are your instincts? I've watched it a dozen times or so. Seems all right to me. We did a good job on the scene, Leah. Collected all the physical evidence we could find."

"I know, I know. It's not that. I'm really not sure what it is." She sipped her coffee.

"Well, you let me know if you figure it out."

"I will."

Leah hung up the phone and thought about canvassing with one of the photographs Dan had left with her. If he was right and his Jane Doe was a prostitute, there was only one area really she'd have to go and that was Oakdale Road on Alvin's west side. That was considered the "bad side of town" in Alvin. Even a town as small as Alvin had a bad side.

And the eyes *were* going to be a problem. They'd be a problem with the identification, but mostly they'd be a problem with the viewing. She'd have to warn everyone before showing them that what they were about to see was pretty damn graphic, even though everyone had seen the images in the *Examiner* and on the television news, she was absolutely sure about that.

She decided to visit the one place Mercy Jo had frequented so much. For anyone who liked their booze, and especially if she ran on the wrong side of the tracks, the Six-Gun Saloon seemed like the place to go. Especially if she really *was* a hooker. The place was like a funhouse for drunks and easy women.

She drove up Oakdale, the sun still over the treetops, fighting its way through the deluge of rain coming down around her. It was starting to set with the sky just beginning to turn dark gray. Parking out front of the Six-Gun, she admired the décor from the outside. It looked like a barn with a large sign on top featuring a girl in a bikini riding a bull. Beside her were the words WELCOME TO THE SIX-GUN SALOON. The words were in two rows and flashed on and off. As they did, the girl on the bull pulled her hat off her head and put it back on.

Leah entered the establishment through a set of saloon doors like you'd see in one of them old spaghetti westerns. The door kept swinging behind her until they finally went back to being still.

Inside it was the same as her last visit. Booths around the edge, a half-moon dance floor around one side of the central bar. She immediately recognized Margaret from before and approached, having to wait until Margaret finished with a customer before she could talk.

"You again. The woman who brings me nightmares."

Leah sighed. "I'm sorry, and I'm 'bout to do it again."

"What do you mean?"

"I have another body I need you to ID for me, and this time I don't even have a name. Once again, her eyes have been sewn closed. Do you feel up to it?"

"You say this killer is in Alvin and takin' out my girls . . . girls who come to *my* bar?"

"That's right. At least so far."

"Then I'll give you all the time in the world, honey. Show me the picture."

Leah handed over the Polaroid. She saw Margaret wince for a second and then study the picture for probably almost a minute. "It's tough to identify someone without their eyes. It's so weird. But I'm willin' to bet this is Faith Abilene. But I haven't seen Faith in months."

Reba McEntire belted something about Little Rock over the loudspeakers.

Leah took a deep breath. "She's been missing for months? The body was found up in Birmingham. Is Faith her *real* name or her stage name?"

"I'm not sure. I think she worked, so it could very well be her stage name. She had a few close friends. One, named Bamby Dearest, comes in quite often. I could give her your number."

Leah reached into her pocket and retrieved her card. "Please do. Make sure you tell her I'm not 'bout to bust her for hooking."

"I will. I know how to handle these girls. Besides, I think she's just a stripper. Works the Rabbit Room some nights."

"Thank you, Margaret." Outside came a giant roar of a thunderclap, followed by a downpour of rain.

"Starting to look ugly out there," Margaret said.

"Yeah, and to top it off, it's a cold, bitter rain."

"You take care of yourself."

"I will," Leah said, and with that she walked back outside to her car, thinking about how much Margaret treated these women as though they were her children. In a way, they were. They were children of the street and they'd found a home here. And now they were being slowly taken out of that home and being shown the harshness of reality.

One thing for sure, Leah was going to put a stop to it.

Back at the station, Leah immediately called Detective Truitt. He'd gone home for the day. Then she remembered he'd given her his home number, so she tried that. Once again, he answered on the first ring. "Truitt."

"Do you just sit, waiting by the phone?" Leah asked.

"Um, this is . . . don't tell me . . . Leah. I knew you wouldn't be able to avoid my charms forever."

"I got a name for your Jane Doe. It's her street name, I think, but at least it's a name. I also have a lead on getting her real name."

"So what's the street name?"

"Faith Abilene."

"I like it. And I'm betting it's not a street name. It sounds too normal."

"Well, we'll see. Anyway, sorry for bothering you at home. Have a good night." ·

"That's it?"

"What?"

"You call me at home and that's all I get?"

Leah had been nervous when she called and had no idea why, and now her nervousness just went up a notch. "Um, what do you want?"

"What are you wearing?"

She laughed. "You're a funny guy."

"I am a funny guy. Have a good night, Leah."

"You too . . . Dan."

She hung up with a feeling in her stomach she hadn't felt in years.

CHAPTER 24

W e didn't have much time Wednesday for watching Isaac Swenson on account of my mother made me go to church, but we had two good hours of surveillance we could get in. Despite the downpour and the rolling thunder and the lightning, we kept our vigil.

Surprisingly, even Bubba became part of Isaac Swenson's routine. Bubba came home from work at the same time both days (twenty after four), put the horses away at the same time each night, and even went in for dinner at the same time as his father. This whole family followed an extreme pattern every day. I started thinking they must all be serial killers.

Me and Dewey watched all this from the golden grass that had long ago been painted from green to gold by the winter sun. We were both dressed in greens and browns. That was my idea: Earth tones would help us blend in better with our surroundings. Had the grass still been green, I would have blended in perfectly. Luckily for us, though, the days were short this time of year and it started to get dark fairly early. It didn't take long before we began to disappear into the darkness and what we were wearing became meaningless.

We also stayed quite a ways back from the actual ranch. Dewey had gotten a set of binoculars for Christmas last year—which he *never* used; in fact, they were still sealed in their box before we took them on our scouting trips—so they allowed us to watch things from a distance.

"I can't imagine *anyone* following a pattern more than Isaac Swenson," Dewey whispered to me on the second night while the Swensons were inside eating supper.

"I know," I whispered back. "I think we solved the case on our first try."

We both had pocket-sized notebooks we used for jotting down activities and events and the times they happened. We had filled them up during the two days of watching Isaac Swenson and his family.

"My notebook's full," Dewey said. "I need a new one before we go watch anyone else."

"Me too," I said. We were still whispering as we got back to our bikes. Then we headed down the hill toward town.

"Friday and Saturday can we stay out later doin' this? With school over for the holidays and everythin' else, we should use the extra time. We'll have an entire week's worth of holidays!"

"I guess," I said. "As long as I tell my mom . . ."

"What?" Dewey asked. "Why did you just stop talking?"

"Because one night during the holidays I have to go out and Saturday's Christmas Eve, which I normally spend with my family. My mom would never let me go out Christmas Eve to spy on people. She makes us go door-to-door singing carols and dumb stuff like that. And this year she's talkin' 'bout goin' out for two nights. Christmas Eve *and* the night before."

"What's the other thing?"

"My sister's stupid birthday. It's on December twenty-ninth. I'm forced to go to some fancy restaurant and eat steak. I hate it. I'd much rather sneak around and solve mysteries with you."

"They both sound like fun!" Dewey said. "Can I come?"

"To what?"

"To both? Carolin' with your family and goin' to Carry's birthday party."

"You can't just go on invitin' yourself to do stuff with my family,

Dewey," I said. "You got the manners of a Brahma moose. "Carolin' is sort of a family thing. You will feel like an outcast. Same as Carry's birthday. Why in the *world* would you wanna come to *that?* It'll just be her eatin' and openin' gifts."

"I don't care. I wanna come."

"Okay, I'll bring it up with my mom, but don't feel too dejected when she says no."

"I won't. I'm used to feeling ejected. Or whatever you said."

We rode along in silence a while until Dewey said, "You know, I really can't believe Isaac Swenson's a serial killer."

CHAPTER 25

It was a Wednesday, which, sometimes, meant it was a church day. My mother decided today would be a church day. So around a quarter to six in the evening, we pulled into the parking lot of the Clover Creek First Baptist Church. I was wearing my white-and-blue-checkered shirt that I was pretty sure I'd outgrown last year. It was too tight. And the black slacks my mother forced me to wear. I had also outgrown them at least a year ago. They only came down to about four inches above my shoes. I felt like such a geek.

"Don't *ever* feel like a geek going to church," my mother told me. "God loves everyone. Even the boys who look like they're ready for the flood."

The way it was raining, I figured there could be a flood any minute. There had been thunder and lightning all afternoon.

I didn't like her making fun of me when I was already mad about my clothes. So I told her just that.

"Tell you what, Abe. This weekend, I'll take you to the mall and buy you a new set of church clothes. So this will be the last time you'll ever have to wear these ones—deal?"

What choice did I have? "Deal," I said, grudgingly.

At least when you're sitting in a pew nobody can really see you.

So as we entered the church, I quickly shook Reverend Matthew's hand and pretty much raced to a pew that was about a third of the way back from the front. This was where my mother liked to sit. Not so far back that you can't hear anything and not so close that you look like what she called a "God Hog."

As usual, the choir sang as we took our seats. After attending Full Gospel—the black church—my opinion of the choir at Clover Creek had gone down significantly. The singers at Full Gospel were amazing. The singers here at Clover Creek First Baptist were just normal singers. I had wanted to go back to Full Gospel ever since we went last summer, but my mother and Carry refused, telling me that was a once-in-a-lifetime experience.

I swore that once I got older, I would be attending the black church every Sunday and Wednesday.

My mother and Carry squeezed into the pew on my left.

"So what made you bolt through the door like that?" my mother asked.

"I didn't want no one to see my clothes. They don't fit me."

"They fit you fine," she said.

"No, they don't."

"What?" my mother said. "I can't hear you over the choir."

Carry was sitting between us and so I leaned forward over Carry's lap so she'd be able to hear me better. That's when it happened. And there was no question. Even over the sound of the choir, my mother heard it, too. It was a loud ripping sound, coming from right beneath me.

I'd ripped the rear end right out of my black slacks.

My eyes went wide. My mother and Carry both tried to hold back laughter, which just made the situation worse. "Oh my God!" I said. "What am I gonna do now?"

My mother couldn't stop laughing. "How bad is it?" she finally managed to say. "Reach down and feel."

I reached down and all I felt were my bare legs and underwear. "It's bad!" I practically screamed. "There is no rear end left in the pants! It's all just skin and underpants! What do I do?"

"You can start by taking a chill pill," Carry said. "Do you think you're the only one who's ripped the rear end out of their pants in the house of the Lord?" And with that, she busted a gut laughing.

My mother laughed even harder.

"Come on, you guys, I'm serious here. What do I do?"

My mother's mouth would not stop displaying that stupid grin. "I don't know, honey. I really don't. This is unfamiliar territory for me. I'm sure Jesus loves you just as much in your underwear."

"Maybe you should just announce it to everyone before you get up to leave. That way it won't be such a shock when they see it," Carry offered.

"You guys are the worst support in the world," I said.

"I know," my mother said. "We can sit here until everyone else has filed out and make sure we're the last to leave. Then the only one who might see it will be Reverend Matthew, and you can explain it to him. I'm sure he'll understand."

"Yeah?" I started calming down. That plan sounded reasonable. Then another thought hit me. "Wait! We have to stand to sing and stuff! I can't stand!"

Carry started laughing again and I realized I was doomed.

Reverend Matthew walked up on the stage and took his place at the pulpit. The choir sang a while longer, filling the building with their powerful voices. Sunlight shone through the stained glass windows, bathing Reverend Matthew in beautiful swatches of red, yellow, and green. He stood there welcoming everyone to his church on this rainy Wednesday afternoon looking almost angelic with the big empty cross on the wall behind him.

Then we did a series of hymns from the hymnal before the church prayer. We had to stand for these, so I quickly untucked my shirt so it hung down the back of my pants. I wasn't certain it hung down far enough, but I had to have faith that it did, and I supposed if there was one place to have faith, then church was the best one I could think of.

Other than my underwear showing, things went pretty near the way they always went at Clover Creek. Just like always, I tried to pay attention to his sermon and understand it completely, and just like always, I got lost about fifteen minutes into it; then I just got bored and wished Dewey were sitting beside me and we could whisper stuff about serial killers to each other. That would certainly be better than the geek pants with the ripped-out rear end I was stuffed into today.

After church was over, I rushed straight to the car, but my mother didn't follow me. She surprised me by approaching some people's pickups in the parking lot and looking at their tires in some very suspicious ways. Carry sort of hung around behind her, looking a little lost, taking in the tall oaks that surrounded the churchyard and continued on behind it circling the graveyard.

The rain hadn't stopped. In fact, if anything it was coming down harder and heavier. I watched it bounce off the ground around the car. The sky was full of dark, low-lying clouds, most of which had moved in while we were inside church.

The first pickup my mother checked out belonged to Jacob Tyne. Me and Dewey already knew all about Jake Tyne on account of we'd been going around town trying to find out on our own who the serial killer probably was. The day wasn't as cold as the days had recently been, so, when Jacob walked over to see what it was my mother was doing, I rolled down the car window so I could hear what they were saying. I started thinking her questioning technique could use a bit of work.

"What're you doin' with my tires?" Jacob Tyne asked. "I don't like you lookin' at 'em that way."

"What way?" my mother asked.

"Like they up and killed someone."

Jacob Tyne was the rancher who owned both Superfeed and K's Bait & Tackle. Me and Dewey had written him off as we were pretty sure he was too busy to be a serial killer.

"Do you mind if I ask you a few questions?" my mother asked him.

Right away, I could tell Jacob Tyne *did* in fact mind her asking some questions. Suddenly, I didn't trust him one bit.

"What *sort* of questions?" he asked back.

"Well," my mother said, "see, I'm followin' this murder case and it involves a pickup truck very much like your own. An' I was just wonderin' if you'd mind if I take pictures of the tread on your tires? I have a Polaroid camera in the trunk of my car."

He looked at her like she'd suddenly turned into a crawfish. "You want pictures of my tires? What, did this person you're looking for run over someone?"

My mother smiled. "Not exactly. But I am trying to match treads with the ones found at the crime scene."

"Are you kiddin' me? Am I a suspect? If I am, you better arrest me, but you ain't takin' no pictures of my truck."

"Okay," my mother said, suddenly taking an interest in Jacob Tyne's shoes. "I understand."

"Now why are you starin' at my shoes?" he asked, getting madder by the minute.

"Those Hush Puppies?"

"I dunno. My wife bought 'em. Suppose they *could* be."

"What size do you wear?"

That was about all the questioning Jacob Tyne could take.

"Detective, I ain't givin' you any information unless you got some sort of warrant. I do a lot of things, but I'll tell you what I *don't* do. I don't break no damn laws. Next you'll be wantin' to see my gun collection."

My mother had her pad and a pen out. "So . . . for the record, you're statin' that . . ."

"I ain't statin' nothin'. This is ridiculous," Jacob Tyne said. "If you want to ask me any more ridiculous questions, you'll have to arrest me. And I don't think you're gonna arrest me on the grounds of I won't let you take pictures of my truck tires or my church shoes."

With that, he got into his truck and tore out of the church parking lot in a burst of gravel and mud, leaving my mother coughing in his wake. In my opinion, that was the sort of behavior only a guilty man would display. I figured me and Dewey maybe should definitely check out Jacob Tyne after all.

"I could ticket you for that!" my mother hollered out behind him, but I don't think he heard her.

Then my mother approached the second pickup truck owner

in the lot. It belonged to Bubba Swenson, who worked at Aunt Bella's Burger Hut and whose pa was at the top of my and Dewey's suspect list. Bubba had stuck around, listening to her whole exchange with Jacob Tyne, laughing. Now he was just getting into his silver Ford pickup as my mother walked over to the door. He was just about to close it, when he said, "Don't even bother. I'll just repeat everything Jake said. An' you *really* need to work on your detective skills, I reckon." He started up his truck. "Or at *least* your bedside manner." To me, he even *sounded* like the son of a serial killer.

I knew we had the right guy. If it weren't Isaac Swenson, then it was Bubba. One or both of 'em were serial killers.

Then, just like Jacob Tyne, he drove away, only without all the rocks and mud bursting up behind him.

Carry had disappeared. I think she'd gone around to the back to look at the graveyard. It was full of pretty gardens.

Despite the split in my pants (which I covered pretty well by pulling out my shirt), I exited the car and walked over to my mother, looking up at her. She was standing there, discouraged; her gaze still fixated in the direction Bubba's truck had gone. "Don't feel too upset," I said. "You *were* askin' 'em to do a bunch of stuff that would make 'em look guilty."

"I never even got to the part where I ask for their alibi," she said.

"What's an alibi?"

"Like where you were or what you were doin' when the body was taken away."

"Who's gonna remember that?" I asked. "I can't even remember what I had for breakfast."

She looked off somewhere in the distance. "You're right, nobody's gonna remember, unless they're guilty, and if they're guilty, they ain't gonna tell me, not even when it comes to someone's life being tragically brought to an end."

"What do you mean?" I asked, getting wet from all the rain pounding down. Just then lightning flashed across the western skies, followed a few seconds later by the roar of thunder.

She squatted down and answered. "Nothin'," she said. "Just

enjoy every day you're alive, Abe, because you never know when somethin' might come along and just sideswipe you."

I wasn't sure I understood exactly what she meant, but for some reason, it made me think of my pa and all them stories I heard about how he collided head-on with that other car that night on his way home from work. I was only two, so I didn't remember it.

But I certainly did miss him.

CHAPTER 26

The next day, Leah got a call at the station.

"Hi, this is Peggy Arnold. Margaret at the Six-Gun asked me to give you a call?"

Leah racked her brain, unsuccessfully trying to come up with a Peggy Arnold. "Peggy Arnold?" she asked.

"Oh," the woman on the other end laughed, "she probably referred to me as Bamby Dearest."

"Oh, hi, Bamby—I mean, Peggy. I was callin' 'bout Faith Abilene."

There was a pause. "Haven't seen her in months. Is something wrong?"

"We think we may have found her body."

"You mean she's dead?" She had the sense that Peggy was trying to hold herself together on the other end.

"Were you two close?"

"Well, you never get too close when you work how we work, you know? But it's just that . . . wow, I can't believe it. Hang on a sec, 'kay?"

Leah listened to her cry a bit and then Peggy blew her nose. When she came back she sounded a lot more put together.

"Okay, okay," she said with a big sigh, "I think I'm fine. What do you want from me?"

"Any details you might have that we don't. First off, was Faith Abilene her *real* name? Or was it a stage name like yours?"

"No, it is—I mean, *was*—actually her real name. She didn't believe in hidin' behind anythin'. That was something I loved 'bout her. She was the real deal."

"The last time you saw her, did she seem any different to you? Was she scared? Paranoid? Neurotic? Any sort of panic?"

There was yet another sigh on the other end. "Let me think back. Like I said, it's been at least a couple months. . . . No, I don't think I've ever seen her anythin' but happy. She had a unique charm 'bout her. Made a lot of friends. Apparently one too many."

"Are there any women you haven't seen in the last two months or more that you would consider 'regulars'?"

A long hesitation before she came back. "Not that I can think of."

"Well, you have my number. Please call me if you think of anythin' that might be of help." Then it was Leah's turn to pause. "There's one other thing."

"What's that?"

"Did Faith have family here in Alvin?"

"I'm not sure. We never talked 'bout family much. I think her dad ran off when she was just a kid. I really don't know anythin' 'bout her past."

Leah immediately thought about her dead husband, Billy. So many things reminded her of him all the time.

So many husbands run off.

Billy got into a head-on collision before he even got his chance.

CHAPTER 27

Ethan Montgomery called Leah into his office. She could tell right away he was peeved about something.

"Close the door and take a seat. Now before we start, let me just say I'm not pissed off. I'm just exhausted and tired of takin' the brunt of all these calls that are precipitated by you."

"What did I do now?" Leah asked.

"You accosted people at church. And this isn't the first time this has happened. It seems like it's one of your favorite places to try and question people."

"I simply asked a few folk some questions."

"Leah, you can't go round just accusin' folk of killin'. It isn't a nice thing to do. Especially at church. Folk go to church because it's a holy place of salvation. They don't want to be assaulted. If you try to do it, folk aren't gonna take it. It ain't like you're saying, 'Oh, the weather's sure cleared up. What a great day for a walk.' You're sayin', 'Oh, the weather's sure cleared up and by the way, did you slaughter two people and throw their bodies away?' Surely you understand why this is goin' to get a rise out of folk."

"It was only two people."

"Only two. Thank Christ."

She looked at her feet, then at the wall of legal books. "All right, I'm sorry. It won't happen again."

"It will. We've gone down this road before. But I have to reprimand you when you do it. It's part of my job."

Leah couldn't help but smile. She looked down as she did, so the police chief wouldn't see it.

"So, now that you have two victims, tell me more 'bout their similar attributes," Ethan said. "Anythin' in common there?"

Leah had cross-references for all of the information in both her and Detective Truitt's reports.

"They say it's a pretty good chance that the same gun was used in both killings," she told Ethan.

Ethan interlaced his fingers and put them behind his head while leaning back. His chair gave out a loud squeak.

"And this is the old Beretta, right?" he asked. "Trouble with looking for guns is that you're in the Land of Guns. Everyone down here owns at least one. Some people own ten. People round here like exercisin' their constitutional rights."

"That's right."

"So you've got yourself someone who likes old guns. What else did you find out?"

"Not much. Everything was the same. Definitely the same killer. Almost the exact same MO. Two of the tire tracks came up with forty percent matches. Problem is, both Ford and Chevy use that same tire."

"And of course," Ethan said, "just like the gun, you live in the Land of Chevy and Ford pickups."

"Right. And to make matters worse, actual dates for the vehicles couldn't be established. As far as shoe imprints go, the experts said it was near on impossible to give anything exact."

"Hair?"

"Long, full, and blond. When I was first shown a picture of the crime scene in Graysville, I thought it *was* our girl."

"How tall are the two victims?"

"One is five eight, the other five nine."

"And when they did the autopsy? What did they find?"

"Near-fatal levels of alcohol, and traces of Rohypnol, same thing they found in our vic."

"So our killer likes blondes. And judging by what we've seen, he tends to prey on the loners."

"Maybe they are easier to catch?"

"Maybe. You said Truitt mentioned he thought this Jane Doe— what's her name?"

"Faith Abilene."

"Right. Faith Abilene. You mentioned he thought she might be a streetwalker?"

"That's his theory," Leah said.

"That would certainly make her an easy target."

Leah's head was swimming. "Yeah, it certainly would."

"And there was *no* sign of sexual contact with either victim?"

"None. That's the part that gets me."

"It doesn't mean the murders weren't sexually motivated, though," Ethan said. "Remember that. Killing and sex are both about power."

"I know, Ethan." She sighed.

The fan above them slowly turned, the way it always had as far back as Leah could remember. Both she and Ethan sat there a moment lost in thought. The fan kept turning.

"He's gonna do it again," Ethan said.

No shit, Sherlock. "I know."

"It will be sooner than two and a half months. Serial killers almost always accelerate their rate of murders. They start to crave the excitement."

"So we're under the gun, so to speak."

"So to speak."

"I honestly think he's trying to get our attention," Leah said.

"Could be. He probably has a hard-on for cops. The crazy part for him is, he's damn well gonna get his attention. And it ain't gonna be the kind of attention he likes. Let me tell you that."

CHAPTER 28

"Do you think we *need* to look for anyone else?" Dewey asked me.

"I think we should, just to be sure," I said. "At least one or two more."

We were riding our bikes, turning down Hunter Road from Cottonwood Lane. It was Thursday after school and we had both decided Isaac Swenson was the serial killer my mother was looking for.

"Who should we try now?" Dewey asked as we raced down Hunter Road.

"I don't know, but before we do anything, we need notebooks. So one problem at a time." We rode up onto the sidewalk and pulled to a stop in front of Mr. Harrison's five-and-dime. We leaned our bikes against the window.

The bus ride home from school had been dreadful. It was always awful, but today it had been particularly annoying because of this big kid who I swear looked like he was in his twenties (I am sure he shaved) wouldn't let anyone sit on any of the seats beside, behind, or in front of him. His name was Scott and, behind his back, everyone called him Snot.

Finally, the bus driver yelled at him and Scott let people sit in the seats. Me and Dewey took the ones in front of him, which was a mistake because he wound up kicking the bottom of it all the way home. I decided from now on I was also going to call him Snot behind his back, too.

At least we had a few days off now for Christmas. We wouldn't be going back for a week, until after New Year's. That made me happy.

"Who should we try next?" Dewey asked as we entered the store.

The notebooks were behind the till, so we had to ask for them. Mr. Harrison kept all the small things behind the till. I wasn't sure why. It wasn't like they were expensive. They were fifty cents each.

We walked in and got in line behind a guy delivering three boxes to Mr. Harrison. Mr. Harrison had his reading glasses on and was signing for them.

Dewey grabbed my arm in what felt like a panic and yanked me down one of the aisles. It actually hurt my arm where he grabbed and pulled.

"What the hell, Dewey? What's wrong with you?"

He spoke in a whisper. "Wasn't Mr. Harrison getting three boxes delivered when we bought our *first* notebooks?"

My pulse quickened. "You're right. And we came straight from getting home from the bus to here, so the time would be the same."

We went outside and stood by our bikes, occasionally casting subtle glances into the store.

"Are we watching Mr. Harrison now?" Dewey asked.

"I reckon we are."

"We have no notebooks," Dewey pointed out. "We need new ones. Maybe AppleSmart's has 'em."

"No, I don't want to leave and miss anything. Write on the back pages of the notes we took for Isaac Swenson."

Inside the store, Mr. Harrison finished signing and the delivery guy came out of the store as Mr. Harrison set the three boxes exactly where he'd set the three he received on Tuesday when we bought our first notebooks. Then he went through the store, aisle by aisle, tidying things. "He started with aisle seven, just like he did before," I said.

"I can't believe Mr. Harrison's a serial killer," Dewey said.

"We don't know that yet. He's still got a long way to go before he beats out Isaac Swenson."

We watched for another fifteen minutes. Mr. Harrison finished tidying shelves and swept, exactly like we'd seen him do a hundred times. He started with aisle one just like always. And when he was finished, he went back behind the counter, picked up a book, and started reading. We'd seen him do that way more than a few times, too.

"This is getting freaky," I whispered to Dewey.

"Yeah," Dewey said, although he didn't sound as excited.

"What's wrong?" I asked.

"I got a problem."

"What kind of problem?"

"I need to use the toilet."

"Great," I said. Truth was, I did, too. I thought about this. "Okay, well, it looks like Mr. Harrison will be reading a while. I think the closest public toilet is at Fast Gas. Why don't we head down there and we can take turns with one of us standin' sentry while the other one goes inside?"

"What do you mean 'standin' sentry'?" Dewey asked.

"Looking for anything weird. People following patterns."

"Oh, okay."

"At least then we're not just wastin' our time goin' to the toilet."

"That makes sense."

When we got to Fast Gas, the only person on shift was a twenty-year-old guy with bad acne, messed-up hair, and the most reflective braces I've ever seen. The good part was I don't think he minded us using his restroom at all. I was worried we'd need to drive in and get gas or something.

Dewey went to the toilet first while I kept an eye on Main Street. I was very careful to not act suspicious. Dewey worried me. He wasn't so great at not acting suspicious.

Turned out my worries were for a good reason.

"What y'all doin'?" I heard the guy with the braces ask Dewey while I was in the restroom. I kept repeating to myself: Please don't tell him the truth. Please don't tell him the truth.

Then, of course, Dewey told him the truth. "We're tryin' to help the Alvin Police Department. We're lookin' for people who live with the same sort of pattern every day."

I quickly finished up as fast as I could and came out, heading straight toward them. "What Dewey here means is that we have a school project to do involvin' patterns in people's lives, and we have all of Christmas break to do it and we thought we'd get a jump on things and start right away."

"So how are the police involved?"

I laughed. "They aren't. But we might be usin' the patterns in class to make fake victim and perpetrator sheets and try to learn forensic psychology." I was pulling every bit of everything I could remember out of the television show *Criminal Activity*. It's a show I'm not supposed to watch, but my mother isn't always home to tell me I can't.

"You boys got homework over Christmas break and y'all startin' it on day one? Who *does* that?"

I shrugged. "I s'pose we're just keen on gettin' a good grade is all."

There was a pause, during which I guessed the attendant thought over what we had just told him, wondering who to believe. Then he said, "You know, come to think of it, my days follow a pattern. Pretty much exactly the same every day."

Dewey flipped to a new page in his notebook. "Tell me about it."

I rolled my eyes. I couldn't believe he was doing this.

"Well, I get up to the sound of my alarm clock at seven o'clock. By then my cat will be calling me for food. So I give her some. By the way, my name is Earl Sims." He stuck out his hand.

Dewey ignored his hand, and asked, "What kind of cat and what kind of food?"

"What the hell does *that* have to do with anythin'?" I asked. Earl Sims's hand still stayed there, waiting for Dewey.

"You know," Earl Sims said, "when a man offers his name, you should acknowledge it and, the very least, return your name, preferably with a handshake. You just did the rudest thing I've ever seen anybody do in a conversation." Then he turned to me. "And *you* shouldn't go round saying *hell*. You're too young to cuss."

"Oh," Dewey stammered. "I'm sorry. I didn't know. I'm Dewey." He finally shook Earl's hand.

"And I'm Abe." Me and Earl shook hands.

"Now you," Earl said to me, "you have a nice grip on you." Then, turning his focus back to Dewey, Earl said, "Anyway, my cat is named Weapon One. She's a big Persian that I love to death."

"I see," said Dewey.

I don't at all, I wanted to say. *How does this tie in to our pattern discussion?*

My gaze wandered to the old gas pumps that looked like they'd been standing where they were for near on a hundred years. This serial killer wasn't like the one I watched from time to time on *Criminal Activity.* This serial killer was much different. Much, much, much, much different. According to my mother, this serial killer tried to comfort his victims before he killed them. She wouldn't tell me *how* the victims were comforted, just that they were.

I had already asked my mother if either of the two victims had been wearing gold neck chains when they found them. Those could've easily been taken by the killer and been the motive for the whole thing. But my mother had little regard toward this theory. She always did that to my theories. It was so annoying.

It still all made no sense to me. I wished I had my mother's background in police work. I was almost sure I was on the brink of sorting this one out, even without her years of knowledge.

The first body had been found washed up in Willet Park in the lake. Well, actually that was the second body. My mother just hadn't known about the first body yet. It had been found in an abandoned mine in Graysville just outside of Birmingham. According to my mother, the perp (which I knew was short for perpetrator) never made any mistakes. She didn't think the killer kept any mementos like a lot of the perps on *Criminal Activity* did; he didn't talk to anyone about his killings; he just led a normal life—well, as normal as you could after watching someone die— and waited two months or so before doing it all again with a new victim.

Dewey had finally finished his ridiculous line of questioning with Earl Sims.

"Okay," I said, "thank you for being so patient with us, Mr. Sims. We really do appreciate it."

"Ah, you guys were a nice distraction from my day-to-day routine, which by the way involves getting up at the same time every morning, putting on nothing but a pair of sweats, eating a full bowl of Corn Flakes, working out on my treadmill for about thirty-five minutes, showerin', dressin' for the day, and headin' out the door to my job.

"Once I get here, from about nine to ten, I play a game on the computer called Slither."

Me and Dewey shared a knowing nod. We knew Slither. It is on my mom's computer at the police station. In the game you have to keep a snake from hitting any obstacles or itself and the whole while, the snake is growing longer. It's annoyingly addictive.

The clerk continued. "I play that, oh, well, that depends on how late the boss is. Then I print out all outstanding reports from this here keypad. If I am going to start on a new job, I enter it manually. If I'm already on a job, I check the computer for any updates that may have been called in from other gas stations or even the public."

I looked over at the bright green letters on the dark green background. "Sounds complicated."

"It's really not."

"Anything else you do?" Dewey asks.

"I make a list of people who need questionin' and put it into my pocket. I then check the magazine on my Smith & Wesson 3904 and make sure it's completely loaded."

"How many bullets does it take?" Dewey asked.

"Eight, but you can throw one in the pipe if you'd rather have nine."

"What does that mean?" I asked.

"It means I'm not 'bout to explain the concept of firearms to you two."

"So you bring your gun to work?"

"Hell's right I do. You know how many freaks out there stop to get gas or to take a leak?"

Both me and Dewey shook our heads, and said, "No," at the same time.

"Well, I'm not sure of the exact number. But it's a *lot*. I just live by the credo 'Better late than never. And even better if you're armed to the teeth.' I know it don't rhyme, but it works for me. Anyway, let's talk some other time. I've got to make it look like I at least *tried* to get some work done today."

"Okay," Dewey said, happy as a clam. We wheeled to the road side and Dewey stopped and waved over his head. "Thanks again!"

Earl completely ignored him. God, Dewey could be so weird sometimes.

We had already started very quickly to fill our pads with lists of different people around town and what they did at certain times of the day. We only wrote down the significant stuff, like eating lunch or going to a certain store. Things like heading to the toilet didn't seem to me to be worth listing. It's hard to control those types of things.

All of this turned out to be hard work with just the two of us, especially on account of we were on bicycles and most of the other folk were in cars, but we started to discover disturbing patterns right away. Our suspect list would grow to eight people by our third day. I figured we'd wait a few more days—maybe even a week—until we had a good list of suspects before presenting our findings to my mother.

"So," Dewey said as we moved on. "I guess we can safely write off Earl Sims," he told me happily.

"What the hell are you talkin' 'bout?" I asked him. "He's one of the weirdest people I've ever met and I even got a 'serial killer' vibe off him, if there is such a thing."

"I reckon he was fine folk," Dewey said. "Very gracious and understanding."

"Maybe he's addicted to killing?" I asked out loud even though the question was directed more at myself than anyone else. The more I thought about it the more that answer was stuck in my head.

"Who?" Dewey asked.

"Our serial killer."

"Oh, I thought you meant Earl."

"I just may have."

"I reckon you're the crazy one," Dewey said.

"Listen, I'm sort of exhausted. Earl Sims sapped the life outta me. Any chance you'd disagree if I said we should ride home and take a little nap before quittin' for the day?"

"Nah, that's fine. Maybe I could do some myself while you're sleepin'."

Oh, dear baby Jesus up in heaven. "Please promise me you won't, Dewey?" I asked.

"Why not?"

"Because these people take things weirdly, and they're used to two people comin' to their door for church reasons and that. If you go by yourself, you'll immediately make them defensive."

Dewey hung his head. "I guess you're right. Okay, I will wait until you're done. In the meantime, maybe I'll go and create some more inventions."

"There you go. A perfect use for your time."

We finished pushing our bikes up the hill of Hunter Road, something we did about half the time. The other half we actually rode up it, but our legs felt so painful afterward. I was completely out of breath and startin' to wheeze when I breathed.

"This can't be good for you," Dewey said.

CHAPTER 29

Leah called Detective Truitt up in Birmingham. "Manage to dig up anythin' new with our evidence?"

"No, we've drawn pretty much the same conclusions."

"Oh, by the way, Faith Abilene is not a street name. It's the real McCoy. I tried to find family here in Alvin but came up short. Apparently she's been living here awhile."

"How did you find that out?"

"Made friends with a hooker."

"Nice."

"Did your medical examiner find any usable DNA on the body? There was none on ours because the lake water would've washed it away."

"None on ours either. This guy was careful. Not even a usable fiber."

"So what do we got to go on?" Leah asked.

"Well, let's see," Truitt said while simultaneously sighing. "Basically our best leads come from the fingernail scrapings. And I suppose if we could somehow link the two messages."

"The ones written across the bodies, you mean?"

"Yeah."

"I've been thinkin' 'bout those, too. I think they're there to taunt us. In the first—on your victim—he's basically telling us that he's the thorn among the lilies. He's the one bad guy who won't get caught at his game. In the second, he simply replaced 'law' with 'Lord,' making it a pretty obvious poke our way, I'd say."

"Could be. So it's someone who has some reason to hate us. And this reason came up around three months ago. What happened in Alvin three months ago, Miss Leah?"

She hated being called Miss Leah, but, for reasons she'll never know, let it go this time. Besides, she figured if she told him she hated it, he'd just do it more often. "I don't know. We're not a very busy town crime-wise. I can't think of anythin' big or small that happened three months ago. Hang on, let me ask Chris."

Chris was just coming back from the restroom. "Ask me what?"

"Can you think of anything that happened three months or so ago that might give someone a reason to have a chip on their shoulder against the police. In particular against the Alvin Police Department?"

Chris thought about this. "I threw Willy Beaumont's kid, Jerry, in the lockup for the night around then for bein' drunk and disorderly on Main Street. But I gave him the benefit of the doubt first. It wasn't until he pulled down his pants in front of two old ladies that I cuffed him and told him I had a nice, cold, stone bench for him to sleep it off."

"I don't think Jerry Beaumont's a serial killer," Leah said.

She lifted the telephone receiver back to her mouth. "Who's Jerry Beaumont?" Truitt asked. "Don't rule anyone out!"

"No, no. He was just a kid picked up for the night so he could sober up after pulling down his pants in front of some old folk."

"Oh. Yeah, I think you're safe taking him off the killer list. Even *I've* done that. What 'bout the crosses?"

"Right. The crosses. I near on forgot 'bout them. Maybe religion does play a role in this after all. Maybe the cross is there as a form of recompense. Sort of like the killer's givin' the victim a ticket to heaven. Could be ritual killings."

There was a pause. "I think you're reachin'."

"Well, hell, Dan, I dunno. This whole thing is a big bag of goose turd. Of course I'm reachin'."

Leah stared at the stuffed dog with the blue ribbon wrapped around its neck that sat on her desk beside her computer monitor. Abe bought it for her for Mother's Day a few years back. She wished it could talk. Maybe it could tell her where to find the answers.

"Let's go back to the nails," Truitt said. "What do we have?"

"Dirt and clay, the type of which appears in the northern parts of Alvin and up in the wooded areas for about a hundred square miles. Most of that land is desolate. Then we have sawdust. Lots of sawdust. Sawdust don't appear that frequently. It takes someone to make sawdust."

"Good point. So where do we find lots of sawdust?"

"Sawmills. Ranches. Most farms, actually. Construction sites. Um, I'm runnin' out of ideas."

"Alvin has a lot of ranches around it, don't it?"

"It certainly does. Twenty-seven major ones last time I counted. And pretty much every one of those ranchers owns a Ford or a Chevy pickup. Thing 'bout Alvin: Folk round here, we buy American."

Leah still clearly remembered one of her last big cases, the Mary Ann Dailey and Tiffany Michelle Yates case. She hadn't managed to save Mary Ann, but she had found Tiffany Michelle before it was too late. Both girls had been hung from a hook in a barn and . . . well, the rest of it Leah had spent the last year trying to push out of her mind. Eventually, Leah shot the killer while he was fleeing through the cornfield. Because of that, the newspapers had dubbed him the Cornstalk Killer.

Leah didn't like the name.

"Maybe you should do a bit of questioning around some of your ranches?"

"Me and Chris could try that. Might piss a few people off. But I'm kind of used to that."

"I could come down and help if you want."

"Nah, why don't you poke around up there. I mean, it's only my *theory* that the killer's from Alvin. He could just as easily come from

Birmingham. I just think it makes sense that the more confident he gets, the closer to home he'll drop the bodies. Why waste a tank of gas and all that time for no reason? Especially if he's out to make fun of cops. But then, of course, there's the Six-Gun Saloon connection."

That was Leah's big clue right now. That both girls frequented the same tavern.

"Between you and me, I actually agree with you, Leah," Truitt said. "And don't take that lightly. I rarely agree with anybody."

Leah laughed. "Thanks for the vote of confidence. I'll get back to you if anything pops up." There was a hesitation, then, "Oh, and, Dan?"

"Yeah?"

"Merry Christmas."

"Merry Christmas to you too, Leah. I hope you and your family have a wonderful holiday."

She hung up the phone and Chris turned to her. "So," he said, "what is it that 'me and Chris' are tryin' that might piss a few people off? I didn't rightly like the sound of that."

"We're goin' on a search for our unsub. Knockin' on farmhouse doors. Checkin' out ranches. Anywhere there's lots of sawdust. Lookin' for places you could keep a body stashed away for six or seven days."

"Unsub?"

"Unknown subject."

Chris put his face in his hands. "I'm gonna get yelled at a lot, ain't I?"

"Yep, most likely."

"You know, some days I really hate my job." He turned to Leah, a beseeching look on his face. "Can we at least wait until after Christmas to do it?"

"Yeah."

CHAPTER 30

It was two days before Christmas, which also meant it was the first day off for Christmas break. Me and Dewey spent the day spying on folk and then in the evening, we joined everyone to go out caroling. There was my mother, Caroline, and my Uncle Henry. I didn't find caroling all that fun. It was a lot like church—something I did to keep my mother happy.

My mother planned on caroling twice this year. Tonight and tomorrow night. She told me she thought it would expand Christmas Eve to go two nights. She really loved caroling. I didn't. I always felt like we were bothering folk.

This year we were collecting for the Empty Stocking Fund. Dewey said, "If their stocking ain't getting filled by now, I doubt Santa's gonna fill it no matter how much we bribe him. He won't have enough time."

Me and my mother just looked at him. I could tell she wanted to say something about his ridiculous belief in Santa Claus, but she held back. "This is for *next* year, Dewey," she said instead.

"Oh, I think I understand."

No, but by next year you should. Hopefully.

We actually started out caroling from the church, where other groups came to gather. Reverend Matthew had been standing in the churchyard giving out books of Christmas carols, I guess in case people didn't know the words. What I didn't understand was if you didn't know the words, there was no way you'd ever know the song, so what was the point? We had already decided to stick to the classics like "Jingle Bells," "Frosty the Snowman," and "Rudolph the Red-Nosed Reindeer," so we didn't really need the books. We all took one anyway. My mother made us. I think it was to be polite.

At first I thought we were all going to go together in one big throng of thirty people, but we soon broke away from each other into smaller groups.

I always try to harmonize with my mother. She has a nice voice and I always think I have a pretty good low voice, but every time I try to harmonize it seems to throw her and she gets mad at me after.

"How come you can't sing like a normal person?" she asked.

"What do you mean? I was singing harmony."

"You was singing a completely different song."

Dewey, who couldn't carry a tune in a bucket, laughed. "You try too hard, Abe. Just sing along. Don't try to go along with anyone else."

This from the guy who once tried to invent a flying hat with a propeller on the top. If the hat actually had flown (and, of course, it never did), you would have to hang on to these little handles sticking out of the sides to fly with it.

"So," Uncle Henry asked between houses, "I assume everyone's excited 'bout the big day?"

"Sure am," Dewey said.

"What did you ask . . ." I had to pause so I didn't laugh. ". . . Santa for?"

"Plutonium."

"What?" Uncle Henry asked.

"Plutonium. I have this great idea for an invention, but I need a piece of plutonium. Just a small one."

"Is that so?" Uncle Henry looked at me.

I just shrugged.

"What 'bout you, Abe?"

"More Dungeons and Dragons stuff."

"I reckon you boys are turnin' into recluses playin' that game," my mother said. "It's all you ever do."

"No, Miss Teal," Dewey said. "I still make inventions. Wait until you see this next one."

"The one you need the plutonium for?"

"Just a small piece."

"Can't wait."

"That Dungeons and Dragons—is it really the work of the devil like those church groups have you believe?" Uncle Henry asked.

"I've stood in the kitchen listenin' while they play at the dinin' room table," my mother said. "It's more like filin' the devil's taxes." She laughed. "I actually think it's pretty educational and, hey, it keeps 'em off the streets. Dealin' with what I've been dealin' with lately, that is a *good* thing."

We got to the next door and Dewey ran up in front of us. We all took a minute to look at each other. "What's he gonna do when Santa doesn't deliver his plutonium?" my mother asked.

"Maybe stop believin'?" I offered.

"That will be sad."

"I think it's time, Leah," Uncle Henry said. "A year, maybe two from now and the kid'll probably be shavin'."

"I doubt it," I said. "He'll invent something to do it for him. Only it will require a Tesla coil to make it work."

CHAPTER 31

I woke up to a very early pink and blue sunrise Christmas morning, despite the fact that I don't think I actually got to sleep until after midnight the night before. I was too excited. It's hard to go to sleep when you're excited or when you're scared. I find both emotions give me the same sort of feeling, sort of like a knot tied up in my stomach. It's not a good feeling, even for something as great as Christmas.

Our tree in the living room had had wrapped gifts beneath it for at least the last two weeks. Five were for me. I'd counted them and shaken them every day, so I knew. But there always seemed to be extra ones once Christmas actually came.

I checked my watch—the one Uncle Henry bought me—and looked at the time. It said quarter to six. Now I had a problem. I had to decide if quarter to six was too early to wake up Uncle Henry. I didn't really care if I woke up Carry or not, and my mother could sleep through a hurricane, but Uncle Henry was sleeping in the same room as the tree and all the presents. It would be impossible to go in there and *not* wake him up.

I decided to do the right thing and lie here until seven o'clock. Seven o'clock was fair. Lots of people got up at seven. But that meant I had to find a way to entertain myself for an hour and fifteen minutes. I wasn't very good at entertaining myself. Here was a perfect example of where Dewey would come in handy. Dewey could entertain himself in the desert where there's nothing but sand. He'd find some way to make that entertaining while he slowly died of dehydration.

I could just see him now, skipping across the Sahara, building sand castles as he meandered his way past the dunes.

Suddenly a loud noise rang out from somewhere in the house, making me practically jump right out of my pajamas. It was a *clang!* that sounded like someone had dropped a big metal ball onto a big metal floor. I started wondering if maybe what I heard was a car accident outside, when I heard the sound again. This time, Uncle Henry's voice followed the sound. "Christmas morning! Ho ho ho! Everybody out of bed and on your feet! You've overslept!" He made the clang again. I couldn't figure out how he was doing it, but I was certainly happy he was up already.

I quickly got out of my bed and put on my slippers. Then I put on my housecoat and wrapped it around my pajamas and tied it tightly. It was a cold morning.

I opened my door and almost raced straight into Uncle Henry, who was standing right outside it with a pot lid in each hand.

"There's one little trooper. Now we're just two short."

He clanged the pot lids together again. They were even louder out here. He was standing right in front of Carry's door when he did it. "Come on, sugar plum, it's time to rise and see the dawn."

"And open presents!" I added.

"And open presents," Uncle Henry repeated.

"Can't you go away and come back in two hours?" Carry complained from behind her bedroom door.

"Nope, Christmas has started. Now there's no stopping it."

He made another clang. This time in front of my mother's door. "Come on, Leah, get up and get festive!"

"You better have coffee brewin' or I'll show you what you can do with your festive," she said from behind *her* door.

"What's with women and sleep?" Uncle Henry asked me.

I shrugged back. "I reckon they're ugly if they don't get enough."

"I heard that," my mother called out.

"Are you two comin' or what? If you aren't out in the next five minutes, Abe and I are gonna start openin' presents without you."

I heard my mother yawn. "I'm comin'. Geez, you're like the friggin' Gestapo."

"Yeah, but they didn't have pot lids." He clanged them together again in front of Carry's door.

"All right! I'm getting up! Go away and I'll be faster."

"Shall we go start on the coffee?" Uncle Henry asked me.

I only got to have coffee on special days and I could think of no day more special than Christmas. "Sure!" I said. I couldn't believe Carry didn't want to get up. I would've just got up an hour after going to bed if I'd have been allowed. Women *were* weird. Uncle Henry was right.

While me and Uncle Henry sat at the kitchen table drinking our coffee, the rest of the family slowly slunk out to join us. Christmas was one of those special times I was allowed to drink coffee. When I first started a couple years ago, my mother gave me maybe two cups a year. I didn't really like the taste, anyway. But now, the special times she lets me drink it happen more and more often and I must say, the taste is growing on me.

This morning, though, I didn't taste the coffee at all. I just waited, full of anticipation and a stomach full of tinsel waiting for my mother and Carry to finally come out of their bedrooms.

First came my mother, who looked like she hadn't slept at all. She had just thrown a robe on over her pajamas like me. Then came Carry, whose blond hair was all tangled and matted. She looked like a homeless person in an extremely oversized Alabama Crimson Tide football jersey and her slippers.

"Too bad, you guys," Uncle Henry said.

"What?" Carry said, her eyes only half open as she zombie-walked to a seat at the table. "Please get me a cup of coffee too, Mother. I hope to God it's strong."

"What do you mean what?" Uncle Henry asked. "You missed Christmas. Abe and I already opened all the presents. Even yours."

"Was that supposed to be funny? It's too early for funny," Carry said.

We all sat and finished our coffees; then we headed to the living room. Uncle Henry had already turned on the tree lights, casting the room in an array of red, green, blue, and gold. It looked so magical. It *felt* magical. But then, Christmas *was* magical, to me anyway.

"Who wants to play Santa?" my mother asked.

"Not me," Carry said with a frown.

"I hate playin' Santa," I said. "You don't get a chance to look at anythin' you got."

"Fine," Uncle Henry said. "I'm Santa. I just hope none of you made the naughty list."

Nobody laughed.

"Okay," he said, reaching for the first box and reading the tag. "This one's for Caroline." He handed her the gift. It was wrapped in paper covered in reindeer.

"And this one's for Abe." He handed me a square flat one, wrapped in paper with pictures of Christmas presents on it, which for some reason seemed weird to me.

I quickly opened my gift. It was a copy of the *Advanced Dungeons & Dragons Player's Handbook*. Even though I figured I was getting it, it was still awesome to actually hold it in my hands. I smelled it. I love the smell of books. "Thank you!" I said, smiling. "This is great!"

"Did I get the right one?" my mother asked, looking like her head was pounding. Her voice sounded lost because she woke up too early.

"Totally! This is super neat! Thank you!"

Carry's gift turned out to be clothes of some sort. She seemed to like it, but I would feel ripped off. Who wants clothes for Christmas?

My next gift turned out to be a Magic 8 Ball. That was kind of cool. I asked it whether or not Dewey was going to get plutonium for Christmas, shook it up, and read: "VERY DOUBTFUL."

"Wow!" I said. "It even works!"

Then I opened a lava lamp for one of the bedside tables in my room. It sat there all bubbly and purple, slowly dripping lava around and around. It reminded me of Slime, my favorite comic book character.

Then Uncle Henry passed me a fairly long, narrow box covered with shiny silver paper and tied with a red ribbon. This one felt different than the rest. Maybe because the paper was so nice or that someone had taken time to wrap it so pretty. It just felt like a lot of effort had been spent on it. I opened it with care, not the way I usually did by just ripping into the paper. At the end, I came to a blank white box. Setting it in my lap, I pulled off the top.

I couldn't believe what I was looking at.

I lifted my eyes to my mother. "Is this . . . ?"

"Six months ago you wanted a sword so bad you made me feel awful for not gettin' you one. Well, I was eavesdropping on your little game the other day and heard your character uses one of these."

I gently pulled it out. "Is it *real?*"

"Better be for what I paid for it. And yes, it's real. Be very careful with it. I bought it at a huntin' store."

"Shh," Uncle Henry said. "Santa's elves made it. They can make anything."

"You've got the wrong guy," I said. "Go down the street six houses."

I couldn't believe it. I had my very own real, honest-to-goodness bow, and farther down in the box was a quiver and six arrows. The arrows were beautiful, with multicolored feathers on their ends.

"I don't know what to say," I said.

"Just tell me you won't kill anyone. These arrows have blunt tips, but they'll still do a lot of damage to someone if you hit 'em hard enough."

"I'll be super careful, I promise." I couldn't believe it.

"I thought it might get you boys outside for a while," my mother said.

There were two more gifts for me under the tree. I could pretty much guess what they were, but I acted surprised when I opened them anyway. One was the *Advanced Dungeons & Dragons: Monster Manual* and the other was the *Advanced Dungeons & Dragons: Dungeon Masters Guide.*

"Looks like you got a lot of reading to do," Uncle Henry said.

"That's what the game's all 'bout," I replied. "Reading. There is no board. You just read and imagine stuff."

"I'd never understand it. Well, pardner, that's it for you, I'm afraid. Oh, except for this."

He handed me the gift from him. It felt like a big round pillow, and turned out to be an archery target. It had white with concentric rings on it and a small wooden stand. "Thanks, Uncle Henry!" I said. "Now I can become a great archer!"

Uncle Henry gave Carry a small camera. She seemed pretty happy with it.

My mother opened my present for her. I spent a long time looking for just that perfect special item. I wanted to buy her a new gun, but they wouldn't sell it to me. My mother also hadn't given me enough money for a gun, so I bought her a knife sharpener instead.

"Thanks, Abe. Now I can make sure all our knives are good and sharp."

"It's almost as good as a new gun. That's what I wanted to get you, but at least with these, you can still use knives to kill people."

"Yes," she said. "But we don't. Do y'all like what you got?"

"Do I? I have to call Dewey!" I said, and ran for the phone.

"Whoa!" my mother yelled. "Hold up there a minute."

"What?"

"It's twenty minutes after six. Don't phone anyone at that time unless it's an emergency. At *least* wait 'til seven. Preferably eight. Normal people sleep in a bit later than we do, and nobody calls anyone at this hour."

Right at that moment, the phone rang. I quickly answered it. It was Dewey.

"What did you get?" he asked excitedly.

"All three Advanced D and D books and, get this, a *real* bow and arrows. Like one used for hunting."

"Neat! But wait 'til you see what I got. You're gonna be so jealous."

"You got your plutonium?"

"Nah, this is better," Dewey said.

"What is it?"

"A sword. A *real* one, like we wanted last summer. I *told* you Santa's elves could make anythin'."

"Apparently as long as it's not radioactive."

"Now we can go outside and pretend we're really playing D and D," he said.

"Our mothers musta got together on these presents."

"What do you mean? Santa brought mine."

"Oh, yeah. I forgot. I can't wait to see it."

"I'm not showin' it to you until I've had some practice with it, so give me a few days," Dewey said.

"What? Why?"

"On account of warriors need to practice and learn The Way before they go into battle."

"What have you been watchin' on TV now?"

"Nothin', it's just somethin' I heard."

"Okay, well, I can practice, too. I'm gonna be a crack shot with my bow."

"Not nearly as good as me," Dewey said. "'Sides, you have a lot of readin' to do with those three new manuals you got."

"You gotta read the *Player's Handbook,* too. And probably the *Monster Manual* isn't a bad idea," I said.

"Anyway, I gotta go," Dewey said. "I still have presents to open!"

"All right. Bye, Dewey!"

And with that, I hung up, thinking the kid was nuts. *Warriors need to practice and learn The Way before going into battle.* He probably thought The Way was some sort of map to a shop on Main Street or somethin'.

CHAPTER 32

Even though it was the day after Christmas, Leah couldn't settle her mind. She decided since the kids were going to be busy all day playing with the stuff they got, it was the perfect time to sneak out and do some research. Also, this day was usually pretty dead at police stations, so it would probably be easier for her to gain access to the file room. They'd either just give it to her or have to call their superiors at home, and nobody wants to bug their superior on the day after Christmas.

Before heading out, she ate breakfast with her family. Hank was still here, but leaving as soon as breakfast was over.

"Can't you stay a little longer?" Carry whined at him.

"Nope, sorry, my little sugar plum," he said. "Gotta get to my boys' house. They're cookin' me up quite a spread; it should be a delicious turkey supper!"

"But you had turkey last night."

"My dear," Hank said, setting a plate of eggs, bacon, and hash browns down in front of Carry, "one can *never* have enough turkey."

"I'm really gonna miss you, Hank," Leah said.

"Oh, I'm gonna miss you guys, too. I always do. But don't worry, I'll be back soon as I can." He turned his attention to Abe.

"How 'bout you, my little wrangler? You gonna miss your Uncle Henry?"

"I'm not your 'little wrangler,'" Abe said. He had his bow in his hand. Leah was pretty certain he had slept with it, but she wasn't about to say anything. She was just happy he was enjoying his gift. "I'm Luciheed, Elf Prince of Newpyr."

"Oh, I'm so sorry, Lucihead," Uncle Henry said. "Please forgive an old fool like me and don't shoot me to death."

"You're forgiven. And it's Luci*heed,* not head. And of course I'm gonna miss you."

Carry said, "Does he *really* have to wear that bow and arrow while we eat?"

"One day you'll be happy I have it. It might be just the power you need for me to save your life," Abe said.

"You ain't got no power, other than the power to hang around with your dimwitted friend. Where is he, anyway? I haven't seen him yesterday or today. That's like a world record, I reckon."

"He's been busy," Abe said, sounding a bit let down.

"Doin' what?"

"Practicin' bein' Black Blade, his favorite comic book hero. Says he wants to get real good before we fight again."

Carry laughed. "He has a sword? You have a bow with just six arrows I bet you can't aim at all. That's *your* power. You're gonna get so walloped by him. I can't wait to see it."

The rest of breakfast was quiet. Afterward, everyone shared in clearing the table. Then they all said good-bye to Uncle Henry and waved to him out the front window as he backed his car onto the street and headed out of town.

"So what are we doin' today, Mother?" Carry asked.

"Well, y'all got fine new gifts to keep you busy. I thought I might slip out and get some police work done. I have a few things that I have to work on and today's a good day to do that."

"So you're abandoning your family on the day after Christmas?" Carry asked.

"Look at it more like I'm lettin' you do whatever you want."

"Oh, that *does* sound better."

"She can't beat me up!" Abe squealed. "Tell her, Mom! Tell her she can't beat me up!"

"Okay, anythin' you want other than beatin' up Abe."

"Thank you," Abe said.

Actually, Leah hadn't completely run out of clues in her case. She *did* still have the weird videotape she had gotten from Dan. Every time she ran it, she had the same reaction. *Something about it is wrong.*

She wondered if it was worth researching newspapers from all the major towns in the Alabama areas, looking for news reports in the last few months about finding bodies with sewn-up eyes.

Then she thought, *If that were true, someone would've put two and two together by now.* But then, it took Chris to do it with the newspaper from Birmingham, so who knew?

If this was a serial killing, and it certainly was chalking itself up to be one, shouldn't there be more murders happening? Shouldn't there be a trail of them? What made the killer start with Graysville? And did he really live in Alvin? And did two killings make a serial killer? Leah thought somewhere in the back of her mind that the number had to be three before it was official. Oh, but that was the Feds talking.

And there was another thing that had been bothering her lately. Should she bring the Feds in on this? She knew Ethan's stance on the whole thing, but maybe this was a case that was too big for her. Even with Ethan's help and his forensics analysis, she felt somehow out of her league.

Pulling a map of Alabama from her drawer and laying it on the table, she examined all the small towns in the vicinity of Alvin: Satsuma, Chickasaw, Grand Bay, Stapleton, Le Moyne, Semmes, and Atmore. There were more, of course, but those were the handful that jumped out at her. If a killing similar to the one Luanne Cooper had found in Willet Park had happened in any of these places, would she hear about it? She was pretty sure she would.

CHAPTER 33

Me and Dewey spent the morning practicing with our new weapons. Before he left, Uncle Henry didn't just set up my target for me, he created a big body bag out of canvas, stuffed it full of old newspapers, and hung it from the boughs of one of the cherry trees for Dewey to hit with his sword and pretend it was a person.

I turned out to be a naturally terrible shot with the bow and arrow. Not only could I not hit the center of my target, I couldn't hit the target. Anywhere.

Dewey fared much better with his body bag.

I was getting so frustrated that by lunchtime I was ready to call it quits and start on our real mission: finding out who the serial killer was in Alvin.

Me and Dewey were pretty certain it was Isaac Swenson, but my mother was still searching all over town for someone else; she was searching for someone she considered to be the *real* killer. We had to find out for sure if we were right, and that involved some closer investigation. I didn't dare go to my mother until we knew for certain. We'd just be given heck.

So, we decided to sneak into Isaac Swenson's barn and search for clues. We figured if there were any to be found, that was where they'd be. We knew his patterns very well—he'd be out with his cattle for another half an hour. That gave us plenty of time to do a thorough examination of his barn.

Like most barns in Alvin, Isaac Swenson's was painted red. We approached the front doors from our hiding spot in the long golden grass and the two of us pulled one side of the large doors open. The door squeaked so loud, I figured they could hear it in Birmingham. "That's far enough, Dewey! If we keep pullin' this thing, we'll have the entire Swenson family out here with shotguns."

"Okay."

We actually hadn't opened it far enough, so we had to suck in our guts really hard and turn our heads to push ourselves through the opening. But we did make it inside. Once we were there we decided to leave the door partially ajar rather than close it and make all that noise again.

The barn stank like horses. Mainly because there were horse stalls down each side. Four of the stalls actually had horses in them. The rest of the horses must've been out in the fields. "So what do we do now?" Dewey asked.

"Investigate," I said.

The floor was covered in sawdust and it was dark. The only light came through a bank of paned windows on the back wall of the barn that looked like they'd never been cleaned since the barn was built. They caused the sunlight falling through to cast weird, eerie shadows that I didn't like. They looked like they belonged in some kind of spooky funhouse. There were also holes between some of the boards in the walls and the roof that let a little light in, and that light sliced down like bright sheets. The whole thing was really eerie.

"I'm sure glad I've got my trusty sword," Dewey said. I told him to shut up and just whisper. And only talk about things that are important.

"Look," Dewey said in a clipped whisper as we approached the back wall where Isaac Swenson kept his tools. There was a workbench that ran the width of the barn. "He's got an ax!"

I checked out the ax. It did look mighty suspicious. It even appeared to have dried blood on it. My mother had to see this. It was definitely a major clue to her case. He had many other tools, but what gripped my attention next was his collection of shovels. They were even more suspicious than the ax. He had five of them. Who needs five shovels unless they're burying a lot of bodies? I figured only serial killers would be collecting shovels.

Then I saw it. At first I thought I was imagining it, but then I realized it was real. It was rolled up and hanging from a hook just beneath the workbench. For a second I froze there, just staring at it. My heart started bouncing like someone was kicking a hacky sack into my guts. "Dewey!" I whispered, trying to keep my voice down even though it was hard when it was full of excitement. "Look!"

There in the darkness with a splinter of light casting across it from a slice in the ceiling was a big roll of rope, the kind you'd use to tie people up with. It was yellow, but parts of it were splattered red that I knew had to be blood. Even the spool had flecks of red on it.

We'd found the clue my mother had been looking for.

We found more clues, but none as incriminating as that rope, that ax, or that shovel collection. We were about to start investigating the stalls when, from outside, I heard the sound of whistling and footsteps approaching in the mud.

"Oh, no!" I said to Dewey, trying to keep my voice low. "He's coming!"

"Why did he break his pattern?" Dewey asked, lowering his voice, too.

"How the heck should I know?" I looked around for any exits, but there were only the large front doors of the barn. "We're trapped!"

"Don't worry," Dewey said to me in a very calm voice, "we have Icarus. We'll be fine." Dewey had named his sword Icarus because he read somewhere that all great swords had names. Why he picked Icarus, I would never know.

This just raised my panic and added a bit of anger to it as I stared at him for a second in disbelief. "Dewey," I said. "What are you going to do? Swordfight him? Other than giving you that ability, the sword don't *really* give you any powers. It's all just make-believe. Please tell me you know that, right?" I remembered he still believed in Santa Claus, so anything was possible.

"'Power is in your heart,' Abe," he replied. "'Believe in it and it will come to you.'"

I shook my head clear. "Where the hell did you get *that* from? Did Yoda say it?"

"No, it came from a comic book. Captain Defender number fifteen, I reckon. But I believe it's true. If you truly trust in yourself, you can do anything."

Right now I was pissing my pants scared. "Well, comic books ain't real either, Dewey. We're in *real* trouble here."

Slowly, Isaac Swenson pulled the left side of the barn doors open, casting sunlight into the darkened interior. Dust motes floated in the air. I realized too late that we should have at least *tried* to hide in one of the horse stalls or something, but we didn't. We were just standing there at the end of the barn in front of Isaac Swenson's tool bench, squinting into the sudden burst of sunlight, Dewey with his sword held with both hands at the ready and me with my bow in my left hand, an arrow ready to be loaded in my right.

CHAPTER 34

While knocking on the door of her seventh farmhouse, most of which were decorated very nicely with Christmas lights (some even had a blow-up Santa and baby Jesus in the yard) and wreaths, Leah realized this was an exercise in futility. Near on every single visit went the same way. Number seven included.

The door was answered by an elderly man, tall and lanky, with a beer belly that the rest of his body didn't quite know how to support, making him lean forward. He wore spectacles and had age spots on his head, and what little hair was left was combed over the top. Black suspenders held up his brown trousers, and he had on a blue collared shirt that was barely tucked in. In his hand was a walking cane.

"Hello?" he asked.

"Hi, sir, I'm Leah Teal, the detective for the Alvin Police Department?" She flashed her badge so he would know she wasn't making this up.

"Eh? What? I can't hear you. My hearing aids aren't in. You need to speak louder."

She wound up screaming at him. Right away that made a bad start.

"You sayin' I have sawdust and clay somewhere? What are you

talkin' 'bout? 'Course I've got sawdust. And God put the clay in. I got lotsa clay if you want clay."

"No, sir. I'm askin' if you've . . . can I see your barn?"

"You wanna look at my alarm? I don't have no alarm. You don't need no alarm round these parts. Folks round here are good people."

She screamed louder. "I want to look at your barn. You know, where you keep your horses?" She made horse sounds and tried to make herself look like a horse. She felt as though she looked more idiotic than anything else.

"One minute." The man turned around and Leah thought she finally got through to him, but a minute later he appeared back at the door with a short, portly woman wearing an apron. She had creases around her blue eyes and her hair was pulled tightly into a bun.

"Hello. Zacharias tells me you are alarmed about our horses. Did something happen? Did one get out again?"

"No, ma'am." Leah couldn't help it. She laughed. It wasn't a smart thing to do. Neither of the elderly people laughed along with her. They were looking at her like she just stepped out of the Twilight Zone.

"I'm sorry," she said. "I'm the detective from the police department? I'd like to see the barn. Where you keep the horses and stuff."

The woman's hand came to her mouth. "Oh, why?"

"There's been a report of a missing girl. We think she's a runaway." Leah rehearsed this story beforehand and gave it to Chris to use, too. It was a good story because it didn't indict anyone. "I just want to make sure she's not hiding back there anywhere."

"Well, I don't think she is; we'd have seen her," the woman said.

"What's she want?" Zacharias asked his wife.

"To see if there's a girl in the barn," the wife screamed back.

"I sent her home already."

The woman looked at Leah. "He's talking about Molly. She comes to help sometimes in the mornings."

Eventually, Leah was led to the barn, where she saw exactly what she expected to see. Horses, straw, a bunch of tools, a workbench, but no blood. No sign of foul play. "Do you mind if I check the hayloft?" she asked the woman.

"No, by all means go ahead."

"Why's she goin' up there?" Zacharias asked his wife.

"To check for the girl," his wife screamed back.

"I told you. I sent her home."

After she was finished with searching that barn, Leah took pictures of the tread on the couple's Chevy pickup. "One last thing," Leah said to Zacharias's wife. She turned and looked back at Leah, expectantly. "What size and type of footwear does your husband have?"

"That's a weird question," she said.

"Just tryin' to whittle down all my suspects, is all."

"We're suspect?"

"No, no, ma'am. Just . . . please answer the question and I will be out of your hair."

"He rarely leaves the farm and when he does, Zacharias wears the same thing he's always worn. Size-eleven galoshes. That good enough?"

Leah jotted this down in her pad. "That is more than helpful. Y'all have been saints with your patience today. I can't thank you enough."

And with that, Leah returned to her car and radioed Chris, telling him to abandon his search. It wasn't working. It was a dumb idea.

There had to be a better way.

She must've missed *something*. There was always *something*.

Then, an hour after getting back to the station, Leah got a call.

Another woman, Scarlett Graham, had disappeared.

CHAPTER 35

"What're you two doin' in here?" Isaac Swenson asked as he slowly walked down the sawdust-covered floor to murder us.

My heart felt like a professional baseball pitcher was using it to fire fastballs at my ribcage. I began to sweat; beads of it ran down the side of my face and continued down my neck. My fingers trembled. Beside me, Dewey whispered, "Abe, I'm scared." And I heard the trembling in his voice. The tension all got worse the closer Isaac Swenson came, until, finally, he was just a few feet in front of us.

"Well, I s'pose I should say hello," Isaac Swenson said, holding out his hand. "I'm Isaac. Isaac Swenson. I own this ranch. Who might you two be?"

I tried to keep the shakiness out of my voice as I answered. "Abe," I said. "Abe Teal." Putting the arrow in the same hand as the bow, I took his hand and shook it. I was sure he felt my hand trembling.

"And I'm . . . Dewey," Dewey said, nearly forgetting his name. "Abe's ma is a police officer," he added, almost as some sort of threat. He also shook Isaac Swenson's hand.

"Is she now? Come to think of it, I reckon I've seen her around. Nice lady. So, tell me, what can I do for you boys?"

"We were just playin' around," I said. "Pretendin' we're Dungeons and Dragons characters."

"Or *real* D and D characters. We're playin' the advanced version now. Abe got all the handbooks for Christmas from Santa!" Dewey added, and I really wished he hadn't.

I quickly cut him off with, "I'm sorry we got into your barn. It won't happen again. We were just looking for interesting places to pretend fight."

Isaac Swenson batted my statement away. "Oh, that's okay. I reckon this place could use some superheroes sometimes."

"Anyway," I said, looking at my watch, "I reckon it's time we got goin'. I'm s'posed to be home for supper in twenty minutes."

"Are you sure, Abe?" Dewey asked. "I thought we didn't need to be home 'til—" Dewey started, but I elbowed him in the ribs, making him shut up.

"All right, then," Isaac Swenson said. "It was a pleasure meetin' you boys. And seriously, I don't mind you playin' on my ranch, as long as you are careful with those weapons of yours. I know those arrows are blunt and that sword ain't really so sharp, but you could hurt one of my horses with them. To be honest, though, I kinda miss my own son playin' out here, but he's all grown up now. So feel free to come back up this way any time you like."

"That's mighty kind of you, sir," I said.

We left the barn and found our bikes where we'd hidden them in the long grass we'd previously used for lying in while we spied on Isaac Swenson. With a wave good-bye, we headed down the steep hill of Fairview Drive. It was definitely easier going home than it was coming up.

Dewey pulled up beside me, and said, "Well, I reckon there's no question at all anymore."

"What do you mean?"

"We found our serial killer: Isaac Swenson."

I looked at him. "What are you talkin' 'bout? He turned out to be one of the nicest folk I ever met."

"Exactly," Dewey said. "It's the perfect disguise."

"So, let me get this straight," I said. "You're sayin' we should be lookin' for nice folk now?"

"Clearly the pattern thing didn't work. Isaac Swenson changed his pattern today. So, yeah, I guess I am. Someone really nice is unnatural and that means they're obviously hiding something. And I'd say that *something* is likely to be that they're a serial killer."

We came to the place in the road where Bogpine Way forks off and heads up to the bog of stench and toads. That was a direction we definitely wanted to avoid at any cost.

"You wanna know what I reckon?" I asked.

"What?"

"That you're an idiot."

CHAPTER 36

Scarlett Graham was another loner with a penchant for alcohol and going to bars. Like Mercy Jo Carpenter and Faith Abilene, she hung out at the Six-Gun Saloon. She had just moved into a new apartment with a roommate named Layla Redmond, and was supposed to meet her at noon to drop off a set of keys. Scarlett was a no-show. Now it was almost five and still no sign of Miss Graham.

"Five hours ain't exactly what we'd call a missin' person," Leah said to Miss Layla on the phone.

"Well, I certainly would," Miss Layla replied. "I've been waitin' here half my day."

"Okay, we'll look into it. You wouldn't happen to have a picture of her, would you?"

"Now why in the hell would I have a picture of her? I only met her a week ago. It's not like we went to college together or anythin' like that. She just seemed like she'd make a good roommate. I got her name out of an ad in the *Examiner*."

"Her parents live in Alvin?"

"Hell if I know."

"Can you describe her for me, Miss Layla?"

"Sure. She has long blond hair that comes down past her

shoulders, I reckon her eyes are blue. She's about five foot eight, I reckon. Just a bit taller than me. I dunno, what else do you want? She wears lotsa makeup."

"Does she like to drink?"

"What does that have to do with anythin'?"

"It may have a lot to do with everythin'."

"Yeah, she seemed to like her booze. I noticed a stockpile of empties when she gave me a tour of the place. So what? It's not a crime."

"So tell me 'bout her apartment."

"It's nice. Scarlett is very spiritual and decorates accordingly. This was the first place I looked at and I liked it so much I just decided this was it. I moved most of my stuff in on the weekend and was just waiting for Scarlett to give me my keys, but she never turned up."

"So when you say she was spiritual, she had incense and candles and that sort of stuff."

"Yeah, she even had a Buddhist shrine set up in the corner of one of the rooms."

Leah scratched it all down on the pad in front of her. It was the long blond hair that caught her interest. "Okay, I got it. We'll look into it."

"Thank you. Please make it a priority. I need my key."

"We'll do our best. In the meantime, I'd suggest contacting the landlord."

She sighed. "I'm not certain she's supposed to have a roommate."

"Well," Leah said, "I'm afraid there's not much I can do 'bout that."

Leah got back into her car and back on the street. She headed to the station with a head full of questions. Was this number three? Or had this woman simply passed out in some bar somewhere? Leah's stomach told her it was the worst of those two cases, and she'd learned to trust her instincts. With a brief pause for thought, Leah called Detective Truitt. He had given her his direct line and he answered on the first ring.

"Truitt," he said.

"Hi. It's Leah, from Alvin."

"Hey! How the hell is life treatin' you down there in the armpit of the world?"

"Good. Listen. I think we just lost our third victim."

"What do you mean?" His tone had changed dramatically. Now he was all business.

"I just got a call from someone telling me that they've been waiting five hours for someone to show up at noon."

"Leah, five hours ain't exactly a missing—"

"She described her as having long blond hair and having a thirst for alcoholic beverages."

"Oh, shit. This really could be number three. That means we got what? Six or seven days before she winds up in some pond in some back-ass town somewhere. Sorry, no offense meant."

"None taken."

She hung up and, after checking the time, turned to Chris. "Listen, Chris, I've promised my kids I'd take them out for hamburgers tonight. Any chance you could do me a favor?"

"Sure. What's up?" He pulled out a pad and poised a pen, ready to write.

"We've got a missing person. Name's Scarlett Graham. I need you to find her parents. Mom or dad. They may be separated, they may still be together. I have very little to go on. They may be livin' in Alvin, or they may not."

"How long she been gone, and who reported it?"

"Five hours, and her new roommate who's been waiting for her to drop off the key to their new apartment."

"Five hours? Ain't exactly a missing person yet."

"Just humor me on this one, okay?"

"All right. I'll call you if I find anything."

CHAPTER 37

Leah took the kids to Vera's Old West Bar & Grill, which brought back thoughts of her meeting here with Dan Truitt. She found herself thinking often about Dan Truitt. Maybe a little too often. The man had obviously made an impression on her. Those thoughts were accompanied by feelings she hadn't felt for a long time. Not since Billy had died in that fatal crash back when Abe was just two years old.

It was something about Dan Truitt's eyes. They were an intense steel blue that seemed to look straight inside her, as though allowing him to read her thoughts while simultaneously he said something completely ridiculous.

But, of course, Dewey, who had to come along, pulled Leah out of her memories.

"I reckon this is the best steak I ever ate," Dewey said.

Leah was a little put out when everyone was supposed to be ordering burgers and when it came time for Dewey to order, he asked for a "ten-ounce sirloin, medium rare, please."

"How many steaks you ever ate?" Abe asked.

"Well," Dewey said, looking up at the ceiling, which was covered in old license plates from all the different states. "I reckon this is my fifth."

"Best out of five," Leah said. "That's not bad. How're your guys' burgers?" she asked Abe and Caroline.

"Good," Caroline said.

"Same as ever," Abe said with a full mouth. "Good."

"So did everyone have a nice Christmas?"

Everyone said they did except Dewey, who seemed slightly disappointed in Christmas.

"What was so bad 'bout your Christmas?" Leah asked. "Didn't you like your sword?"

"My sword is fine. I love my sword. But I didn't get the *one* thing I asked for."

"Which was?"

"A piece of plutonium. See, I have this invention that I—"

"Wait," Abe said. "You asked Santa for the plutonium?"

The waitress came around and asked if anyone wanted refills on their sodas. Everyone except Leah said yes.

"I only asked for a small piece," Dewey said, answering Abe's question.

"And it didn't show up under your tree Christmas morning?"

Dewey stared back blankly. "You know it didn't. I already told you."

"You didn't tell me you asked Santa for it. I thought his elves can make anythin'. So . . ." Abe said, leading into the vital question. "Why didn't you get your plutonium?" Across the table, Leah gave him a dirty look.

"My mother told me them elves won't make anythin' radioactive on account of it's too dangerous."

"Sounds plausible," Abe said, nearly laughing as he took another bite of his burger. "It is, after all, plutonium."

"That's why I *need* it. My invention takes the plutonium and converts—"

"Wait," Abe said, again speaking with his mouth full. "I'm not so much interested in *why* you needed the plutonium, more that you expected to get it. Where would Santa get it from?"

"His elves can make anything," Dewey said. He took a bite of steak and washed it down with Coke.

"You don't *make* plutonium, Dewey. At least I don't think so. It's an element."

"Elves are magical. They can make elements."

Leah looked to Caroline. She could tell her daughter was on the brink of breaking under the strain of this demented conversation. When Caroline went off, she tended to go off like a neutron bomb.

"I don't think they're up at the North Pole hammering out weapons of mass destruction, do you?" Abe asked.

"Well, my invention isn't a WMD; see, my invention uses the plutonium as a nuclear power source to drive—"

"Wait," said Abe again. "I don't even want to hear the rest of it. This invention is one of your worst to date. I can already tell. Can we just skip it?"

Dewey looked at Leah and Caroline. "Y'all don't wanna hear 'bout my hover boots either?"

They both shook their heads. "I just wanna enjoy my burger," Caroline said. "With my feet on the ground, thanks. And can we seriously change the subject because I'm gettin' ready to snap."

Leah held back a laugh.

"Fine."

Most of the rest of the meal was pretty quiet.

Almost as soon as they got home, the phone rang. As was usual, Abe raced to answer it. "Hello? Yep! Just one sec."

"Mom, it's for you. Officer Chris!"

Leah took the call on the kitchen phone, knowing it would be about Scarlett Graham.

"Has she turned up yet?" Leah asked.

"Nope, but I managed to track down her parents."

"So you told them she was missin'?" Leah was absently wrapping the telephone cord around her finger.

"Did more than that," he said.

"What do you mean?"

"Call me Super Chris. I saved you a whole bunch of time and drove over there and took a statement and everythin'. Turns out they didn't know she was missing. I emphasized that we actually don't usually count people as missin' until they're gone at least twenty-four hours, but in this case it seemed weird considerin' she was supposed to drop off keys to her new roommate."

"And they said?"

"They said that is truly out of character for her. That we should take this very seriously. They were quite concerned."

"So we may very well have just proven that Alvin's got a serial killer runnin' round the neighborhood. Did you—"

"Get a picture? 'Course I did. And her telephone number."

"How old is she?"

"Twenty-seven. Long blond hair, blue eyes, five foot nine. A pretty good match for the other two victims."

"Okay, I'm comin' in."

"What for?"

"I want to take the picture around, see if anyone's seen her. Main place I wanna take it is the Six-Gun Saloon. So far, both of the other victims spent a fair amount of time there."

CHAPTER 38

Leah dropped by the station and got debriefed by Chris. He had talked to Scarlett Graham's mother. Her father had been at work. The picture he got from Scarlett Graham's parents showed a woman who looked nearly exactly like the other two victims, only in this picture her eyes weren't sewn up, of course. It made for a much nicer shot to show around for identification purposes. This would make Leah's job that much easier.

The woman in the picture looked so innocent. If she matched the profile and turned out to be a hooker, Leah would be surprised.

"Did her mother tell you how old she was in this picture?" Leah asked Chris.

"No, I didn't ask. I'm assumin' it's quite recent, she looks to be in her late twenties."

Scarlett had been living by herself since she was nineteen. She was now twenty-seven and had just lost her job. She worked as an office assistant. In order to make ends meet, she put an ad in the local paper looking for a roommate. Layla Redmond had been the only person to answer the ad.

According to Scarlett's mother, her daughter liked to keep things clean and organized and was very spiritual, so her place was filled with candles and incense and things like that.

" 'It's completely out of character for her to just disappear like this,' Scarlett's mother told me," Chris said to Leah.

"Did her mom mention her drinking?"

"Not a word of it."

"Ah, so either her mother's delusional or just puts her head in the sand or Miss Scarlett's good at hiding things." The possibility of her being a hooker popped back into Leah's head. "When I spoke to Layla Redmond, the woman moving in with her, she said there was a stack of empty wine boxes and bottles by the door that looked near on ready to topple, it was so high.

"Anyway," Leah continued, "I'm gonna go show this picture around the Six-Gun Saloon. I'm startin' to like that place."

"Good luck!"

Scarlett Graham actually was well-known by the staff and some of the patrons of the Six-Gun Saloon, although everyone Leah talked to was adamant that she was not a "working girl."

She'd pop in maybe two or three times a week, the bartender told her. Margaret wasn't working tonight. Instead, it was someone whose name tag read TOM. He was a tall, skinny black man with brown hair, high cheekbones, and long fingers like a pianist. He had stubble on his face, as though he hadn't shaved in a day. A black vest covered his starched white shirt, keeping in theme with the rest of the décor of the Six-Gun. Leah couldn't see his feet, but if she could, she was willing to bet he was wearing cowboy boots.

This must've been the brother Margaret told Leah about on one of her visits.

"Do you know where she worked?" she asked, after showing Scarlett's picture to Tom.

He shook his head. "People come here to forget 'bout work, not talk 'bout it, I'm 'fraid. Is she in some sort of trouble?"

"She's gone missing," Leah said. "We're hoping to find her."

"Oh my God."

"Can you think of anything that might help the investigation? Anything unusual lately? Had she been talking to anyone unusual? Anything?"

The bartender thought about it. He continued to think about it as a waitress came up and asked for four pints of beer. He poured them for her, still obviously lost in thought. Turning back to Leah, he said, "I'm sorry, I just can't get over her bein' dead."

Hesitantly, Leah took in Tom, head to toe. "That's funny," she said, "I didn't *say* anythin' 'bout her bein' dead. Just that she was missin'."

"Oh," the bartender stumbled. "I just . . . I just assumed that since you was askin', she must be . . ."

Leah took down all the man's particulars and once again asked if he could think of anything unusual involving her disappearance.

"I don't *reckon* there was anythin' unusual, but if somethin' pops into my head, do you have a number I can reach you at?"

He just beat Leah to the punch on that one. "Here's my card," Leah said. "My emergency number's on the bottom, but call the station's line first. Emergency calls forward to my home."

"Okay . . ." the bartender said, "and I really do hope you find out whoever did this."

"Oh, we will, Mr. . . ."

"Gherkin. Like the pickle."

Thank you, Mr. Gherkin.

Leah spoke to some of the regular staff members and even some of the regular patrons and took more notes, trying to keep things as light as possible. She didn't want anyone to know she was conducting official police interviews. As soon as she left, she immediately pulled out her pad and started jotting down everything she remembered. Especially about the bartender. She didn't want him to think she was suspecting him of anything, but the way he substituted "dead" for "missing" had stuck with her. She also thought there were things he was holding back or not quite telling the truth about. It could be he was just one of those people who give out a guilty vibe.

Despite being dead tired, when Leah got home that night, she popped the videotape she had gotten from Detective Truitt into her VCR and watched the crime scene again. It showed the dark inside of the mine with the body lying there being tended to by cops. She could make out Dan Truitt. She saw the forensic team.

Then the image panned the onlookers. There were probably twenty, maybe twenty-five. And again, she got that feeling in her stomach.

Something about the tape was wrong.

She watched it twice more, but each time, she couldn't place what it was that was giving her the feeling that something on the video was trying to tell her the secret to everything. She decided she'd bring it into the station and let Ethan take a look at it. He had a VCR hanging below that television in his office. Maybe he had keener senses than she did. Maybe he could spot what she could only feel.

CHAPTER 39

Deciding the mayor should know about a potential killer in his town, Leah told Chris she had decided to drive out to Mayor Robertson's house and give him a surprise drop by, that was, if he was home. She didn't call first and hoped she wasn't being too rude.

On her way over, she remembered the mayor had lost his wife in a motor vehicle accident a long time ago. She shared some history with him; her husband, Billy, had also died in a motor vehicle accident. Leah couldn't remember the details of the mayor's wife's accident—she only knew that anytime you lost a loved one was bad. You never really got over it.

The mayor lived in a log cabin–style home on a winding road called Maple Drive, which ran between Blackberry Trail and Main Street. The area was highly wooded, mostly with maples, and driving around the curving streets made you feel like you were a hundred miles from home. Up here, there were no other houses around, so you didn't see any traffic on the road either. The mayor's closest neighbor on Blackberry Trail lived about four miles away. To Leah's knowledge, nobody else lived anywhere closer.

His house was beautiful. Something about log cabins had always appealed to Leah. She guessed it was on account of when she was a little girl, her family used to rent one every summer up in Mississippi. The memories of those trips were good ones, and they were tied in to her memories of log cabins.

Leah came up the hill that always took her breath away. The wooded area was to her right. To her left, Clover Creek ran lazily along. In the spring and summer, it could rise to quite a height and become dangerous, but this time of year there was hardly any water in it. What little there was rolled slowly down its twisted route. The sun had just fallen behind the hills of sage and brush on the other side of the creek, but it still cast an aura of orange, red, and yellow over the sky above Leah's head.

It reminded Leah of a song. It was something the band The Eagles would probably call a "Tequila Sunset."

When she came to the cabin belonging to Mayor Robertson, Leah pulled into the wide, circular driveway and parked near the end closest to the road. The driveway was just dirt, but very hard, packed dirt.

Getting out of her car, Leah walked up to the mayor's doorstep. She gave the door a couple of raps. When nobody answered, she began thinking nobody was home. She knocked again, a little louder this time—just to be sure—and waited a tad longer. Then she saw the doorbell button and gave that a try. She really didn't want to have to go home having come all this way for nothing.

Sure enough, a minute later, Mayor Hubert James Robertson opened the door wrapped in a towel and possibly not wearing a stitch of anything else.

Hubert James was a large man. Tall and broad with a bit of gray hair around the edges of what was once black. He still looked like he could beat anyone in a wrestling match. But his most distinguishing feature—to Leah, anyway—was his eyes. They were a bright blue with black specks in them that literally captivated her.

During the few conversations they'd had, she'd always managed to just catch herself before she started staring into his eyes instead of listening to the man speak. Frankly, she found politicians boring. Every one of them said the same thing; they just wrapped it in a different package.

"Leah!" the mayor said, taking her hand.

Leah kept glancing discreetly to his waist, hoping the towel wouldn't slip.

"Sorry, I was in the hot tub. As you can see, you have me at a disadvantage." He looked down at the red towel wrapped around him.

"I'll come back some other time," Leah said, managing to hold her composure together. "When you're not so . . . busy. Sorry for botherin' you. Next time, I'll call first."

"Oh, nonsense. I've got the rest of my life to sit in hot tubs. Come on in. I don't suppose you brought a bathin' suit?" He smiled. Unlike his eyes, she didn't like his smile one bit. He had a politician's smile—it sort of reminded Leah of the mouth of a shark.

"No." She didn't laugh. She tried to keep *some* semblance of decorum.

"Didn't think so. I might be able to dig somethin' up for you if you're interested."

"I'm not really interested."

"Okay, then you come on in and have a seat in my livin' room." He gestured to the wide, expansive room the foyer opened into. You had to walk up four polished maple stairs to get to it, but it certainly looked worth the effort. Everything was polished maple and glistened in the sun, which, from up here, you could still see going down.

"And I'll go change into somethin' more appropriate," the mayor said.

"That sounds great." It sounded great to Leah because deep inside, she wanted him to sit and be interviewed wearing that red towel all night. And that couldn't be a good sign.

Mayor Robertson went upstairs to change. Leah sat down on one of the most comfortable sofas she'd ever sat on. One thing about this living room: You could tell right away only a man lived here and that he was single. There was a bearskin rug on the floor in front of the stone fireplace, along with a four-and-a-half foot amberjack mounted on a plaque above it. He also had four mounted buck heads around the room: three six pointers along one wall, and a five pointer on another. His coffee table looked completely carved from one big stump of a tree, with the top shaved flat and the roots curved to create legs. However, the main tip that there was no feminine input into how this house was decorated was the smell. Leah couldn't place it, but something about it just smelled "manly."

When she saw all the dead animals everywhere, a voice inside of Leah spoke up and told her something she hadn't thought of before. The northern parts outside of Alvin are a hunter's paradise. Maybe it wasn't the farmers and ranchers she should be interviewing, but the hunters (even though in most cases, they were the same).

"You look comfy," Leah said.

"You like this?" The mayor was wearing a red hoodie and gray sweatpants. He took a seat on one of the two wing chairs sitting kitty-corner from the sofa. Strangely, there was no television in the room. Leah only now noticed.

He pulled the hoodie down tight so Leah could see the logo. It had an Alvin Alligator logo on it showing a gator with a football in its mouth. Alvin didn't have a high school, but they did have a high-school football team. "Isn't this great?" he asked, looking down on it. "They gave me this for kickin' the first ball of the season out last year." He laughed. "Funny part was: I have no idea how to kick a football. I think my kick went ten yards—sideways." And then that smile came back. That white, toothy, shark grin.

"So," he asked, "what brings you out this way? Oh, first I shouldn't be so rude. Would you like a tea? Coffee? I think I have some juice, or a soda."

"No, I'm fine. Do you mind if I ask you who these pictures are of? I recognize the ones of your son, Paul, and your daughter, Ginger, but I don't recognize the other lady. Do you have *two* daughters?"

He laughed. "Does she look that young? I guess she does. She'd be fourteen to sixteen or so years younger than me in most of those pictures."

Leah didn't know what to say. She laughed along but was kind of lost.

"No, Leah, those are pictures of my wife, Susan Lee."

She hesitated. "Oh, of course. Actually, I did know you had a wife."

The mayor let out a breath. "Well, *had* is the big word in that sentence. I lost her three months ago. Well, actually, I lost her twice. Three months ago *and* I lost her near on thirteen years ago."

Leah tried to figure out what he meant but couldn't. She just stared back at him. "I . . . I'm sorry, I don't understand."

The mayor slapped the arm rests of the chair he was in. "She drove to the store to get a quart of milk for our baby. That would've been Ginger."

Leah smiled. "She's a very sweet girl."

"She is. Practically everyone in town knows her. She so much reminds me of her ma."

"So what happened to your wife? If you don't mind me askin'? I was quite young when she had her accident."

"A drunk driver came roaring through the stop sign at Sweetwater Drive and put an end to my marriage."

Leah's hand came to her mouth. "Oh my God. I'm so sorry. I remember hearing of the accident. I didn't make the connection."

"No, it's fine. It took a lot of time, but I can talk about it now." He sort of drifted off for a minute and stared at the tops of the trees rising up over the hills. "Yeah, well, it was pretty bad. The details are even worse. Susan Lee was on her way back from Fanta's Main Street Five-and-Dime—it's not there any longer, can't say I was upset to see 'em tear it down—and I guess, from what police could tell, a car just ran the stop sign doin' 'bout forty over the speed limit and slammed into the side of her vehicle. Broke both her arms and severed a portion of her spinal column. She didn't have her seat belt on, they figure, since she was thrown through the windshield in a shower of glass that got into her eyes and blinded her."

"Oh, Jesus, how horrible," Leah said.

"The blindness was no big deal on account of she was in a coma and they couldn't wake her up. They put her on life support for twelve years before finally pullin' the plug. Her eyes never opened again anyway. So that part was almost a bit of a blessing."

Leah was at a loss for words. She tried searching for a way to react but came up at a loss. This was such a terrible thing to be sharing with someone. Her own Billy was killed in a car crash, but nothing this horrific.

"She was in Providence Hospital down in Mobile," the mayor said. "And I made that trip near on every day to sit at her bedside on the off chance she might wake up. Of course, she never did." He looked away as he said this, staring at the carpet. Leah could tell he was starting to tear up.

"So, Miss Leah, when you ask me about my wife, I count the twelve years on life support as being part of the time since I lost her. For me, she died the day she went through that windshield."

"Oh my God," Leah said. "I'm so sorry."

The mayor slapped the arm rests again and continued looking away to the floor. "Yeah, it wasn't very easy. I didn't deal with it well. I'm still not dealin' with it well."

"I *guess* it wasn't easy. I would be worried if you *did* deal with it well."

"Anyway, she managed to survive for twelve years in that hospital until they finally decided it was long enough. And it was."

Leah couldn't believe what she was hearing. "And then what?"

"They pulled the plug on the machines keepin' her alive." He gently closed his eyes and Leah could tell he was holding back tears. "It was time. I didn't want to make the decision. But it *was* the right decision. I see that now. I kind of hoped she might wake up in those final moments, but she didn't. She did die in my arms, though. I take some solace in that."

"Oh my God. What happened to the person who hit her? How drunk was the driver?"

"Zero point one two. Probably shouldn't have been *walkin'* home, never mind drivin'. Originally, the court basically gave her a slap on the wrist, but that all changed when my wife actually died. Then the driver got five years for reckless manslaughter. That's the maximum sentence in Alabama, can you believe that? Had it happened in Georgia, she'd have gotten ten years. Before that, she'd only gotten a first-offense DWI and revocation of her license. But the minute my wife died, it became vehicular homicide."

"Well, at least there's a tiny bit of justice left in the world."

The mayor was still looking away. He lifted his hand and rubbed his eyes with his knuckles. "I'm sorry. Talkin' 'bout this still gets to me. I thought I was over it."

"That's okay. I totally understand. You know I lost my husband in an automobile accident. I don't reckon you ever get over it."

"Oh, yeah, that's right. I forgot. So you *do* understand. Was his a drinkin' and drivin' thing, too?"

"No, I imagine yours is worse, because you can actually blame someone. I can't. The only one at fault was him."

"And you're okay with it now? How do you get past the anger?"

"I'm starting to accept it now. It took eleven years and the influence of my son to get me to this point. I dunno if I'll ever fully accept it. And for me it was less anger and more me having to forgive him. For years I was unable to forgive him for leaving me alone to raise two children. How nuts is that? Like he meant to have that car accident?"

"My daughter and son helped me, too. We all deal with death different ways. The main thing is that we get through it, whatever it takes. You see the other picture?"

Leah wondered why the sudden shift of topic, but looked at the mantel. There were two pictures that looked like the same woman, only younger. She was standing with another woman. They looked very similar. "Is this your wife, too?"

"Yeah, but that's from before I met her."

"Who's the other woman, if I may ask?"

"Her sister."

"They look alike." And something about the one on the right looked somewhat familiar, but Leah couldn't place her. Both women had dark hair down to their shoulders, blue eyes, and the same smile.

"Everyone says that." He was still looking away from Leah. Now she heard him sniffling as he rubbed tears out of his eyes. Finally, he turned his face to her, his eyes swollen and red. "So tell me, Leah, what brings you here today? I think I've had enough conversation 'bout my dead wife."

"So, you're quite the outdoorsman, I take it," Leah said. There was a picture of a cabin out in the woods on his wall, too.

"Yeah, I like my huntin'. Fishin' too."

"Is that your cabin?"

"Certainly is. My little home away from home. Built it about eighty miles north of here. I like to just go there when I want to relax. You know, take my mind off things. I'm actually in the process of renovating."

"Making it bigger?"

"Adding what I like to call 'an annex.' Give me a place to hang meat while I'm waiting for it to cure. Right now it's just an open room with two walls waiting to be built and badly in need of a floor. Last I was up there, it was all just sawdust and mud."

Taking note of all the sawdust and mud that would be created from such a procedure as adding onto a cabin, Leah admired some of the heads in his room. "You got some nice bucks. If you're into that sort of thing. My pa was. That's the only reason I know. I'm not. Not really."

Once they were both sitting, she told him about the case, leaving out the part about the psychic.

"What should we do?"

"Well, there's been a major development."

"What's that?" he asked.

"A third person has gone missing."

"*Another* one? Where? Who?"

"Her name is Scarlett Graham. This means the killer has really accelerated his rate. It's bad."

"You've got to stop him."

"That's what we're all trying to do, Mr. Mayor."

"Shouldn't the FBI be called in at this point?"

"Police Chief Montgomery wants us to hang on to this one as long as possible. Bringin' the Feds in just makes a mess of it for everyone. But you're right—if it goes much further, it will have to become a federal issue sooner or later."

"Well, what information do you have on your killer? Surely you've profiled him."

"He's very predictable and organized. He chooses certain women over others. They all look similar, and are of similar ages. They are all loners who like to drink. We think he picks loners to buy himself some time; in most cases, people won't realize they've disappeared until long after he's taken them. Then he keeps them confined for up to a week before killing them and getting rid of the body. But he's meticulous 'bout not leaving any evidence behind." She didn't tell him about the eyes or the crosses in the pocket, or even the writing across the chest.

"How do you know these two women were all taken and murdered by the same person?"

"The MO—the modus operandi—was the same. I don't know how gory you want me to get, but you've seen the images in the paper."

"You mean with the eyes and the sewing?" he asked.

Leah nodded. "Those are done with the victims still alive."

"Oh my God," the mayor said.

"He keeps them alive six or seven days like that before finally killing them with a shot to the temple. He uses the same gun every time. A very old Beretta. We figure it must have sentimental value or something to him."

"You can tell all that from a body you just found?"

"So far, both bodies have not been buried. One washed up on the shores of Willet Lake, the other was found a hundred miles away just outside of Birmingham in a town called Graysville. It was in an abandoned mine." Something shot off in the back of Leah's mind. She wasn't sure what it was, but it was something she'd have to think about later.

I see a body in darkness . . .

Welcome to Graysville . . .

Writing on the body . . .

"Is there anythin' I can do, or anythin' we can rally the town into doin', that will help you with your job?"

Leah thought a moment. "I don't think so. If you think of anything, you can call me. Here, let me get you—"

She was about to pull out a business card, when the mayor produced a pen and paper. He held the pen in his *left* hand.

"You're a lefty," Leah said.

"Yes, the bane of my existence. So, what's your number?"

CHAPTER 40

"Here, let me just give you one of my cards." Leah passed it to the mayor and again, he took it with his left hand.

"This guy sounds like a real bad character," he said.

Leah thought for a second. "Tell me something, Mayor Robertson," she said, "what was your life like growin' up?"

"Does this have any bearing on the case?"

"No, it has bearing on how I raise my boy. You have showed me today that you can be strong and still show weakness. I want to imbue him with these qualities."

The mayor sat back in his chair. "Well, I dunno. I guess I owe my upbringing to my pa on account of my ma dyin' when I was five."

"I'm sorry to hear that."

He looked out the window. "Lots of death. You learn to cope, but you never learn to get over it."

"I understand that," Leah said. "Or at least I'm startin' to."

"My pa made sure I went to school every day, even though he had to miss mornings at work sometimes and even some afternoons."

"What did he do?"

"He was a tailor and a shoemaker. A craftsman. Back then, everyone was a craftsman."

A maniac tailor . . .

"He didn't make a lot of money, but what he did make he made sure got spent on the right things. He didn't drink, didn't smoke. We'd go to church every Wednesday and Sunday come hell or high water."

Leah blushed. Her church schedule was more erratic than consistent.

"But mainly he taught me 'bout morality. How to keep your word. How to stand up for yourself and earn the respect of others. He would always say, 'Hubert, you're only as good as your word. If your word ain't worth nothin', then you ain't worth nothin'.'" He stopped talking and looked out the window again. "I'd say that's the most important thing he ever taught me."

"All right. I appreciate the advice. Thank you."

"Don't thank me," the mayor said, "thank my pa. It's just too bad you can't. I think the two of you would've got along famously. He always respected authority."

"I see." She looked up at all the deer heads hanging on the wall, then down at the bearskin rug. "Where did the huntin' gene come from?"

"My grandfather. I guess that one skipped a generation." He smiled.

"Where do you usually hunt?"

"All over the place. Usually nearby. Places like Le Moyne, Prichard, Semmes, Bay Minette, you know. Anywhere there's good huntin'. And of course I do all my fishing in Mobile Bay."

"That where you caught the amberjack?" It hung over his stone fireplace and must've weighed in at sixty pounds at least.

He looked up at it, smiling. "Yeah, ain't she a beaut. Almost snapped the line on that one. But to answer your question, my pa wasn't no hunter, my granddaddy sure was. I reckon my passion for it came from him. He was also a very intelligent man. Made a lot of good investments."

"Maybe he'd be smart enough to help catch our serial killer," Leah said.

"It was certainly sad to see him go," the mayor said. He paused and looked away the same as he had done so many times since they met. "So much death in my life. You start to wonder if it's all worth it."

"Now don't go thinkin' stuff like that," Leah said. "Those kind of thoughts are contagious, and I just pulled through something like that."

"I'm sorry."

"What 'bout your wife's parents, they still alive?"

"Yeah, they are. Her pa's got dementia, though. Lives in a special place where they take care of him. It's nice there. I actually reckon for him, the dementia is almost a blessing."

"That's good. And your ma?"

"Well, her ma is. I lost mine a long time ago. But hers is still here and in great shape. She still beats me at cards twice a week," he said, and smiled again.

"Well, I just thought I'd give you an update on where we were on the case. If you read the paper, you'll just get more and more confused." She gave him a false grin.

"I rightly appreciate that. And I hope you solve it quickly."

Leah stood. The mayor followed. "I should get out of your hair," Leah said.

"You mean what's left of it," the mayor laughed.

They shook hands at the top of the stairs leading down to the door. "Don't be a stranger," the mayor said. "And if there is any more advice I can give you, please don't hesitate to ask."

"Oh, by the way," Leah said, "a word of warning. The Ladies' Auxiliary wanted to thank us for a wonderful Christmas parade this year and award us with some sort of plaque. I told them it was all your doin', so I just wanted to give you a heads-up that you'll probably be the center of their attention for a while." She smiled. It wasn't a lie. The Ladies' Auxiliary *did* have a plaque for him.

He laughed. "That's great. That's what makes the people of this town so wonderful and it's the people who make a town. So without the goodness of the common folk, our town would be just like any other. But you know what? I think Alvin's somewhere special. And I ain't just sayin' that cuz I'm the mayor. I'd say that if I were cleanin' up garbage in the streets for a livin'. Don't you agree?"

God, she hated politicians. They believed their own bull crap.

"Yeah," Leah said, "I guess I do. We do have some pretty great folk livin' round here. Thank goodness the odd one turns out to be a homicidal maniac or a drug pusher or I'd be out of a job."

He laughed, but it wasn't a real laugh. "Mostly we have good folk, though, that's all I'm sayin'. I just hope you catch whoever is responsible for these deaths."

"Oh, don't worry, we will."

Leah walked down the stairs to the door and was about to open it to leave when the mayor stopped her with one last thing.

"Oh, and, Leah," he said, "next time, remember to bring a bathing suit."

She just shook her head and left. Politicians really did believe in their own bull crap.

CHAPTER 41

Leah may as well been flying when she got to the station. She went straight to the coffee machine. Chris watched her with dismay as she quickly filled up her mug, came to her desk, sat down, pushed some papers to the side, turned on her computer, and then swung her legs around so she was facing him.

"I need you to work some of your magic for me today," she said.

"Sure. What do you need?"

"I want a list of everyone who signed up for the fishin' derby and the huntin' contest at the last Harvest Fair. Not just the people who participated, but everyone who signed up. If you can get me the year before last as well, that would be even better."

Chris wrote both these items down. He sat, watching, pen poised, ready for the next task. "What else?"

"That's it," Leah said.

"That's *it?*"

"You sound let down."

"I thought you was gonna give me somethin' hard to do."

"Oh, there actually *is* one more thing. Can you call Luanne Cooper back in for questionin'? I wanna make sure I didn't miss anythin' the first time around."

"She was the one who called in the Willet Lake murder, right?"

"Right."

"Will do."

One addition to the Alvin Police Station in the last six months was a small interview room behind Leah's desk. They still had the doors that led to the lockups behind Chris's desk, but now they had a nice little room to take witnesses and suspects to talk to them. It also acted sometimes as an action room when the team wanted to get together and go over some specific thing. Chief Montgomery's office was getting a little small even for just the three of them.

The room had the obligatory one-way mirror, although the one in Alvin wasn't very large. Inside was a table with three chairs—two on one side and one on the other. The rest of the room was the same mustard color stonework as the cells.

Leah sat in the interview room on one side of the table, Luanne Cooper sat on the other side.

"Why am I here?" Luanne asked, after she'd been escorted in and given a cup of coffee. "I told your other officer out there everythin' I knew that day at the lake."

"Well, I just wanna be sure," Leah said. "What time did you come across the body?"

"I already told you this."

"Humor me."

"Must've been going on seven o'clock. Sun was just coming up. Park was beautiful that time of morning."

"Were there any other witnesses?"

"Not at that time, no," Luanne said. "The park was still too cold. Too cold for most people, anyway. Why am I being asked all this again?"

"We just want to be thorough. Now, I found your boot tracks down by the body. . . ."

"Right. I told you I went down for a closer look. I'm sorry. Look, I ain't never seen a dead body before."

Be happy about that, girl. . . .

"Okay, Luanne, we're almost done. But I ask myself," Leah said, "someone with the skills you got for photography probably has a good eye for detail. See, we're comin' up with very little to go on for this case, and I need any details I can find."

Luanne just shrugged. "I've told y'all everythin'."

"Can I ask you somethin', Luanne? I promise you won't get in any trouble no matter how you answer it."

"Sure."

"Did you take any pictures of that body that mornin'?"

Her eyes looked to the table for just a minute. Just enough for Leah to know the woman was about to lie. "Of course not. You told me to stay away from the scene and make sure others did, too."

"Right. Which you did a very good job at, by the way, thank you very much. But what 'bout before you called me? Did you take any pictures then?"

Luanne shook her head. "No, none. I ran to the nearest pay phone and called the police as soon as I saw the body. It was quite disturbin', to be honest."

"I bet it was. You okay now?"

"What do you mean?"

"You don't seem too shook up 'bout it anymore."

"No, I'm fine. I've had some time to get over it."

Leah looked up at the mirror where she knew Chris was watching. The interview was also being taped and recorded, just in case Luanne said anything worthwhile. So far, she hadn't, but taping and recording interviews was simply just standard practice.

"Can I go now?" Luanne asked, setting her empty coffee mug down on the table.

"I don't see why not. You answered my big question. Just remember, if you think of anything else, you call me, okay?"

"I will. I already told you I will."

Leah escorted the woman out of the room and she and Chris watched as Luanne and her spiky red hair walked outside and turned down the sidewalk.

"How do you think that went?" Chris asked.

"Hard to tell. I think she's holding somethin' back."

"Somethin' like what?"

"I dunno. Just somethin'."

* * *

There was a bang on the outside window and Leah looked up to see Abe and Dewey leaning their bikes against the glass.

Oh, Jesus, she thought, *why are they here?* Her boy and Dewey coming to the station to see her was rarely a good thing. In fact, thinking back, she couldn't recall one time when it was.

"What's goin' on?" Leah asked, not getting up from her desk as they walked in, Abe leading the way and Dewey trailing behind. Chief Montgomery was locked away in his office doing what he referred to as "official police business." It involved watching his television. Even through the closed door, Leah could hear some sort of sporting event. She thought it sounded like hockey.

"Me and Dewey have been investigatin' for you!" Abe said with a big, wide grin.

"Oh, dear Jesus," Leah whispered under her breath. Leah's boy had a tendency to take things a little far and to misinterpret stuff a lot of the time. She started wishing she'd never had the talk with him about serial killers.

"Is that so?" she asked. "And how have you been doin' that?"

"We've been followin' people," Dewey said matter-of-factly. "Watchin' for anyone with patterns."

"That's on account of you tellin' me serial killers followed patterns," Abe said, still beaming.

He had a paper bag in his hand and he upturned it onto Leah's desk, dumping at least a dozen pocket-sized notebooks all over the place. "These are our top twelve suspects," he said. "All of these people follow the exact same pattern every single day."

"At first," Dewey said, "we were near on positive Isaac Swenson was our prime suspect, but it turned out he don't always follow the same pattern, so he got dropped from our list. His son, Bubba, is still on it, though."

"Bubba's pattern is simple, but it never changes," Abe said.

"We're pretty near on certain all these folk are serial killers," Dewey said.

From beside her, Leah could hear Chris trying his best not to laugh. Leah held her face in her hands, considering that never again would she tell her son anything that related to her work. "Are

you two insane?" she asked. "And let me guess . . . you did all this
with your bow and arrow and your sword on you."

Abe looked down at his bow, strapped across his chest, and
then to Dewey with his sword in its scabbard at his side. "What's
wrong with our weapons?"

"You look like fools."

"I think we look like superheroes with super powers."

"But you're not superheroes," Leah said. "And you certainly
have no super powers."

"Power is something inside of you . . ." Dewey started, but Abe
shushed him.

"These weapons ain't stupid," Abe said. "What if we'd been
attacked?"

"You followed people around while dressed in Halloween
costumes," Leah said. "It's not the *weapons* that are the stupid part."

"*D and D* characters," Abe corrected.

Leah sighed. "You know what? I don't even want to *have* this
conversation."

"Anyway," Dewey said, gesturing to the notebooks as though
he completely missed the last five minutes, "these are all serial
killers we're pretty certain, but the one you're lookin' for is *this*
one." He pulled a yellow notebook from the mess. "Miss Noelina
Waters from Frankie's Bakery. She's a total pattern follower, ain't
she, Abe?"

"She most certainly is. She never changes a thing from day
to day."

"And," Dewey said, "the one time she does break her pattern is
so she can drive through town in a pickup sometimes."

"Yeah," Abe concurred. "It's a blue Ford."

For a brief moment this actually caught Leah's attention. Then
she realized she was listenin' to facts gathered from her twelve-
year-old boy and his best friend and how ridiculous it was. "Now,
how did you boys know about the pickup clue?" Leah asked.

Abe kicked one shoe into the toe of his other. "I overheard you
sayin' it to Officer Chris."

"You mean you was eavesdroppin' again? How many times do
I have to tell you it's not your job to listen to my conversations?"

"I'm sorry. It's just that—"

"It's just that you found it interestin'. I *do* get why you do it, Abe. But you shouldn't be doin' it. Was the truck for certain a Ford?"

Both boys looked at her questioningly and nodded.

"Okay," Leah said. "Now I want you boys to listen closely to me. I don't know how many times I gotta tell you this, but I do *not* want you two spyin' on or followin' any more people in town, do you understand? It's ridiculous enough that y'all is runnin' round with weapons. Catchin' the bad guys is *my* job, not yours. So, *please* leave it to me? Besides, all the two of you are fixin' to do is get hurt. There is a real killer out there. This isn't make-believe. This isn't your Dungeons and Dragons."

Abe looked down at the pile of notebooks. "So you ain't gonna follow up any of our leads?"

"No, Abe, I'm not."

"Why do you always think my ideas are dumb?"

"You just answered your own question."

"I don't understand."

"Because, Abe," Leah said, "your ideas usually *are* dumb. Not always, sometimes they can be very smart. But when they're dumb, they seem to be extra dumb to make up for the very smart ones."

Abe examined the carpet. "Oh."

"So promise me," Leah said. "No more spyin'?"

Abe and Dewey both hung their heads. "Okay," Abe said, "I promise."

"And, Dewey? What 'bout you?"

"What if I just look out my window at people?" he asked.

"If you're doin' it to keep tabs on what people is up to, then it's spyin'. No more spyin'."

"Okay," he said reluctantly. "I promise."

"Now go home and play D and D or whatever you do in the backyard like normal kids," Leah said.

Abe and Dewey turned and slunk out the door. Before it closed behind them, Leah heard Dewey say to Abe, "See? I told you we shouldn't show her our work."

"Just shut up," Abe replied.

"Don't take it out on me," Dewey said.

They got on their bikes and rode away down Main Street.

Inside the station, Leah scooped all the notebooks off her desk and into one of the drawers. All of them, that was, except for the yellow one containing the information regarding Noelina Waters from Frankie's Bakery. When the boys spoke of that one, it had brought a feeling to Leah's gut she'd been waiting for in this case; a feeling she usually got when she began to get close to solving a mystery or uncovering an important clue.

But this was something she purposely kept to herself. There was no way she would ever tell those two boys they had done something good by spying on townsfolk.

CHAPTER 42

In order to be discreet, Jonathon and Carry met each other at the theater to watch the new movie *Beetlejuice,* featuring Michael Keaton, who was pretty much the funniest guy in movies these days.

Carry arrived first, which was a welcome change for her. She wore her favorite winter jacket—she had three—but this one was yellow and she absolutely *adored* the color yellow. She'd made sure her hair was perfect and she had on the cutest snowman earrings. She felt more confident than she could ever remember.

It didn't take long before she saw a tangle of red hair coming down the sidewalk toward her. *He even looks good at a distance,* she thought. She was finding more and more how much she liked him. He was wearing a different jacket from yesterday. This one looked like an English schoolboy's jacket with a wide collar and togs instead of buttons going up the front. He was actually wearing sweatpants and suddenly Carry wished she had gone with sweats. They would've been a lot warmer than the capris she decided on, even with the long underwear she was wearing underneath.

When they finally got to the box office and the rest of the people waiting to go in had entered, Jonathon's hand found Carry's and their fingers interlaced—and Carry's butterflies instantly returned.

He turned around and bought them both tickets to the show. "Oh, you don't have to pay for mine," Carry said. "I brought my own money."

"Listen, here's the rules: When we go on proper dates, *I* pay. When we go on freaky girlish things, like, say, you drag me to the opera or something—then *you* can pay. Deal?"

"Deal." They shook hands and Carry took her ticket from the plump woman behind the ticket booth.

"I hear this movie is pretty good," Carry said.

"Me too, but then only from TV reviews. I haven't really kept in touch with any of my friends over the break."

Carry looked at her white booted foot and crossed it over the other. "Yeah, me neither."

"Oh, well, one more week and it's back to school."

"Don't remind me."

"You really hate it *that* much?"

"Actually, no. I hate going to and coming home from school because *this* is the year my little brother had to start coming to Satsuma, too. He attends the middle school, but I'm stuck on the same bus ride with him and Dewey. So I have to walk to and from the bus stop with him and his brain-dead friend and listen to them talk about the most inane things along the way. You wouldn't believe what they find interesting. Then, once on the bus, I try desperately to sit as far away from them as possible, but usually, since we're the last pickup on the route, we wind up sitting together. It's a horrifying experience I wouldn't even wish on my worst enemies."

Jonathon laughed as they entered the lobby to the theater. The smell of popcorn swelled in the air. A big smile appeared across Carry's face. "How 'bout *I* buy the popcorn?"

"Okay. We can throw that into the rule book, if you like."

They were about tenth in line at the concession stand when Jonathon asked her what time the movie started.

"Three-ten," she said.

He checked his watch. "We have fifteen minutes. I hope there's no popcorn disaster between now and then. I wonder how long the movie is? What time do you need to be home?"

"At five for dinner. But if I'm a bit late, my mother won't care."

Okay, that was a wee bit of a lie. The last time Carry was a bit late, her mother whiled away the time by showing Abe and Dewey how to take apart her gun and teaching them how to shoot with it. Then things got really bad once she got home. Luckily *that's* never happened since.

"Okay, I doubt it's two hours long. You should be fine."

They held hands while they stood in line. Frogs were hopping all around the insides of Carry's stomach. They'd replaced the butterflies.

"So what sort of stuff do your brother and his friend talk about that bothers you so much?"

"Oh God, what *don't* they talk about? 'Hey, Dewey, I wonder how many LEGO bricks it would take to remake our exact houses so we could live in LEGO versions?' 'Um,' Dewey says, 'I'm guessing at least ten thousand, but it would be so much better. Imagine the flexibility. If you didn't like a wall where it was, all you'd have to do would be to carefully unclip it from the floor and move it. I'm gonna ask my ma if she minds if I try to redo our house as a LEGO house. I can build it in the backyard and then, when the time came that it was finished, knock down the existing house and move the LEGO house forward onto its same spot. Brilliant!'"

"You're kidding," Jonathon said with a laugh.

"Why in the name of everything holy would I kid 'bout somethin' like that? That was a conversation they had a day or two before Christmas break on the way to the bus stop. There I was, half asleep, having to listen to them recite the glories of LEGO architecture."

"Wow. It is kind of a brilliant idea, mind you."

She elbowed him. "Don't you start."

"Tell me another one."

"Geez, I try to block these things from getting *into* my brain. Now you're askin' me to remember 'em?"

"Just one more."

Carry sighed. "Okay. 'Abe, I came up with the greatest invention in the world.' 'Really, Dewey?' Abe asks. 'What's that?' 'Reusable wrapping paper. You make it out of stretchy, almost rubbery material that sticks to itself and you can buy it in different sizes. You never cut it or anything, and it's completely reusable and good for the environment.' 'Who cares 'bout the environment?' asks Abe. 'One day you will. I was watching this show on TV by this guy called David Suzuki and . . .' And it just keeps going on and on and on and on . . ."

"I think you should paste them all in a book, and Dewey is right. David Suzuki *is* brilliant and one day soon everyone will be forced to worry 'bout the environment."

"Oh God, please stop. Don't be a geek." She looked up. *Please, God, don't let him be a geek.*

"How does knowin' stuff make you a geek?" Jonathon asked.

"It's *what* you know. Knowin' stuff is fine by itself."

"Okay, I think I'll have to ponder that one later. For now, I think you better order whatever you want to eat and drink." They had come to the front of the concession stand.

"Wanna just share a large popcorn and soda?" Carry asked Jonathon.

"Sure."

"Diet okay?"

"Rather not. That same guy—David Suzuki—talks about how bad aspartame is for you. Your brain can be tricked into thinking it's being given sugar—which it likes—when it's actually being given aspartame—which will kill it."

"Oh, how sweet. God, I asked very politely that you not make him a geek," she said, glancing up. The person on the other side of the counter just waited for them to order. She looked like she was growing more and more impatient by the minute. "Okay," Carry said. "Large Coke and large popcorn." She looked at Jonathon, and said, "With extra butter?"

Jonathon said, "Of course."

"With extra butter."

The movie turned out to be hilarious. It had so many good lines, Carry was repeating them all the way back to her place. Jonathon was nice enough to walk her home. They got to the end of her driveway and she asked him the time.

"Five-forty," he said.

"Oh God, I'm late."

"Will you get in much trouble?"

"I dunno, this is new territory for me, just being a *bit* late. We'll have to see."

"Okay, well, I hope you don't and if it's any consolation, I had a terrific time today. Do you mind if I hug you again?"

Carry tried not to look too disappointed. She was hoping for a kiss.

"I would expect nothing else, you big geek," she said, and smiled.

"I am *not* a geek."

They embraced and the warmth of his body pressed into hers. Time stood still. Carry lost all concern of being late, of school, of . . . of anything. Even the frogs in her tummy took a breather.

When they broke apart, Carry said, "Wow."

"Yeah, I was gonna say that," Jonathon said. "Wow."

"When do I get to see you again?"

"Well, you'll probably see me around school and, if you do, don't be afraid to come up and say hi or even give me one more of those," Jonathon said. "Otherwise, I have your number. I *will* call you."

"When do I get *your* number?"

"I wasn't sure you wanted it."

"I want it."

"I have a pen but nothing to write on."

"I have a hand but no pen to write on it with."

Jonathon gave her the pen and recited his number while she copied it onto her hand. "Good night, Jonathon. Dream of me."

"I have since the day we met."

God, that boy knew the right things to say.

He began walking down Cottonwood Lane. Carry watched him with an almost-full moon hanging high above his head and a clear blanket of stars draping down over the world around him.

There could be no question: She was falling down the rabbit hole.

* * *

Walking into her house, Carry braced for impact. But she was surprised to find her mother not even mad. "You're forty minutes late for dinner."

"I'm sorry; I just got to talking with . . ."

"Don't make up a story. I don't mind forty minutes. Forty minutes late is normal high-school behavior. We didn't wait for you to eat dinner. Yours is in the fridge. You'll need to microwave it."

And that was that. Carry couldn't believe it. It was as though her mother took a double dose of Prozac today or something.

CHAPTER 43

Leah came into the station.

Chris immediately started reading from a report he held in his hands, the paper looking bright white on his dark brown fingers.

"Turns out, in the last two years, the Harvest Fair had a lot of folk sign up for the Huntin' Contest and the Fishin' Derby," he told her. He handed her two pages of printed paper. "Of course, a lot of them were duplicates. I didn't bother listin' the same names twice. Reckoned that was a waste of time."

Leah scanned down the names. "The mayor didn't attend?" she asked, surprised.

"Not if he ain't listed," Chris said.

"Strange. See as how he seems like such an avid outdoorsman."

Chris just shrugged. "Whatcha gonna do with that now that you got it?" he asked.

"I'm not too sure," Leah answered. "But it's a lead. One of these guys—or women (there were three females listed)—could be our killer. There's gotta be a way of narrowin' this down. If this guy's really leaving a message for us, we should be able to cross-reference this list with anyone who had any legal squabbles in the past two years."

Chris scratched the back of his head. "Not sure how we'd go

'bout doin' that, to be honest. We could get background information on every one of 'em, but you're talkin' 'bout doin' fifty-seven background checks. Mobile will want to kill me if I call 'em up and ask for that."

"At least it's you and not me. Do it. It's quite possibly our best lead right now. While you're at it, add the mayor to your list."

"Mayor Robertson? You seriously want me to ask for background checks on fifty-seven—wait, scratch that—fifty-eight different people?"

"Yes."

"They'll bring back lynchin'."

"You're bein' overly dramatic."

"I'm being realistic."

"Just run the checks."

"Okay, Commander. And the mayor? Why the mayor?"

"Yeah, the mayor. I want background on everything you can get me on him and his dead wife."

"The mayor had a wife?"

"Apparently she was hit by a drunk driver thirteen years ago."

"And you want their background info, why? Especially someone who's been dead thirteen years?"

"Just call it one of my hunches."

"I hate your hunches."

CHAPTER 44

Leah was still waiting on the background checks to come in. In the meantime, she figured she may as well follow up on the one good lead Abe and Dewey happened to stumble upon: Noelina Waters.

After looking up Noelina's address, Leah got in her car and went to pay the lady a little visit.

Noelina Waters lived on Thompson Drive, which made for a short but rather pretty trip from the station. A mixture of evergreens and deciduous trees lined the sides of streets between houses, and grasses and sedges grew amongst them. There were even clumps of hollies, junipers, and berried shrubs that glistened in the afternoon sunlight. Two mockingbirds dipped in and out of a batch of white violas.

When she arrived at the house, there were two cars in the driveway, a red Volkswagen Bug and a dark blue Dodge coupe. What there wasn't was any sign of a blue truck like the one the boys had said they saw her driving.

Leah got out of her car and followed the concrete path to the door. The front yard was well kept, with evergreen sweet flags lining the path. Even in the winter they were in bloom and looked very pretty. A large willow practically filled the front yard, its branches draped heavily with Spanish moss. The winter sun shining through it made everything take on an almost mystical glow.

The path ended at the steps leading up to the porch, but a garden continued on beneath what was probably a bedroom window. The front tire of a Big Wheel stuck out from around a small shrub and Leah guessed that Noelina must have kids. At least one, anyway.

She checked her watch. It was half past one. That was good, she shouldn't be interrupting lunch or anything like that.

Ringing the doorbell brought the sound of tiny feet running on hardwood. When the door opened, the boy on the other side was all red hair and freckles. He wore a red shirt almost completely tucked into black sweatpants and had bare feet. His eyes were blue and looked polished, like the stones Leah and Abe sometimes pulled out of the Anikawa River.

He stood there staring at Leah in silence, just the screen door between them.

"Is your mother home?" Leah asked.

The boy nodded, but didn't move or say anything. He started hanging off the brass doorknob.

"Can I talk to her?"

More nodding. Still no moving or talking.

"Can you get her for me?"

The boy turned, took two steps into the foyer, and yelled, "Mom! Someone's at the door! They want you!"

"Who is it?" came a call back from somewhere in the house.

"I don't know!" It sounded like the boy was getting fed up. "Ask them!"

With a sigh, the boy took the two steps back to the door and his stony eyes stared into Leah's. "Who are you?"

"My name is Detective Leah Teal," she said. "I'm with the Alvin Police Department."

He took his two steps away again, and yelled, "It's the police!"

"The police? Tell them I'll be right there!"

It wasn't quite the introduction Leah wanted, but it worked. Sure enough, within a few seconds a dark haired woman was at the door. She had her hair tied back and wore an oversized shirt and purple sweatpants. On her feet were purple fuzzy slippers. Leah guessed this was her "housecleaning look."

"Hi," she said, hesitantly and out of breath. "You don't look like no police."

Leah flashed her badge. "That's cuz I'm a detective. I don't wear a uniform. I don't get the fancy car either."

The woman looked past Leah at the brown sedan parked on the side of the road.

"You're Noelina Waters?" Leah asked.

"Yeah, but folk just call me Noel. I have no idea why my folks called me Noelina. Apparently it was my daddy's idea. Anyway, may I ask why you're here?" she said, sounding a little anxious. "Somethin' wrong?"

"I wouldn't say somethin' was necessarily wrong, I would just like to ask you a few questions concernin' a case I'm workin' on is all. If that's all right with you?"

"Certainly."

There was a huge hesitation while Leah waited for the woman to invite her in until she realized Noel Waters was expecting her to ask the questions out here.

"Do you mind if I come inside and ask 'em? Be a mite more comfortable, I reckon," Leah said.

"Oh, no, not at all. I'm sorry. I just ain't had no police showin' up at my door before, Miss . . . I'm sorry, what was your name again?"

"Detective Teal."

"Detective Teal," Noel Waters said.

She brought Leah into her living room, which was right off the foyer. "Can I get you anythin'?" Noel asked. "Cup of tea? Coffee? Glass of water?"

"No, I'm fine."

Leah took a seat on the long green sofa that ran beneath the picture window. There were two matching chairs in the corners of the room and everything faced the television, which stood on a back stand in front of a faux walnut wall. Above the TV was a framed picture of Santa Claus, and, from where she sat, Leah could tell right away there was something weird about it.

"Actually," she said, "maybe I will take that glass of water after all."

With a smile, Noel left to get the water and Leah took the opportunity to get up off the sofa and examine the Santa picture more closely. Just as she had expected—the whole thing was made from tiny stitches. There were also little beads used in parts of it. She couldn't imagine how tedious something like this had to be to make.

Noel returned and handed a glass of water to Leah. She noticed Leah looking at the picture. "You like that?" Noel asked. "It took me near on six months to finish. It's the biggest cross-stitch pattern I've ever done."

"Looks very complicated and difficult," Leah said, searching through the picture for any part where the stitching pattern might match the pattern they were seeing on the eyelids of the victims.

"It's really not, once you get the hang of it. It's more frustrating than anything. Especially if you lose your count and miss a stitch or put in one too many."

Leah went back to her seat on the sofa. Noel took the chair to her left.

"So," Leah said. "I couldn't help but notice you have two vehicles in your driveway. They both belong to you?"

Noel laughed. "No, I only need one. The other's my husband's. Mine's the Bug. I just think it's so cute."

"So your husband's home today?"

"No, he's actually up in Montana on a business trip. He'll be back next Friday unless things change. They tend to change a lot with his work."

"What's he do?"

"Handles the buying and selling of ranch land. Deals a lot with foreclosures and banks, but also with personal sales."

"I see."

"He's up looking at a piece of property that his company is thinkin' 'bout buyin' for themselves just to sit on as an investment. Six hundred acres or something like that. I can't recall the exact size. But it's pretty big."

Leah took a sip of her water, setting the glass on a coaster on the coffee table in front of the sofa when she was finished. "You work at . . . Frankie's Bakery," Leah said. "That right?"

Noel gave her a huge smile. "That's right. It's my bread and butter, I like to say."

"How come you ain't at work today?"

"I don't go in every day, or sometimes I just go in for a couple hours and make sure things are runnin' fine."

"Doesn't the boss mind you workin' that way?" Leah asked.

Noel laughed again. "Oh, I thought you knew. I *am* the boss. I own the place. Frankie is my husband."

Leah felt dumb. She should have at least done enough research to know something as basic as that before coming to question someone. But this might also explain the truck.

"I assume, bein' the boss an' all, occasionally you must need to buy supplies, probably on a regular basis. Do you go get those from somewhere, or are they delivered?"

"Usually they're all delivered, but sometimes I'll go pick up a load of flour and sugar and yeast and whatever else we might need if we have a big week or something special like Christmas. I just had to go do my own pickup a few days ago, in fact."

"And there's enough room in your Bug for that? Seems like it would fill up pretty quick."

Another laugh from Noel. "Gosh no. I have access to a pickup I borrow from a friend when I need it. She lends it to me and in exchange I give her more baked goods than she can eat in a month."

"Where's this friend from?"

Noel's eyes narrowed slightly. "Why? Is she in trouble? Are you lookin' for someone with a pickup? There's lots of people with pickups, you know."

Leah took a deep breath. Should she lie? She never liked lying. Should she stretch the truth? It was better than lying. Actually, the best response is to just omit part of the truth. Then she's not lying at all. She's just avoiding.

"I'm involved with a case right now where we believe the perpetrator used a truck as a getaway vehicle. It happened in Alvin. I'm just trying to strike everyone I know with access to a pickup or who owns a pickup off my list."

"Well, you can definitely strike Cassandra off your list. She doesn't live in Alvin and she doesn't drive her pickup here. Only I do. I drive up to her place, leave my car there, take her pickup, and later return it and get my car back."

"Okay, that's great, thanks." Leah had pulled out her pad and written all that down. "Now, if you don't mind and for the sake of me not getting screamed at by my chief of police, could I please have Cassandra's last name and where she lives?"

"Sure. It's Cassandra Benson. And she's up in Birmingham. Has the cutest little cottage-style house you've ever seen. And boy, if you want to see someone who can cross-stitch, she's your girl. . . .

When Leah got back to the station, she immediately called Detective Truitt.

"Hi, Dan, it's Leah. I have a potential I need you to check out."

"It's what I live for."

"I know."

"Who is it?"

"Name's Cassandra Benson. Lives in Birmingham. Apparently an expert at cross-stitching and owns a blue Ford pickup."

"That hardly implicates her as a serial killer."

"I know. I just have a feeling."

"I know feelings. Okay, I'll check her out."

"Thanks."

"And, Leah?"

"Yeah?"

"What are you doing for New Year's Eve?"

"Um, what? Why?"

"Can I come down there and take you out? I'll let you order your own steak and everything."

She smiled. Of course, he couldn't see it. "Okay. I know a great place in Willet Park, and they always have fireworks at midnight in Willet Park. The restaurant's right on the water."

"Isn't that where Mercy Jo was found?"

"Other side of the lake."

"Kinda creepy," Truitt said.

"Too creepy?"

"No, that was excitement. I like creepy."

"Okay."

"What's the place called? I will make reservations."

Leah felt dumb, she was smiling so hard. "It's called Waves on Willet."

"Sounds great. I'll get back to you on Cassandra Benson."

"Thanks, Dan."

CHAPTER 45

It was the twenty-ninth of December. The day Carry would say is the greatest day of the year because it was the day she came into this world. It was her birthday. Jonathon even had a dozen roses delivered to Carry's house; although when her mother asked her who sent them, Carry just got tongue-tied, and said, "A friend from school." She was still a little gun-shy (and a little embarrassed) to talk to her mother about her love life, despite what Madame Crystalle had told her.

Even Abe and Dewey seemed to give her a gift today: the gift of quietness. Other than wishing her a happy birthday, when they came in for lunch (Carry's mother made grilled cheese sandwiches—one of Carry's favorites), Dewey didn't talk about atom bombs, antigravity boots, ray guns, or anything stupid and dorky all the way through the meal. It was the most delightful lunch Carry could remember having all year.

She even received three happy birthday phone calls from girls at school she didn't think really liked her. Maybe she'd have to reassess her popularity status after all.

After lunch, the boys raced outside to play with Abe's new bow and arrow. Carry tried to watch television for a while, but all the birthday attention had her too hopped up. She went into the kitchen, where her mother stood at the sink cleaning up the lunch-time dishes.

"Hey, look who it is," her mother said. "The number-one birthday girl. I hardly get to see you that often anymore."

"What do you mean? I'm always here. Just usually watching TV."

"Not true. You were out just a day or two ago. Even stayed forty minutes past curfew." Carry wondered if she was going to get reprimanded now. Her mother was always slamming her for something.

"So, are you gonna tell me, or do I have to pry it outta you?" her mother asked.

"What?"

"About the boy."

"What boy?" But Carry felt her face growing pinkish. Stupid face.

"Caroline, do I look like I just fell off a turnip truck? The boy you've been seein'."

"What makes you think I've been seein' a boy?"

"Mothers know these things. Is he cute?"

Carry blushed completely. "Mother, I am not discussing my love life with you."

"Oooh, your *love* life. Is he good to you?"

"He's very sweet and very cute. Can we leave it at that?"

"He sent the roses?"

Carry just nodded. They were on the coffee table in the living room. They were beautiful—twelve velvety red, long-stemmed roses with baby's breath in a beautiful crystal vase her mother gave her.

"I just have one more question that's vitally important."

"What's that?"

"How old is he?"

Carry hesitated. "Seventeen."

"An older boy." Her mother went back to washing dishes. Thank God. Still, Carry felt the conversation was left dangerously unfinished.

"Mom, this isn't like last time—"

"It better damn well *not* be like last time." Then her demeanor changed. "I suppose you're only two years apart. That's less than me and your pa was. I'm okay with two years. So when do I get to meet him?"

"I dunno." She couldn't believe her mother just approved of her dating.

"I've got an idea. Why not invite him to your birthday dinner tonight?"

"Seriously? You don't think that would be . . . awkward?" Carry felt like she was walking into a trap.

"What's a little bit of awkwardness among family?"

She decided to spring the trap. "Okay . . . I'll call him and see if he's free."

Carry ran to her mother's room to use the phone in there. At least you had a modicum of privacy on that phone. She quickly dialed Jonathon's number. He answered on the second ring.

Carry asked, "Hey, what're you doin'?"

"Homework. Why do you sound so excited?"

"My mom wants to meet you. She asked me to invite you to my birthday dinner tonight. We're going to the Waterhouse. It's gonna be awesome."

"I love the Waterhouse. But are you sure nobody minds me tagging along?" he asked.

"My mother said she'd love it if you came along."

"If who comes along?" Abe said, wandering into his mother's bedroom after hearing Carry on the "quiet phone."

"None of your business, ass face," Carry said. "No, not you, Jonathon. I was talking to my dweeby little brother. My mom actually *wants* to meet you. She flinched a bit when I told her your age, so try to act maybe fifteen or sixteen."

"What? How?"

"Sorry, that was me tryin' to be funny."

"Should I meet you at the Waterhouse or come to your place first?"

"Come here first. Come as soon as you can. I'm so nervous and excited. This is gonna be great."

"Or a complete disaster," he said.

"Okay, Mr. Negative. Thanks. I hadn't put that option into my head."

"Wait a minute," Abe said, "while we're talkin' 'bout people taggin' along, is it okay if Dewey comes?"

"Absolutely on no accounts is Dewey to set foot in the same restaurant as me," Carry said. She still had Jonathon on the other end of the phone.

"Wait for a second and think this through, Caroline," her mother said, joining Abe and Carry in the bedroom. "If you just have Abe, odds are he's gonna be annoyin'. But if you bring Dewey, he will at least have someone else to talk to."

Carry looked to Abe. "You promise not to be a little Piss Bucket if I let you bring your friend? And keep the level of Piss Bucket comments to a minimum?" She actually expected her mom to go all crazy about her use of language, but, surprisingly, she didn't.

"I promise," Abe said with a wide grin.

"Great!" Jonathon said, hearing the exchange over the phone. "I wanna meet this Dewey I've been hearing so much about."

"I can't believe I'm even entertainin' this idea," Caroline said. "Okay, fine. Invite Dewey. But he's sitting in the back of the car with you, Abe."

"That's fine," Carry's mother said.

"My God, this phone is no longer a privacy phone. See you soon, Jonathon."

"You will. Bye."

Dewey must've been waiting for Abe's call right by the phone all evening because, when Abe called, Carry could tell Dewey answered it on the first ring. Then it seemed like only eight minutes went by before he was knocking on their back door.

"Wow, you must really wanna come to my party," she said to him. "All I can say is: I hope you brought a present."

"Of course I did," he said. "I just have to unstrap it from my bike. What kind of person would show up at a birthday without a present?"

Dewey went back outside to his bike and returned with a nicely wrapped gift that was spherical. About ten inches in diameter. He very gently handed it to Carry. "Be careful, it's breakable," he said.

"What is it?" she asked.

"Open it," her mother said.

Then Carry shrieked. "It just moved. All by itself. Take it away from me!"

"Open it!" Dewey said.

"I'm too afraid!" Carry said.

"Is it one of your inventions?" Abe asked.

"I wish," Dewey said.

Another shriek. "It moved again, Mother. Please take it away from me!"

"Just open it, honey. How bad can it be?"

Everyone looked at Dewey. "Think 'bout what you just said," Carry replied.

"Point taken."

Finally, Carry got her courage up to gingerly open the spherical gift. When she did, she screamed far louder than she had shrieked. "You got me a rat?! For my birthday?"

"A rat in a ball," Dewey said, smugly. "Who doesn't want one of those?"

"I don't!" Carry said.

"Put it on the floor," Dewey advised. "Let it wheel around."

Carry dropped the ball onto the floor. The rat indeed wheeled around the kitchen. It bumped into the stove, then the fridge. Then it came back toward Carry.

She shrieked again. "It's coming at me!"

"It likes you," Dewey said, smiling.

Just then there was a knock on the back door, and Carry's demeanor changed entirely. "I'll answer that."

She opened the door to Jonathon standing there, his red hair bright under the setting sun. In his hands was a bouquet of winter flowers. He was dressed rather smartly in a fancy white shirt and black pants. He even had nice shoes on.

"Jonathon!" Carry said with a big grin. "Come on in." They walked into the kitchen, where her mother, Abe, Dewey, and the rat already were waiting.

Carry took a step back, and said, "You look . . ." *Scrumptious . . .* ". . . nice."

"Am I overdressed?" he said, frowning.

"No," Carry's mother said, coming through the dining room to meet him. "We're just all underdressed. You look perfect. I'm Leah Teal. Just call me Leah." She held out her hand.

"Thanks, Leah," Jonathon said, shaking her hand (he had to move the flowers to his other hand first). "Call me anything you like. But my name is Jonathon." He smiled and Carry's mother smiled back. Carry had a big, stupid grin she just couldn't get rid of. She was eating all this up like ice cream.

Then the rat in the ball came bouncing off furniture into the dining room.

"Whose rat is that?" Jonathon asked.

"Dewey's," Carry said. "Well, I guess, technically, it's mine. Dewey gave it to me for my birthday."

"Lucky you. I've always wanted a rat. I would name it Algernon."

"Well," Carry said, "today's your lucky day. You just got your wish. The rat is yours."

"Really? Wow. Thank you. Oh, and these are for you." He handed Carry the flowers.

"Now let me introduce you to the two most annoying people on earth while I look for a vase to put these in," Carry said, nodding to Abe and Dewey.

While Carry searched through the cupboards for a vase that would fit the bouquet, her mother came up to her with a surprise. She leaned in close and whispered. "Here's a birthday present for you: so far, I really like him."

CHAPTER 46

The Waterhouse Burgers & Steak Grill wasn't as fancy as Vera's, but it was still pretty awesome and it had more of a party atmosphere. When (if) they found out it was your birthday, they made you wear this moose helmet with ridiculous antlers; then the staff took turns drumming on it from behind while they sang "Happy Birthday." Of course, everyone pretended they didn't want the staff to find out it was your birthday, but, secretly, they really wanted the moose helmet treatment.

The restaurant also had a nice view of the courthouse where the town planned for a big fireworks display on New Year's Eve. Carry had heard all of the tickets for that were already sold out, though. The Waterhouse was even going to have rooftop seating and everything. It's too bad she met Jonathon so late. It would have made for a great date.

But tonight was a great date, too. When they weren't in the car, he held her hand, except for when he was careful to open the doors for her and her mother, and do every other thing listed in the *Big Book of First Date Ethics*. Even if her mother hadn't told Carry she liked Jonathon, Carry could tell that she did. Compared to her last boyfriend, Jonathon was fantastic. Carry couldn't imagine a date going as bad with Jonathon as that one had. But that was water under the bridge now. Thank Jesus.

Despite having reservations, they still had to wait fifteen minutes to get a table and, for a Thursday, the place seemed unusually packed. It probably had to do with it still being part of the "festive holidays." Carry didn't mind, though.

When they finally got their seats, one person had to sit in a chair at the end of the booth. There were just too many of them. Carry knew better than to try and separate Abe from Dewey, so it fell to her or Jonathon to sit on the chair. Jonathon offered to take the chair right away—of course—but Carry decided to let him have the booth seat. Their knees still touched. That was good enough for her.

Carry noticed that, when she was with Jonathon, time went much faster than normal. It wasn't fair.

Once everyone was seated, Carry's mother asked who was having drinks and appys so they'd be ready when the waitress came around.

"Mother, can't you just say 'appetizers'?" Carry asked.

"Why? Is 'appy' not an 'in' word?"

"Not coming from someone who's forty."

"Lay off her," Jonathon said. "She's welcome to use any word she wants. I happen to think your mother is completely cool enough to use the word 'appy' if she so desires."

Carry felt her face grow red. "Thank you, Jonathon," Carry's mother said. Carry shut her mouth and said no more about the subject.

Abe wanted a stack of onion rings for *his* appetizer. It was called the Leaning Tower of Oinisa—which Carry thought was a stretch. Carry wanted a Caesar salad. Jonathon said he'd like cheese bread and told Carry she had to share it with him, and Leah just said she'd eat the half of the onion rings that Abe wouldn't be able to finish. "The lower half of the Tower of Oinisa. Where the princess is kept," she said, trying to be funny. Carry thought her mother shouldn't try to be funny, but instead of saying this, she said, "That's the spirit, Mom."

"Can I order a piece of cake?" Dewey asked.

"This is an appetizer," Carry's mother said. "It's a before-meal meal. Cake is a dessert meal."

Dewey started into a speech so jam-packed with Dewey logic, it was deserving of an award. Carry knew Jonathon was loving it: "Is that written down somewhere? I'd like to read it. See, the way I reckon it is like this: Say I order the peppercorn steak, which I currently have my eye on. Now, if I finish all that steak and the fixins and mashed taters it comes with, I'm gonna be too full for cake. But I *want* cake. So I'll have my cake now and bring whatever parts of the meal I don't eat home with me. Takin' dessert home sucks. It never tastes very good. And dessert's cheaper than the rest of the appetizers. Well, most of them, at least . . ."

As usual, it was a Dewey-ism with little room for rebuttal. "Oh, order your damn cake," Leah said.

Dewey's smile ran from ear to ear as the waitress came up to our table.

"Can I start you with any drinks or appys?"

"I'll have the Leaning Tower of Oinisa," Abe said. Carry was happy her mother didn't add, "Where the princess is kept."

"I'll have a Caesar salad," Carry said.

"I'll have a Super-Duper Chocolate Brownie Explosion," Dewey said, as though it were the kind of thing folk order every day for an appetizer.

"You want that *now* or after dinner?" the waitress asked.

"Let me explain this to you," Dewey said. "I reckon it goes this way, say I order the peppercorn steak, which I—"

Leah cut him off. "He would like it *as* an appetizer, please."

Dinner went off without a hitch. Even Abe and Dewey were tolerable despite Jonathon trying to draw them into ridiculous conversations like: *How many dilithium crystals does it take to run the Millennium Falcon anyway? I heard Captain Kirk was actually a robot in the* Star Trek *movie. Did you know Han Solo is a Buddhist monk?*

She didn't think they ever once thought he was joking. He managed to hold back his laughter throughout the entire night. Carry didn't know how he did it. She wouldn't have been able to.

But the greatest thing by far was the last belated Christmas gift he presented her with.

"Guess what I got us?" he asked.

"Oh. It's going to be another dorky lie, isn't it? A stuffed C-3PO doll?"

"Nope, tickets to this restaurant for New Year's Eve at eleven o'clock. Rooftop seating. We have front row on the roof for the fireworks at midnight."

Silence skittered across the table. Carry's mouth dropped open. "Are you serious?"

"Totally serious." Even Carry's mother looked a little stunned. "How?"

"I have contacts."

"What, are you in the mob or somethin'?"

"Or somethin'."

Carry looked at her mother. "Is it okay if—"

"Of course!" She looked just as surprised as Carry.

"What 'bout me?" Abe asked.

"I think you and Dewey are old enough to stay by yourselves until midnight," Carry's mother said. "I won't be much later than that."

"Wait," Carry said. "Mom? You have New Year's Eve plans?"

Her mother gave a wry smile. "Your mother has a date."

"She does?" Carry asked. "When do I get to decide if I approve?"

"You don't get to approve or disapprove. That's my job."

"Who is he?"

"Just a guy. A detective from Birmingham."

"Really. Wow. Is it serious?"

"No, no." She looked away, flushed. Carry wondered how serious it really was. Her mother obviously cared for this man.

"What's his name?"

Her mother hesitated, then said, "Dan. Dan Truitt."

"Detective Dan Truitt. Sounds like a made-up name for a crime novel."

"Oh," her mother laughed, "I can assure you he is not made up. He is definitely different from my usual type, though."

"Your *usual* type? Have you ever *been* on a date?"

She thought about this. "Well, different from your pa, I guess."

"Different's good," Carry said, and smiled.

"Anyway, getting back to New Year's Eve. I won't be late, boys." She gave Carry a look. "Neither will Carry. So one of us will be home by one at the latest, in plenty of time to look after you. You can have Dewey stay over and watch the ball drop on the television."

Carry couldn't believe it. For the first time in her fifteen-year life, she had *plans* for New Year's Eve.

CHAPTER 47

The fifty-seven (fifty-nine if you count the mayor and his wife) background checks that Chris asked the Mobile office for came back. All but three had no real police incidents worth looking at, other than speeding tickets or parking ticket violations.

One, of course, was Preacher Eli, who had gotten out of prison after serving time for accidentally shooting three-year-old Caleb Carson. But Leah had already ruled him out of any bad doings when she solved what had come to be known as the "Orwin Thomas Affair."

The other two, Leah remembered now that she had them in front of her. One was Corwin Strait, a twenty-two-year-old who had held up the Alvin Liquor Store with a .12 gauge sawed off. Within seconds of him leaving the store, the storekeeper was on the phone to the station. Because of where the liquor store is located on Main Street, Leah and Chris were able to cage him like a rat. There was a standoff for about twenty-five minutes that was fairly tense, but in the end the police got their man. He wound up being sentenced to ten years. He got out a year and a half ago. And if Leah remembered correctly, Corwin hated cops. He didn't get out for good behavior, let's put it that way.

But why wait a year before starting to kill people if it was him?

Still, she put him on her suspect list. She would definitely be dropping in unexpectedly for a chat.

It was always better to drop in on suspects unexpectedly because, by using the element of surprise, you weren't giving them the opportunity to fabricate a lie or come up with some sort of alibi. You made them have to do it on the fly, and most people ain't that good at coming up with stuff right off the top of their heads.

The other suspect of the three potentials was Glen Swift, a good ole' boy who liked his beer like he liked his motorcycles and liked them to go together. He had a drunk driving accident involving himself and, of all places, the front window of the Alvin First National Bank. He wound up spending six months in prison and paying some hefty fines, mainly because he pissed off the judge with his attitude. He got out about eight months ago, but Leah didn't see him being someone who would go around killing people. To her, he didn't show that kind of ambition. Still, the dates matched better than they did with Corwin, although there was still a gap of five months between his release and the first body being found. She wrote him down on the suspect list anyway.

The mayor's record was squeaky clean; not even a parking ticket violation. For some reason it pissed Leah off. She wanted to see at least *some*thing sordid in his past. Nobody could be *that* perfect. Could they?

CHAPTER 48

Leah decided to check out Corwin Strait first and leave Glen Swift for dessert. By far, Swift would be the easier to deal with.

Strait lived in a rundown shotgun shack on Abbot Drive, close to Cornflower Lake. It had once been painted red, but had taken on a rust color over the years. Leah noticed there wasn't a single Christmas decoration to be seen. No lights anywhere, no Santa Claus or baby Jesus nativity scenes in the yard. She assumed Corwin Strait wasn't really the festive type.

The porch leaned left, but seemed stable enough as she walked up the steps and knocked on the door. She noticed a mud-covered green Ford pickup parked in the driveway beside the house. There was also a garage that appeared in slightly better repair. Set back from the shack, it had the same rusted red siding and was almost camouflaged in a clutch of firs and pines.

She knocked on the door and, after a minute or two, it was answered. Leah immediately knew the man on the other side was Strait: He had a wandering eye and hadn't shaven in at least three days. He wore a T-shirt that hid the top of the tattoos running down both arms. Tattoos of snakes and skulls.

His eyes squinted as he looked Leah up and down. "I know you," he said, his voice low and raspy.

Leah showed her badge. "Detective Teal, Alvin Police," she replied. "I'd like to ask you a few questions."

"I ain't talkin' to no cops."

"Then I'd like to take a look around. In particular, I'd like to look in your garage. And, possibly, do a quick search of your house."

"You ain't comin' near my place without no warrant," Strait said.

Leah expected this. She sighed. "You sure you wanna do this the hard way? Your attitude makes you look guilty, like you have somethin' to hide. I can easily get a warrant. Whereas if you just comply on your own volition, it looks good for you."

"Looks good for me for what? I ain't done nothin'. What do you suspect me of?"

"If you ain't done nothin', you shouldn't be 'fraid of me lookin' round. And so far I don't suspect you of nothin'.'"

"I ain't 'fraid, Miss Detective, I just don't want cops in my place of residence. Now, kindly remove yourself from my front door."

With that, he calmly closed the door on Leah's face.

She had to bite her tongue from yelling an insult.

Back inside her car, she radioed Chris to apply for a search warrant for Corwin Strait. She put him near the top of her suspect list. Nobody's that paranoid about letting cops in unless they're hiding something.

Then she backed out onto Abbot Drive and headed out to see Glen Swift, happy to have left the dessert for last.

CHAPTER 49

Leah knocked on the door of Glen Swift's house. Unlike Corwin Strait, Swift's place was nicely kept. He actually had a garden out front of his split-level home, obviously planted for flowers that blossomed in the spring and bloomed in the winter. There were three trees in his front yard, all of them Japanese maples. The little blue home with the white accents looked rather pretty to Leah, especially with the small twinkle Christmas lights adorning the trim. She'd only met the man once, but he seemed humble and docile, his only downfall being his love of beer, so this wasn't quite a leap in her head. He did his crime, maybe he was done with the dark side of the law entirely.

Or maybe he just gave up driving. There was no vehicle in the driveway.

A kid answered the door. He couldn't have been older than ten. He was still in his pajamas, despite the fact that it was nearly three o'clock in the afternoon.

"Whatcha want?" he asked.

"Your pa round?" Leah asked.

"Let me go see."

The kid started walking back into the house hollering, "Pa! Someone at the door for you!"

Finally, a man Leah barely recognized showed up in the doorway. He was about six foot one, had a couple of tattoos done in jailhouse blue, wore no shirt, and was wearing Levi's that hung a little too low at the waistline. His hair was curly and fell down the front of his face. He looked very boyish—not at *all* the way Leah remembered Glen Swift the last time she saw him.

Of course, the last time she saw him he was piss stinking drunk and in handcuffs at one in the morning, having just driven his car through the plate-glass window at the front of the bank.

"Hi," he said, with a smile that dimpled perfectly.

Leah collected herself. "I'm Leah Teal, detective for the Alvin police. I was wonderin' if you wouldn't mind answerin' a few questions."

"Sure. What's up?"

Oh, dessert is so much better than dinner. "Do you still own the 1982 Chevy pickup you drove through the Alvin First National Bank window?"

He laughed. "No, it was sort of a bad reminder of things for me. Got rid of it the moment I got out of the can."

"Do you own *any* pickups?"

He leaned forward. "Lady, look around you. I don't own *any* vehicles."

"Would it be okay for me to take a look inside your house and your garage?"

He hesitated on this but finally decided it would be all right.

She looked through his house first. Other than toys littered over the floor pretty much in every room, the place was clean. Working with Glen Swift was a stark contrast after trying to work with Corwin Strait. It didn't take long for Leah to convince herself that there were no hostages anywhere inside Swift's house. He was just a man who lived with a boy he seemed to love very much. Everything about the house showed a father trying to handle raising a son on his own. Made Leah wonder what happened to the mother.

"You own any guns?" Leah asked.

There was a hesitation. "Sure, I use 'em for huntin'. What's that got to do with anythin'?"

"Mind showin' them to me?"

"They're in a gun vault in my bedroom. I have a license and everythin'."

"I'm sure you do, I just wanna see what you got."

They went into the master bedroom where he showed her the guns.

His vault was a rather stylish wooden affair with glass sides so you could see the rifles sitting vertically inside. There was a compartment at the top that had its own key that stored handguns.

"So you own a rifle and a shotgun?" Leah asked, lookin' into the vault.

"That's right. The rifle is a .22 long and the shotgun is .12 gauge."

"Any handguns?"

"No, under the 1968 legislation prohibition, my past makes me unable to buy anything but long guns. But you already know that. At least you should."

"Care to open the top of your vault?" Leah asked. That would be where someone would normally store their handguns.

"Care to show me a warrant, Detective?"

"I'm lookin' for an old gun. Somethin' more like a collector-style thing than somethin' you'd use for huntin' with. It's a Beretta 950, made back in the fifties or sixties. Know anyone who might have somethin' like that?"

He was already shaking his head before Leah finished her question. "No, ma'am. I don't talk to a lot of people 'bout guns."

"You know anyone who collects old guns?"

Swift thought for a moment. "Not really. I don't get out much anymore since returning home from my stay in prison. Most of my time is spent lookin' after Wyatt."

"Okay, well, I guess you've answered all my questions. If you can think of anyone who might have a lead on that Beretta 950, please give me a call." She handed him one of her business cards, both of them knowing it would be tossed into the trash as soon as she left.

He took it. "Are you done lookin' through the house?"

"I think so," she said.

He escorted her to the front door.

"Now can we look in your garage?" Leah asked.

"Sure," Swift said.

The garage was empty of any cars or trucks, but looked like a junk drawer full of children's toys. Swift was beside her when they walked in. "How many kids you got?" Leah asked.

"Just the one," Swift said. "He's enough. What a handful."

"His mom round?"

"No, she left when I got outta the joint. Not sure why she didn't take Wyatt with her, but I'm kind of glad she left him with me. Be awfully lonesome otherwise."

"All these toys belong to him?"

Swift laughed. "Yeah, most of these are from when he was four or five or even younger. I don't like to throw anythin' away. I figure one day he might have a kid and I can give him back all this stuff."

"You still drinkin' beer?" Leah knew she was on shaky ground with this question.

"I have the odd one. Nothin' like before. As soon as I was the only one in charge of Wyatt, I knew things had to change. It's amazing what kids can do for your life."

"Yep," she said, her mind shifting gears to her own kids and everything they'd brought into her life. There are times she thought that, without them, she wouldn't even be here anymore. They gave her reasons for living. "Kids are great . . ." she said, almost to herself, her voice trailing off.

"Sure are. Anyway, feel free to come back anytime."

"Thank you."

Leah returned to her car and drove out onto the street, wondering if there might be more to Glen Swift than he let on. He seemed *too* nice for comfort. And then there was the rifle and the shotgun.

To say the least, they made an impression on her.

CHAPTER 50

"Okay," Dewey said, trying to sound spooky, "are you ready to learn your future?"

"Sure," I replied, not really caring.

Dewey had his mother's scarves tied all over him and looked like he should be twirling around onstage with ice skates on or maybe on one of those TV shows where the men all dress up as women.

Closing his eyes, his left hand fingers shot to my forehead. I thought he was going to poke me in the eyes, so I backed away really quick.

"Don't," he said, opening his eyes. "Come back where you were. Don't move."

"Then don't poke out my eyes."

"I wasn't. I was getting your psychic aura."

"Okay."

I moved back and he did it again, this time ending up with three fingers on my forehead. "I see . . ." he said. "I see that your name starts with an *A*."

"Dewey, you know my name already. This isn't psychic. This is psych*o*."

"Just give me a chance. Your name is Abe and you come from the small town of Alvin."

"You're just brilliant at this," I said.

"Wait! I see something else! You're going to encounter some danger soon."

"Danger of boredom," I said. "Don't you use your cards? I think they'd be better than this."

"I do . . . just give me a sec, I'm still receiving images. Someone is going to kiss you tonight."

"Okay, I'm not listening to this." I started getting up. "You're about as psychic as the Palmers' beagle."

"No! No! Sit back down! We'll use the cards!"

With a huff, I sat.

We were sitting in my bedroom on the floor at the foot of my bed. The hardwood was cold, but it was a nice day outside so we didn't mind so much. Lately the temperature had been bouncing around like a rubber ball. One day it would be sixty degrees, the next it would be forty, the next it would be fifty-five. One day even dropped to thirty-five, if you can believe it. I don't think *anyone* went outside that day.

The only good thing about the weather was that there hadn't been much rain. We'd had a little and the one big rainstorm, but for the most part every day had been fairly sunny with white puffy clouds filling the sky, when there were clouds.

But today, once again, dark clouds had been threatening. They'd started in the east a few hours ago and looked the color of pencil lead right after you've sharpened your pencil and you fill in a picture with it at school. So I wasn't holding my breath about the good weather holding up much longer.

"Okay," Dewey said, having pulled the tarot cards from the deck. He started going through them, looking at their fronts.

"What're you doing?"

"Looking at a card to represent you."

"Madame Crystalle never did that."

"My book uses a different method than she does."

He finally pulled out the Page of Swords and laid it on the floor in front of him. Then he handed the rest of the deck to me awkwardly using his left hand. I went to grab it, and he said, "No! Use your left hand." So I did.

"Shuffle the cards overhand."

I did. Just like Carry did when we saw Madame Crystalle. Then I laid them down in three piles with my left hand and Dewey picked them up with his left. As he pulled cards from the top of the deck he said things like, "This covers you," and "This crosses you," and "This is beneath you," and stuff like that. In total, he put ten cards down. Two went on top of my card, three went around it, and four came down the right side.

Then, with the help of his book (and I'm sure a fair amount of imagination), he read my future.

"I see a new beginnin' in some sorta financial venture where you'll do well except right now somethin' is holdin' you back from startin'."

"Maybe the fact that I'm twelve years old?" I suggested.

"Whatever it is, it's gonna take a bit of strugglin' to get past it."

"Probably not my age, then. That just sort of goes by on its own."

"In your head, money's always been a problem, but the reality is you're unable to see how clever you really are, believe it or not. Which is hard to believe because you think you're pretty clever." He looked up.

"It doesn't say that," I said.

"No, but it should."

"Just stick to the cards."

"You see yourself as havin' a good imagination, and you reckon you're smart enough to keep up with everyone else."

"Who can't I keep up with?"

"I'm just readin' 'em, Abe."

"Fine, go on."

"Other people see you as reckless, with no direction. They reckon you're suspicious by nature, and misuse your energy, which would be better spent in other places."

"I ain't suspicious by nature."

"You are, too. Remember Mr. Wyatt Edward Farrow? What 'bout Preacher Eli? And how much time did we waste lyin' in your front yard staring at Mr. Wyatt Edward Farrow's stupid garage wonderin' when he left to go pee?"

"Okay, then, there's no way it says that."

"Does too," Dewey said, turning the book around. "Look."

"Holy cow."

"Yeah, I told you these work."

"Keep goin'."

"You like to be congratulated for stuff. When you come up with a theory or an accusation, you want to be right. But that's not usually enough. You want the world to know you're right."

"Everyone wants that," I said.

"Not as much as you. Okay, we only have one card left—it's called Temperance and it's in the tenth position. So in that position, it means you will eventually find calmness and balance, but first you'll need to go through a bunch of struggles. Most of those struggles will be over showin' the world how smart you are and then provin' to it that you are right. Which sounds to me like you're awfully stubborn."

"Stick to the book. I don't need your editorializin'."

"Well, there ya go, that's your readin'." Dewey picked up all the cards. I just sat there, thinking.

"You know, Dewey, I think if you could memorize all the stuff in that book? You could make money doin' this. You're actually pretty good at it."

"You're surprised? I told you I was psychic."

"Surprised ain't the word. Shell-shocked would be more like it. I wouldn't wear the women's clothing, though."

"This isn't women's clothing, Abe, it's psychic attire. You know, like pirates and how they wear scarves."

"I'm not sure about pirates wearing scarves, especially on their heads."

"Sure they do," Dewey said.

"Well, they definitely don't wear lace, Dewey. And I'm pretty sure their scarves aren't made from their ma's silky lingerie."

CHAPTER 51

"How good are you at golfing?" Jonathon asked Carry the morning of New Year's Eve.

"Golfing?" she laughed. "Um, I don't know. I've never held a golf club in my hands. There are no golf courses in Alvin."

"There are," Jonathon said, "in fact, two. And today we're going to one."

"Oh, we are, are we? And where might these mythological golf courses be?"

"That's private information, only given out on a need-to-know basis, and you don't need to know. Just make sure you're wearing comfortable shoes."

They were currently at Carry's watching television, only for once Carry's eyes weren't glued to the TV screen, they were fixed on the side of Jonathon's head. He was sort of lying down in her lap. She had found herself becoming more and more fixated on him since they first met that day on the sidewalk with all the pizza.

The golf courses, wherever they happened to be, couldn't be very far away on account of Jonathon told Carry they were leaving on foot and wouldn't be taking the bus. That meant they were within walking distance. Now there was one thing Carry was sure of and that was that there were absolutely no golf courses within walking distance from her house.

She turned out to be wrong.

Sort of.

The only club she wound up needing for golfing turned out to be a putter. Jonathon took Carry to Jolly Castle Fun Park, an arcade with mini-golf located just off Main Street on Sweetwater Drive. Carry hadn't actually been inside the place for years. It was in a giant castle. Like being in the castle, she hadn't mini-golfed since she was, like, twelve, so she doubted she was going to be any good.

"Oh, it's like riding a bike," Jonathon said.

"I haven't really done that since I was twelve either," she said.

"Okay, then it's like falling off a bike. Either way, you'll remember how to do it after the first couple of holes."

Before they actually started golfing, Jonathon took her for lunch at the castle. It wasn't the greatest of lunches—hot dogs and soda pop—but it was lunch with her boyfriend, and Carry loved the way *boyfriend* rolled around in her head when she thought about the word.

Jolly Castle Fun Park had two different mini-golf courses. One had an aquatic theme, the other a jungle theme. Jonathon bought the tickets, choosing the jungle-themed course. The courses were beneath the castle and they had to walk down two flights of steps to get to the entrance.

Inside, everything was dark. There were floodlights (mainly blue) positioned around each of the holes.

"How many holes are we playin'?" Carry asked, kind of hoping he'd say nine.

"You gotta play eighteen. It's the law."

"Whose law?"

"The law of miniature golf."

"Great."

The first hole was pretty straightforward. Just a straight drive from the tee to the hole with a small bump in the middle. At the other end, a purple octopus wrapped around the outside of the hole with its tentacles reaching in toward the cup. It looked like it should make things easier.

"You go first," Carry said.

"No, no. Ladies first."

"You go first, or I wrap this club around your neck."

"Okay," Jonathon said. "There are always exceptions."

Jonathon ended up with a three, which was one over par. Carry ended up with a seven, but it was a sort of cheat seven with Jonathon blocking her ball with his foot as it sailed over the hole, so instead of whipping past it dropped straight in.

"I knew this was going to be a disaster," Carry said.

"It's not 'bout the score," Jonathon said. "It's about the fun."

"I'm not having much fun. I'm losing ridiculously."

"That's not fun?" Jonathon said. "Just relax. By the end of the course you'll be better."

Jonathon's theory turned out to be totally wrong. By the end of the course, Carry was just as bad as she had been at the beginning of the course. In fact, she was worse because her mood had turned so sour. She wanted to club Jonathon to death for choosing this as their New Year's Eve date. She was so happy when she saw the sign for the eighteenth hole coming into view.

On that hole (which, thank God, was the last hole), if you got the ball into the lion's mouth, you won a free game of mini-golf. Jonathon went first and barely missed. His ball ended up dropping to the edge and rolling away.

Then Carry went. *Please don't let me win a free game,* she thought. She whapped her ball, not taking aim at all, and lo and behold, her ball bounced off the top of the screen blocking bad shots, came back down, and fell right into the lion's mouth. She had won a free game of mini-golf.

It was the last thing she wanted. She raised her club, considering bludgeoning Jonathon with it if he even so much as mentioned playing another round.

"Oh my God, that was great!" Jonathon said, brushing the club she was holding up and giving her a great big hug. "Do you want to play your free game now?"

Carry was too stunned over the hug to answer. Her stomach felt like a burst of sparrows had just flown from a tree growing in its center.

"Well?" he said.

"Well, what?" she asked, having completely missed his original question.

"Wanna play again and use your free game?"

"Right now?"

"Yeah."

"No!" Carry said, a little too quickly. "In fact, you can have it." What she did want to do was have him hug her again. Or better yet, kiss her, but she wasn't about to say that.

"No, no. It's yours. We'll use it next time we come."

She sighed. "Okay. Next time we come."

She hoped there wouldn't be a next time. Or if there was, they'd just stick to the hot dogs and the soda pop. By far, that was her favorite part of Jolly Castle Fun Park. Oh, and the hugging. Hot dogs, pop, and hugging. Now *that* would be the perfect date.

"What are we going to do now?" Carry asked.

Jonathon checked his watch. "Our reservations aren't until eleven o'clock. That gives us almost eight hours to find something to do until dinner. Sure you don't want to play another round?"

"Very sure," Carry said. Again a little too quickly.

"Okay. Well, do you rollerblade?"

Carry laughed.

"What?"

"I've never tried, but one thing I'm *not* is athletic."

"How 'bout bowling?"

"How 'bout we go back to my place and see if my mother is out? Maybe we can snuggle on the sofa and watch television."

"I like that idea," Jonathon said.

CHAPTER 52

Leah had found the perfect little outdoor restaurant around the edge of Willet Lake: Waves at Willet. She met Dan Truitt there at ten-thirty, so they'd have time to eat before midnight.

From here, Leah and he would be able to see the fireworks across the lake. Leah had already given permission to let Caroline go out on her own, too. This gave further permission for Abe to be in charge of himself (with Dewey). Leah hoped this wasn't a mistake. She was pretty sure she'd made the right choice, though. As she liked to say, Abe was old for his age. Something she worried about constantly. She hoped her being a cop didn't inadvertently rob Abe of his childhood.

"So, Detective Leah Teal, I know very little about you. You got kids?" Dan Truitt asked, after a sip of red wine. Once again, he'd ordered the wine without consulting Leah. At least this time, though, he'd let her order her own meal. He was having the steak and ribs. She was settling for a flame-broiled tuna over rice.

"Yes, I have two. Abe and Caroline. Caroline just turned fifteen, and I guess she acts like a typical fifteen-year-old. You know, she has her moments. Abe will be thirteen in March, but sometimes he seems so much older. He reminds me a lot of his father."

"What happened to his father?"

Leah's breath caught in her throat. She didn't like discussing Billy's death. "He died when Abe was two. Stupid car accident. He was coming home from working a midnight shift. Thought he could pass an eighteen-wheeler. Ended up in a head-on collision."

Dan reached out and touched Leah's wrist. "I'm so sorry."

Leah looked away so he wouldn't see the tears collecting in her eyes. "Yeah, it was hard. It still is a lot of the time. But I'm slowly gettin' over it. I have my son to thank for that."

"Yeah, children are great, aren't they?" Dan asked.

She met his eyes. "They really are. How many do you have?"

"I don't have any myself. Never been married. Lived with a few women for extended periods of time, though. It always seemed to end up the same way. They'd find something wrong with me and slowly the yellin' and screamin' would set in, and that would turn into them throwin' stuff and me duckin' and coverin' and the police gettin' involved. I mean, I *am* the police, so it was kind of embarrassing. . . ."

Leah laughed. "I guess."

"I s'pose I'm not easy to live with. The common denominator seems to be me in all these awkward relationships. Which is weird because, in my head? All I want is peace and quiet. I want to just get along."

"Yeah, I understand, I reckon."

"Really?" Dan asked. "You're the first person to ever tell me that."

The moon looked huge and the night was lit by thousands of tiny stars. There wasn't a cloud in the sky. It couldn't have been a more perfect night. Somewhere out on the lake, Leah heard a fish jump.

"Oh," she said, "you never told me what happened with Cassandra Benson, did you check her out?"

"I went and paid her a little visit. Got a little rough. Had to really pull my testosterone back."

"Seriously?" Leah asked.

"No, she's eighty-six and in a wheelchair. I don't think she's our serial killer. Not unless she ran the victims down and then knitted them to death. Very nice lady, to be honest."

Leah laughed. Probably more than she should have. Wine had a habit of doing that to her. "Seriously? She's really eighty-six?"

"Seriously. I was ready to go in all Dirty Harry and I meet Grandma Moses."

Leah sighed. "We're not gonna figure this one out."

"Yes, we will. But do me a favor?"

"What's that?"

"Take a break tonight from being a cop? Tell me about your family."

"Well, my daughter's a handful and I don't reckon she means to be. I honestly think she doesn't reckon she's doin' anything wrong even when she is. It makes it very hard to raise her or to give her any guidance."

Leah finished the rest of the Cabernet in her glass. Dan refilled it.

"I'm happy you said yes when I asked you to go out on New Year's Eve," he said.

She smiled, a little bit sadly. "I'm happy you invited me."

"No, you misunderstand. I'm happy because I made reservations at a different place up in Birmingham six months ago just figurin' someone would show up in my life to go to dinner with so I wouldn't look like an idiot. I didn't want to show up alone. This place is much nicer." He laughed.

Leah laughed, too. "You're an idiot." She laughed even more.

"Why are you laughin' so much?"

"Cuz that's what my son would say: 'You're an idiot.' I just find it funny."

Dan checked his watch. "Fireworks should start in ten minutes. We're ten minutes out of 1989. How does that feel to you?"

"Like I'm goin' to be another year away from Billy's death and things should be that much easier to cope with."

"Well, that's positive, right?"

"I suppose."

"What are your kids doin' right now?"

"Oh, probably gettin' ready to walk round the neighborhood smashin' pot lids together. They're a little on the extroverted side. At least my youngest will be. He and his friend have the run of the house. My older one—my girl, Caroline—is out on her first *real* date. Can't say I'm not a little bit on edge about it."

"With you as their role model, I bet they're great kids."

"I hope so," she said, trying to keep the worry about Caroline out of her voice.

People were gathering along the railing separating the restaurant from the lake. "Come on," Dan said, "let's have one more glass of wine and go and get good positions for the fireworks."

"Sounds like a great idea!" Leah said.

The next glass of wine for both of them went quickly. They got up out of their chairs and approached the railing, and while they did, Dan reached out his hand and Leah took it, their fingers intertwining.

Five minutes later, the fireworks started.

Leah stood there, not realizing how beautiful life could be. The lake, the cypress trees, the fireworks glowing red and spreading in the sky, and then white, and then blue, and then pink, and then green and blue all coming together with little sonic booms. It was all so beautiful. She had never stopped to notice the graceful moments of life until tonight and she realized why.

Usually, there were so many fireworks in the sky, it just seemed like daytime. It took someone like Dan Truitt to shake her out of her lonely existence and let her experience life once more from a new point of view.

Inside, her heart beat like thunder. Was she in love? Hardly. Was she enamored? Possibly. It seemed more like a schoolgirl crush than anything else.

But for now, she'd take it.

CHAPTER 53

When Carry and Jonathon got back from mini-golf, Carry's mother had not been home. Apparently, her date had started early.

"This is very unlike her," Carry said.

"She would probably say this is very unlike *you,*" Jonathon replied.

Carry took a moment to consider this, and finally said, "I reckon you're right. I reckon this year is a weird year and it hasn't even started yet."

"What are Abe and Dewey doin' for New Year's?"

"Who the hell cares? I think they're watchin' television and ringin' in the New Year with Dick Clark."

"I kinda like 'em. Abe and Dewey, that is. I don't s'pose you want to invite them with us?"

"It would be worse than miniature golfing and, trust me, that's sayin' a lot."

"Okay, then. By the way, thanks for the rat. I have a great cage set up for him and everything."

"You should really be thanking Dewey for the rat. It was his gift."

"To you."

"I didn't want it."

"Whatever."

They were sitting together on the sofa in Carry's living room. Or to be more precise, Jonathon was sitting and Carry was lying with her head in his lap. Carry wanted Jonathon to make a move on her, but he didn't seem to want to. Or maybe he was scared to. She started thinking this was something she was going to have to initiate.

"So, I have a surprise," Jonathon said, looking at his watch. "And it should be here anytime."

It was almost ten o'clock, an hour before their dinner reservations. What sort of surprise could he possibly have?

There was a knock on the door. "Oh," Jonathon said. "That'll be your surprise now."

They went to the door, Carry creeping behind like an excited little schoolgirl. What she saw took her breath away.

Beneath a cloudless sky full of stars on this crisp New Year's Eve stood a horse-drawn carriage waiting out in the street. The carriage was black and was being pulled by four giant white Clydesdales.

"Oh my God!" Carry squealed. "How did you—"

"I told you. I got connections," Jonathon said smugly.

The driver who knocked on the door was dressed in Victorian style, with a top hat and a tail coat and trousers with a dark waistcoat. He looked anything but cold. From where she stood, Carry could tell his coats were both velvet lined. "I assume you're our driver for the night, my good man?" Jonathon said.

The man nodded. "That I am. You may call me William."

"All right, William, we shall be out the door in no time."

"Yes, sir."

William went back and tended to his horses while Carry smiled what felt like the biggest smile of her life. "You got us a horse-drawn carriage?"

"Only for the way there. We have him for an hour, so I told him to take a very scenic route. For coming home, I'm afraid I'll have to walk you."

"I think I'm falling in love with you," Carry said.

"Holy, that wasn't hard."

And Carry guessed it wasn't, really.

Five minutes later, Carry and Jonathon were aboard the coach and the driver signaled his horses to begin clomping down Cottonwood Lane. It was a very slow but very romantic way to travel.

"Permission to head north on Hunter Road, sir?" the driver called back. "I was considering taking all the forested roads in the south before finally making it down to Main Street. You will reach the restaurant from the east if that's okay with you."

"That sounds fine, William," Jonathon said.

"I feel like a millionaire," Carry whispered, and giggled.

"It actually wasn't *that* expensive. Just hard to book on New Year's Eve."

"How did you do it?"

"I told you, I've got connections."

"Your connections are scaring me a bit, to be honest."

"Okay, then I'll let you off the hook. It's all because of my grandfather who owns the pizza place. He knows *everybody,* and it's like everyone owes him a favor. And as I said before, he's a true romantic, so it's easy to talk him into these sorts of things."

"Make sure you thank him for me."

"My smilin' face is thankful enough, I reckon."

They made it to the restaurant for exactly eleven. Carry didn't see how much Jonathon tipped their driver, but she was willing to bet it was substantial.

The maître d' for the restaurant ushered them right in. "We've been holding your table. And *everyone* has been asking 'bout it," the girl said. "I reckon you've got the best seat in the house."

They climbed the stairs to the rooftop where, among all the busy people, sat one lonely table with by far the best view of the courthouse. And it belonged to Carry and Jonathon. Carry's heart was doing tricks on trampolines.

She barely remembered dinner. "Order anything you want," Jonathon said.

Carry was going to stick with a hamburger and fries, but when

Jonathon went ahead and ordered the prime rib, she decided to go with the sirloin Neptune. She had no idea how much tonight was costing her poor new boyfriend, but she was sure enjoying it.

They finished dinner with fifteen minutes to go before the fireworks. "Just enough time for dessert, I reckon," said Jonathon.

Carry's mother *rarely* let her order dessert when they were out. Jonathon ordered a chocolate tiramisu and Carry ordered a caramel-covered chocolate brownie.

Both desserts came in record time. It was as though the staff wanted everyone done before the fireworks started. Carry had her last bite in her mouth when the music from the courthouse suddenly swelled up, and the first ball of red swirled as it shot way over their heads and exploded into a giant cascade of sparkles that hung there in space as three more came to join it.

Being so close to the fireworks was amazing. The explosions went off like small sonic booms Carry felt in her chest a half second after the fireworks burst in the night sky. There were showers of red, white, blue, gold. Some shot straight up, others arced across each other before exploding. The whole thing was perfectly choreographed to the music being played from the courthouse.

Jonathon moved his chair in close beside Carry's and Carry thought *no night could be any better than this.*

Then he said the one thing that upped the ante: "Caroline Teal? Would you mind so much if I kissed you?"

"Jonathon Mitchell?" she replied. "I wouldn't mind one little bit."

And suddenly, beneath all those gigantic bursts of explosive colors, Carry's lips found Jonathon's and it felt as though the fireworks hung there amongst all the tiny stars in the night sky as time stood still and the night turned into one of the best ones Carry could ever imagine having in her entire existence.

CHAPTER 54

New Year's morning, Carry was on the verge of yelling at us to go play in my bedroom or better yet go play with our new weapons. Mom had decided to go in to work, and Jonathon had showed up around ten o'clock. It looked like today was panning out to be another day of being ordered about by my sister, who liked to rule the house with an iron fist whenever she fought with me.

This time, she surprised me, though. It all happened when Dewey dropped the bomb on Carry that gave us diplomatic immunity. "Ever since Christmas, I've been studyin' to be a psychic. I have tarot cards and everythin'. I'm pretty good at it, too. Ain't I, Abe?"

"I have to admit, he wasn't bad when he read mine," I said, "but it could've been a fluke. And the first part was full of stuff he already knew."

"Do you have your cards here?" Carry asked, actually sounding hopeful or, dare I say, happy we were here—something I don't think I had ever heard before.

"Yep, they go with me everywhere I go. I even sleep with 'em under my pillow. Apparently it's supposed to give you a better psychic bond with your deck. And without a good psychic bond with your deck, you ain't no real psychic."

"Read Jonathon's future!" Carry exclaimed.

The two of them were wound up like a corkscrew together with Jonathon sittin' at one end of the sofa and Carry sittin' practically on top of him. He had his legs up and interlockin' with hers, and his arms crossed over her belly and were holdin' her opposite hands. I wondered if they'd ever sit like this if my mom were home. I highly doubted it.

"Oh, don't make me move," Jonathon whined to Carry. Clearly he had second thoughts about Dewey's psychic abilities.

"It won't take me very long," Dewey said, running for his backpack, which was in the dining room. He'd dropped it there on our way in. "Probably only ten minutes!" he called out while (I assumed) he rummaged through his backpack. I guessed he finally did find what he was looking for because he came bursting back into the living room with the deck in one hand and his backpack in the other. Why he'd brought his backpack with him was beyond me.

Carry untied herself from Jonathon. "Come on," she whined. "All you have to do is sit up."

"What if I don't wanna know my future?"

"Don't worry," I said. "He's not *that* good."

Finally Carry convinced Jonathon to sit up so he was leaning over top of the coffee table. "I'm afraid I have bad news," I said.

"What's that?" he asked.

"The coffee table's not big enough. You have to sit on the floor."

"Are you kidding me?" Jonathon gave Carry a look like a dog about to be put down.

"Please?" she asked. "You're already halfway there."

With a huge sigh, he asked Dewey, "Okay, where do you want me?"

"Right there across from the television. I need 'bout three feet to set up my spread."

"The psychic we saw only had about a two-foot round table," Carry said.

"She used a different spread than me. The one I use is called the Celtic Cross."

"What did she use?"

"I'm not sure. I haven't found it in my book."

"You've read *one* book and you're reading my future?" Jonathon asked.

"Almost," Dewey said.

"You're almost reading my future?"

"No, I've almost read the book. I have 'bout fifty pages to go."

"Okay, then. Let's get this over with."

Like he did with me, Dewey flipped through the cards looking for a special one for Jonathon. He finally found it: The Knight of Cups. He placed it faceup in the center of the imaginary square he had going on between him and Jonathon.

"Wait a minute," I said. "How come he's a *knight?* And why is he a cup guy when I was a sword guy? I only got to be a page."

"I told you," Dewey said. "This card represents who you are. The Knight of Cups represents Jonathon more than any other court card in the deck. The Page of Swords represents you more than any other card in the deck.

"Please explain why?" I asked.

"Please don't," Jonathon said. "Please just get this over with."

Dewey did as Jonathon asked and passed him the deck left to left like he did with me, asking Jonathon to shuffle them overhand as much as he wanted until he felt confident that he had imprinted himself on the cards. Surprisingly, Jonathon shuffled for quite a while, probably double the amount of time I had.

"Does it matter if the card is upside down?" I asked Dewey. Four of Jonathon's cards were upside down.

"Yes, and their position and what the card is. Notice some cards have numbers like regular cards. These are called the Minor Arcana and are just like regular cards with court cards like the king, queen, and jack (except the jack is a knight) and one extra court card called the Page. They also have four suits just like regular cards except instead of hearts, spades, diamonds and clubs, they're cups, swords, pentacles, and wands. There's also a Major Arcana and these have numbers too, but they are special cards that aren't part of the Minor Arcana or like anything in our regular deck. If you see here, Jonathon has three Major Arcana cards in his spread: The Hanged Man, The Empress, and the Wheel of Fortune."

"Wow, and you have to remember what all this means?" I asked, actually impressed.

"It's not that hard. It's like telling a story."

"You mean you make it up?"

"No, no. The cards tell the story. I just read it."

"Guys," Jonathon said, "can we just tell my story and get it over with. I'd like to get back to that sofa."

"Okay," Dewey said, "here goes. You like to take care of people. You feel blessed and balanced, whatever that means. You like to look on the bright side of life. You are an all-around happy guy. The only thing that was missing from your life was a girlfriend and she found you, so now your life is perfect. Your relationship will do well especially if you take chances."

"See," I said. "He's just tellin' you stuff you already know or want to hear."

"Not all of it," Jonathon said. He was starting to get interested. Even Carry had come down from the sofa and was kneeling beside Jonathon now that Dewey had started.

"Your carefree attitude toward life also affects your work, making you not such a good employee. You don't really care about work and you goof off a lot. You'd much rather be puttin' your time into things that are fun. The same goes with school, and your grades suffer because of it."

"Well, that goes for everyone," I said.

Carry patted the top of Jonathon's head. "It's okay if some bad stuff comes out. Nobody's judging. Seriously."

"Despite all this," Dewey continued, "you have an almost 'secret' project you've been working on to make money. Unfortunately, it looks like the project is gonna fail, but if you keep up with it, it won't. Be patient with it and it will make you be successful."

Jonathon's eyebrows shot up in complete surprise to this. I couldn't tell if Dewey had nailed something right on a bull's-eye or if it was just so off base it blew Jonathon away.

"One thing you'll have to watch is that you don't like yourself too much or suffer from a fear of the future. You could easily fall into the trap of thinking about the past when things were good, especially when some of the money you expected to come through doesn't come. You might begin to see yourself as a failure, although other people around you don't agree. They see you as a king who has achieved much. Someone who has a tremendous family, married the woman he loved, and is very happy."

"See," Carry said. "It ain't all doom and gloom."

"In your later years," said Dewey, "you slow down and take a break from everything to reevaluate your life, and you realize it really wasn't so bad. You spend the final years of your life very happy with your wife and grandchildren, occasionally looking back and realizing what a topsy-turvy life you've had. Yet, given the chance, you wouldn't trade it for the world."

They all waited for more, but no more came.

"That's it," Dewey said.

"I can't believe how good you are at this," Carry said. "You're almost as good as Madame Crystalle."

"And you didn't make any of that stuff up?" I asked.

He shook his head. "Not a word of it."

"You sure," I said, not quite believing him.

"He didn't," Jonathon said. "There was enough in there that he doesn't know about to prove he didn't make it up."

"Wow. You really could do this for money. I mean, you're good now. Just wait until you finish the book! Except you have to get cool cards with dragons or something on them like Madame Crystalle has. Maybe you can order them from somewhere."

"And I'd need something like rent money for a place to do it, Abe," Dewey said.

"Oh, yeah, I'd forgotten about that part."

"Anyway, I'm moving back to the sofa," Jonathon said. "You comin', love? Thanks, Dewey."

"Of course I'm comin'," Carry said. "And yeah, Dewey, you're amazin'."

"Absolutely my pleasure."

He was soaking up all this attention like a mop in a bucket. I couldn't believe the guy went out and taught himself how to tell the future. Who thinks of doing that?

I guess the same type of people who think of running two hundred feet of aluminum foil around the house to get better television reception.

"Like they say, there's a fine line between insanity and brilliance," I said as we walked down the hall to my bedroom.

"What do you mean?" Dewey asked.

"I mean that line that you trip over when you get out of bed every morning."

"I have no idea what you're talkin' 'bout."

"Oh, never mind. I'm just jealous is all. Don't let it go to your head."

"Don't worry, Abe. One day you'll be smart, too."

See? It's like he just shifted gears from brilliant to extremely stupid. What were the odds now that I *won't* strangle him in his sleep next time he spends the night?

CHAPTER 55

Leah went back to Corwin Strait's place, this time carrying a search warrant. Once again, the man answered the door and Leah could smell guilt on him. But he had the demeanor of someone who was *constantly* guilty of *something.* Not necessarily guilty in this case.

While Strait read over the warrant, Leah pushed past him and entered his shotgun-style house. It was a disaster area. It looked like a bomb of pizza and Chinese take-out boxes had gone off in his living room. No sign of anything menacing, mind you. Leah was looking for any clues that he might be hiding a woman somewhere with her mouth taped up and eyes sewn shut.

If the living room looked bad, the kitchen looked worse. The smell hit her first. Rotten food that had long ago turned to mold littered the room. Dirty dishes had overflowed from the sink and were stacked beside it on the counter. A bunch of cockroaches skittered away when they saw Leah coming; she almost threw up when she walked inside the room. Again, though, nothing suspicious. The man's allowed to be a slob, providing he ain't stashing away bodies.

She checked the rest of the house and it was all the same. Lots of garbage scattered everywhere. By the time she was through searching thoroughly, she'd almost grown used to the sight of cockroaches and the smell of old food rotting away. Not a single decoration or even a Christmas tree stood anywhere in the house. There wasn't even an empty cross hanging on any of the walls—at least none that Leah could see.

"You a religious man?" Leah asked him.

"Sure, as much as anyone."

"Yet you haven't got a single cross on the wall or a picture of Jesus."

"My religious beliefs don't concern you."

"I s'pose that's true," Leah said. "What 'bout Christmas? You have no decorations up. Not even a tree."

"Once again, Detective, my beliefs don't concern you. Are you just 'bout done?"

"Just 'bout."

Strait was still reading the warrant when she got back to the main entrance of the shack. She wondered how well he could actually read. "Now I need to check out your garage," she said.

"This warrant don't say nothin' 'bout my garage." Strait's voice had a very "hillbilly" sound to it.

"Yes, it does," she told him, and pointed to the clause that read she had the right to search anywhere on the property. "I plan on searchin' the garage and your pickup."

"My pickup ain't part of my residence."

"No, but it's *on* your property." She decided to check the pickup first, before he got the thought to drive it out to the street.

The back of the pickup was caked with mud and dirt. She took a sample of it and bagged it, labeling what it was. There also seemed to be a dark red substance dried in the truck bed. "What's this red stuff back here?" she asked Strait.

"Blood."

Leah cocked an eyebrow.

"Don't get all excited. It ain't human blood. It came from hogs. I sometimes use this truck to take hogs into town for Quinton Russell. Occasionally, I don't let them bleed out long enough before loading them into the truck."

His story sounded plausible, but Leah took scrapings of the blood anyway, bagging them with the tongs from the CSI kit.

"Who's Quinton Russell?"

"Lives down near Oakridge. Has a little pig farm. We go back a while. . . ."

Leah assumed he was saying they met in prison.

Next, she checked the truck's cab. It was also a mess of fast-food wrappers and Chinese take-out boxes. She especially concentrated her investigation on the passenger seat, looking for anything that might be there as evidence. She found a long blond hair on the headrest. Very carefully, she took it and placed it in the evidence bag. It looked like it had the follicle still attached to it. If it did, it would be a tremendous find as far as DNA evidence went. Without the follicle, it was still good evidence, but it couldn't be traced to an individual.

"What's that you're takin'?" Strait asked.

"Just somethin' that I might be able to use as evidence."

"Evidence for what? I ain't done nothin' wrong."

Last thing Leah did was investigate Strait's garage. She figured if she was going to find anything of real value, it would be in here. As she walked inside and fumbled for the light switch, she thought Strait was starting to look a little antsy.

The garage was empty. She supposed Strait only owned the one vehicle.

Compared to the house and the truck, the garage was like a paradise. It was actually somewhat clean. At the other end, running from one side of the wall to the other was a long workbench, above which hung a number of tools. He also had drawers with sorted screws and nails and other things. It was like a completely different person lived out here.

There was no oil patch on the concrete floor like there usually was in garages. "You ever bring your truck in here?" Leah asked him.

"Sure, when she needs a tune-up. Mechanical work is my hobby."

"How good are you at sewing?"

"What?"

"You know," Leah asked, "with needle and thread?"

"Sewing's women's work. Why the hell would I be sewin' anythin'?"

"Just a question."

"Are you just about done?" Strait asked.

"I am, but just so you know, I may be back."

"I'll bake you a cake."

"Baking another of your hobbies?"

"No, it won't be a good cake."

CHAPTER 56

Leah and Chris pored over the background checks Leah ordered on Mayor Hubert James Robertson and his wife, Susan Lee Robertson nee Susan Lee Williams, which came back with the rest of the fifty-seven background checks she'd asked for. It didn't take Leah very long to see there was something fishy-smelling off the Gulf of Mexico.

"Susan Lee was indeed in an automobile accident back in 1976 involving a drunk driver named Anna Marsh," Leah said to Chris. "And just like our mayor told me, she was in a coma on life support at Providence Hospital in Mobile for twelve years."

"That poor guy," Chris said. "I can't imagine goin' through somethin' like that."

"Yeah, and from what I've heard, he came and visited her near on every day. But that's not the interestin' part of all this. The mayor told me the truth 'bout when they pulled the plug on her."

"That would be just horrible," Chris said. "I don't think I could ever get through it. It would drive me to alcoholism or somethin'."

"Or somethin'," Leah said. "I think it did drive him to somethin' actually."

"What do you mean?"

"Guess what date they pulled the plug?"

"How should I know?"

"Just take a wild stab in the dark," Leah said.

Chris shook his head. "Fourth of July?"

"Close. How about September the fifteenth?"

"Which was?"

"The date the coroner estimated the first victim—the one found outside of Birmingham—was taken off the streets. Or pretty much thereabouts."

"What? No, let me see that." She handed him the background check on Susan Lee Robertson and he sat there staring at it in disbelief for a good thirty seconds. "This can't be right."

"It's right, Chris."

"The mayor . . ."

". . . is our serial killer," Leah finished. "He even *told* me the laws of this state had him irked because the person driving the other car only got five years. The *maximum* in the state of Alabama. I think his words were: 'If only she'd been drivin' in Georgia. The other driver would've got ten,' or something to that effect." She looked up. "He may even have used the word 'bitch,' I can't remember." She thought for a moment. "Chris, the timing is *perfect.*"

He just stared at her in disbelief for a moment.

"Can you get a picture of the drunk driving woman who killed his wife?"

"Probably, but it would take a while."

"I bet dollars to donuts she looks like all three of our victims so far. I mean, think 'bout it. They all match. They're all in their late twenties, with long, thick blond hair. They're all heavy drinkers. It *fits.*"

"You want me to go arrest the mayor?" Chris asked.

"Not yet. What's it say 'bout Susan Lee, his wife?" Leah asked.

Chris read from the background check. "Just that she's survived by her husband, Hubert James Robertson, daughter, Ginger Robertson, son, Paul Robertson, her sister, Luanne May Williams, her mother, Gina Williams, and her father, Alistair Joe Williams. Have you talked to anyone at the hospital during the time Susan Lee was in her coma?"

"No, but that's an excellent idea. And while I do that, maybe you could do me a huge favor?"

"What's that?"

"Go to the library and go through their newspapers back around the time of the car accident that put Susan Lee into the coma. I want a picture of Anna Marsh."

"Okay," Chris said. "On my way."

Leah called Providence Hospital in Mobile, where Susan Lee had spent her last twelve and a half years on life support. She managed, after much asking and being passed from line to line, to finally be put through to a nurse who was around at that time. Apparently, she remembered Susan Lee and Hubert quite clearly.

"It will be a while before I forget her," the nurse told Leah. "If I *ever* do."

"Why's that?"

"Because her husband came and sat beside that bed for hours a day *every* day. Or at least *most* days. She didn't even know he was here, yet for twelve years he kept coming, day in and day out. That's some kind of commitment if you ask me."

"What sort of mood was her husband in? Was he angry about what happened?"

There was a hesitation; then the nurse said, "No, if anything, the opposite. His manner was so calm and tender. He was full of love for his wife. He just wanted to see her come back. I think that's what he was waiting for."

"What about when they finally took her off life support?"

The nurse sighed. "Oh, that was a hard day. Many of the nurses cried. He cried, but not a lot. I think he realized it was best to let her move on. You know, he'd made so many friends among the staff—especially the nurses—that many came to her funeral. He's a very special man. How's he doing?"

"He's mayor of Alvin."

"Alvin. Is that in Alabama?"

Leah rolled her eyes. "Yes, we're a small town close to Satsuma. Got some good people." *And one that likes killin' 'em.* "He seems to do a pretty good job of runnin' things."

"Sounds like him. He had a lot of charisma. I'm sure he had no problem getting voted in."

"Well, it seems like you've given me all the information I need," Leah said. "Unless there's anything else you can think of that might be of use to me. Any strange details?"

"I don't know what you're using the information for, so I don't know what sort of details you need."

"I'm working a case regarding a serial killer."

"And you think Mr. Robertson's involved?" the nurse asked. "That's impossible."

"No, no," Leah said. "I think he could be a target. This is why I want to solve the case as soon as possible."

"Hmmm," the nurse said.

"That sounds like you thought of something," Leah said.

"No, it's nothing really."

"Please? Anything might help."

"Just . . . his wife had a sister."

"And?"

"Well . . . you know."

"Pretend I don't."

"She was just a bit . . . quirky. Sort of rubbed me a little strange. I shouldn't even be saying anything. It was my issue, not hers."

"Okay."

"Well, thank you for bringing back those old memories. They are happy in a sad sort of way. And if you see Mr. Robertson, tell him Nurse Sandra says 'hi!' "

"I'll make sure that I do," Leah said. "Thank you for all your help."

She hung up the phone, now more interested in the mayor's sister-in-law.

Later that afternoon, Chris returned with a photocopy of Anna Marsh's picture. Frustratingly, it was in black and white, but that was clear enough to see what Leah needed to see. She could tell the woman was in her late twenties, had light-colored (probably blond) hair that hung thickly to her shoulders.

Surprisingly, the shot wasn't from seven years ago, but from near on three months ago, when Anna's sentence got changed from simply a drinking and driving charge to vehicular manslaughter.

"I originally looked for her picture in the paper at the time of the accident, but they only ran a picture of Susan Lee's body lying in the street."

"Figures," said Leah.

"But Anna Marsh's resentencing was enough to get her own photo."

Leah held the picture away from her to give it her full attention. "What do you think?" she asked Chris. "Think she looks like our victims?"

"I'd say she's an awfully good match."

CHAPTER 57

Leah brought the videotape to the station and knocked on Chief Montgomery's door. He waved her in.

"I got something here I want you to watch. Tell me if it's just me, or is there something quirky 'bout it?"

"What is it?"

"Videotape. That VCR hanging below your TV still work?"

"Dunno, haven't used it for at least a year."

"Well, let's give it a shot."

Leah could barely reach up to slide the tape into the machine. A sparrow was sitting on the branch of the fig tree outside. It squawked, almost mocking her. Finally, the tape slid into the machine and Leah pressed PLAY. Nothing appeared on the screen except the sports channel that was already playing. "You have to turn the TV to channel three, I reckon," she said to Ethan.

Ethan did. It worked and the video started. She knew it by heart now. First the shot of the body, lying in the darkened mine shaft with the EMT and police investigators working all around it. Then we come up to Detective Truitt—who she'd been meaning to call—standing off to the side, talking to some of the officers, probably one of which was the first officer on the scene. Then everything gets brighter as the camera pans out of the mine and across the crowd and here is where the feeling comes, only this time she thinks she knows why. Her hand quickly goes up and presses the PAUSE button when the image shows nearly the whole crowd of onlookers.

"Looked fine to me," Ethan said. "Nothing abnormal."

"No, it *would* look fine to you. I think I just figured it out."

"Figured what out?"

"This woman"—she pointed to a woman in a hoodie with the hood up over her head concealing the spiked orange hair underneath—"I believe she's the same girl who called in our crime scene for Mercy Jo Carpenter. That would put her at both scenes." She looked back at Ethan.

"Way too much of a coincidence."

"Right. I think that makes her a suspect. Probably top of my list."

"Who is she?"

"Luanne Cooper," Leah said. "She lives in Alvin."

"What would be her motive?"

"Not a clue." Killers without known motives were the scariest kind.

"How long has Scarlett Graham been gone?"

"Six days, today," Leah said.

"Then we need to act fast," the chief said.

Leah left Ethan's office and grabbed the phone at her desk and called the number she had for Luanne Cooper. There was no answer. "Damn it!" She pounded the phone back on the cradle, startling Chris more than anything else.

"What's goin' on?" Chris asked.

"I think I know who's got our girl, but I think we might be too late."

"Who?"

"There's no time to explain right now."

Then Leah Teal thought of something else.

She went and checked the background they ran on the mayor again. Sure enough, Leah's instincts were right. She *had* seen Luanne Cooper before, in a photograph on the mayor's wall. She was the sister of his dead wife. Only, she had dark, shoulder-length hair and blue eyes instead of spiky red hair and green eyes (the miracles contact lenses could do these days).

Leah opened the door to the main room, and asked Chris, "What did it say on the background report for the mayor's wife? Who were the surviving members of her family again?"

He shuffled through the pages until he found the right one. "She's survived by her husband, Hubert James Robertson, daughter, Ginger Robertson, son, Paul Robertson, her sister, Luanne May Williams, her mother, Gina Williams, and her father, Alistair Joe Williams."

"Luanne gave me a pseudonym for a surname. We need a search warrant for her house and we need it pronto," she said.

"I'll make the call," Police Chief Montgomery said, picking up the receiver from the phone on his desk.

Meanwhile, Leah called Detective Truitt up in Birmingham. "Truitt," he said, answering.

"Dan, it's Leah. I think we got her."

"Her? Her who?"

"Our serial killer."

"It's a her? Didn't see that comin'. I had this one profiled to a guy."

"It's the mayor's sister-in-law. They pulled his wife off life support around three months or so ago and pronounced her dead. Because the case took place in Alabama, the drunk driver responsible for her death only got five years in prison, which happens to be the maximum."

"Seriously? Wow. I can see why she might be a little pissed."

"All the women she's targeted? They're all lookalikes to the drunk driver, Anna Marsh. They're also all basically hookers or loners, so they're people who won't be noticed missing right away, giving her an element of time. She's basically getting revenge in her own way. And, at the same time, taunting us with the messages."

"I'm coming down."

"We're getting a warrant to search her house right now. This'll all be over before you make it."

"Oh yeah, I forgot. You've never driven with me."

Leah sighed.

"Yet," Detective Truitt added.

CHAPTER 58

"I must say this could be one of the most stupid ideas you've ever had, and that's sayin' somethin'," I told Dewey when I got to his house and he had all these pine boards laid out in his front yard on the grass.

"Why? When we was little we used to do it with lemonade. Fifteen cents a cup, remember?"

"Yeah," I said. "I also remember the only people who bought it were our folks and neighbors. Those were mercy buys, Dewey. Nobody really wanted any of our lemonade. But this is different. You're thirteen."

"Twelve. I won't be thirteen for another three months. And I ain't sellin' lemonade."

"No, what you're sellin's almost worse."

"I'm sellin' them their future. Here. Hold this board up while I nail it to this one."

I held the board even though I was seriously against this idea. Nobody was gonna pay—I didn't even know how much he planned on chargin'—but nobody was gonna pay a twelve-year-old kid to read their future at a lemonade stand on the side of the road. I doubt even our folks and neighbors would show up for this one.

"How much you plan on chargin' for this?"

"A dollar."

"A *dollar?* Have you gone crazy?" I figured he'd gone crazy.

"You just wait and see. Folks wanna know 'bout their future. Okay, now hold this board here. Thanks."

I kept holding up boards while he nailed them. In the end we had the weirdest looking lemonade stand. Well, it was only weird because the shelf was about three times as big as normal lemonade stands—Dewey needed it that big to lay his cards out. Then he threw a dark red cloth over the shelf so it looked like a table and, on the top of the stand, we nailed a board facing outward like a sign. On that sign, with purple paint, Dewey wrote: FIND OUT YOUR FUTURE. I noticed he didn't post his price anywhere. He put three lawn chairs around the stand, one behind it for him to sit in and two in front. I guess he expected people to be coming in pairs.

About twenty minutes went by while I stood leaning against the stand and Dewey sat in the chair shuffling his tarot cards overhand. It was a quiet twenty minutes.

"Nobody's comin', you know," I said.

"Give it a chance," he replied.

Finally, Melissa Delwood and her little sister from down the road happened to walk up the sidewalk toward Hunter Road, probably on their way to Main Street. They stopped at the stand. "What you boys doin'?" Melissa asked. "Awfully cold for lemonade."

Melissa was in the twelfth grade. I wasn't sure what grade her little sister was in, but she still went to school here in Alvin.

"We ain't sellin' lemonade," said Dewey. "We're sellin' your future."

"Whatcha mean?"

"I mean I can tell you what's gonna happen in your life with these tarot cards. And I'm real good at it, too."

She looked to me. "Is he pullin' my leg?"

I shook my head, remaining stone-faced. "I wish he was."

Melissa sat in one of the chairs on the other side of the stand. "How much does it cost?"

"A dollar," Dewey said without missing a beat.

I thought for sure that would end the conversation there and then, but without even trying to negotiate a better price, Melissa reached into her purse, pulled out a dollar bill, and handed it to Dewey. "Okay," she said. "Tell me my fortune."

Dewey went through the cards and pulled out the Queen of Wands and laid it in the center of the table. I still had no idea how he was choosing these cards to represent everybody, and he wouldn't really tell me. He just made passing mention that there was a certain way to do it and that was it. I felt like buying a book on tarot card reading just so I didn't feel stupid while he did this stuff.

Dewey took the cards from Melissa after she shuffled them and laid them out on the table. Then he began reading Melissa's future.

"Melissa, you are very balanced. This is good," Dewey said, and I knew he just said it because it sounded like something Madame Crystalle would say. "Throughout your entire life, however, you feel like you have been judged."

"Hmm," she said, like she was taking this all seriously.

"The biggest obstacle in your life is money and you have a boyfriend who is starting a business. You're hopeful that will work out, but really, deep inside, you don't think it will."

A smile burst across her face. "Wow! You really know what you're doing," she said. "Wait till I tell my friends!"

"But," Dewey said, "I have good news and bad news. The good news is, the business will work out. The bad news is, your family and friends won't believe it until they see it."

"That's so true," she said.

I rolled my eyes.

"Your biggest influence is your mother and father, who have lots of money. You hope to one day be like them and not have to worry about it. You just want to find happiness and love, and not be brought down all the time by your lack of money."

"I can't believe how good you are at this," Melissa said.

And I guess she did tell her friends because, over the next two days, twelve more people showed up at Dewey's stand to get their fortune read. By all accounts, Dewey had managed to start an actual business. He made himself thirteen dollars that, to me and him, was near on a fortune.

"You gonna do this every weekend?" I asked him as he was putting his stand away.

"On the sunny days, I think. I doubt I'll get many customers in the rain."

"This could be one of your best ideas of all time, you know," I said, which was something I rarely did—actually compliment Dewey.

"I know," he said very matter-of-factly. So matter-of-factly, in fact, that it made me want to slug him. "I knew it would work the minute I thought of it."

"No, you didn't," I said. "Ninety-nine percent of the stuff you think of never works."

"But this one was different. I just knew it would work. You know why?"

"Why?" I realized too late I should never have asked this question.

"Because, Abe," he said. "I'm psychic. Remember?"

And once again I wanted to slug him.

CHAPTER 59

After getting an emergency no-knock warrant from the courthouse, Leah and Chris hit Luanne Williams's home. Leah took the front, Chris the back, both coming through their respective doors with battering rams. Quickly, Leah swept the living room with her Glock. "Living room clear!" she announced.

"Kitchen clear!" Chris called from the other side of the wall.

"Hallway clear!" Leah shouted.

They went through the whole house making sure nobody was there. It was empty. No sign of Luanne, no sign of Scarlett. They did find something mighty disturbing, though: one of the three bedrooms had been converted into a shrine with pictures of the victims. They were all black and white, presumably made in the converted darkroom they found in one of the other bedrooms.

The images filled the walls, pinned at different angles. Shots of the victims before their eyes were sewn shut, shots of them with just their feet and arms bound and the tape over their mouths, shots of them with one eye stitched and one eye not. Those may have been the worst, because you could see the fear in the single eye left open. It looked wild and confused, like a caged animal.

Then there were the pictures of them dead, with the bullet hole in the right side of their head.

Pictures of Faith Abilene, of Mercy Jo, and even pictures of Scarlett Graham. There were pictures of Scarlett with her eyes sewn, but none of her with bullet holes in her head. This left Leah with a little hope.

"She's not keepin' the victims here," Leah said. "It's not the right environment anyway. We're looking for mud, clay, and sawdust."

"That could be anywhere," Chris said.

"No, I have an idea."

They walked back out to the kitchen. Chris happened to notice something hanging on the wall of the dining room. "Holy cow. Come look at this, Leah."

It was a framed five-foot-tall white embroidered cross. The stitching was perfect.

"Well, we can attest to her talents."

Leah picked up Luanne's phone and had the operator put her through to Mayor Robertson. She quickly explained what she thought was going on. He wanted more details, but she was frustrated, running out of time.

"Listen, Hubert, I'll tell you more when I can. What I need to know right now is that cabin you have in the woods? The one you're building the annex onto? Where exactly is it?"

"Should I ask why?" he said, sounding like he wasn't quite trusting her anymore.

"Does Luanne know about that cabin?"

"Of course she does."

"Do you know anything 'bout her owning an old handgun? An original model Beretta Model 950 Jetfire?"

"I don't, but that's a pretty old gun. I know 'bout guns. I'm an avid collector myself. That gun would be worth quite a bit, especially if it still worked."

"I have reason to believe it still works."

"Her daddy collected guns. Just a few, mind you. Could've belonged to him."

"Where's her daddy now?" Leah asked.

"Old folks' home," the mayor said. "Got a case of Alzheimer's."

"Does Luanne have a key to your cabin?" This was the big question.

"No, but I keep the key hidden at the cabin. Nobody in Alvin is dishonest enough to break into a cabin, and if they did I have nothin' up there worth takin'."

"Where is the key?"

"It's beneath a little ceramic frog that sits by the door," he said. *More frogs. What is it with frogs?* "When was the last time you were up there?"

"Oh." He let out a big breath. "Let me see . . ." Leah was growing ever more frustrated. "I guess July?"

"Okay, I need directions to your cabin and I need them now."

He told her how to get there. The cabin was about eighty miles north. Dan Truitt may be even closer to the cabin than she was. She quickly called the dispatcher at the Birmingham station and asked her to relay the address to Detective Truitt. "Tell him we'll meet him there. No cowboy stuff."

The dispatcher just laughed. "Why don't I ask him not to breathe while I'm at it?"

Chris and Leah had arrived in the same squad car. "Let me drive," Leah said as they hurried outside.

"Why?" Chris asked. "I always drive the squad car."

"Because I drive faster than you."

"You drive more reckless than me."

"Right now speed is more important than safety."

CHAPTER 60

They took off with the siren on, dodging Alvin traffic all the way north until they were out of the main city limits. Then things started to change. The eighty-mile drive to the mayor's cabin wasn't an easy one. Most of the roads were old mining roads, and some of the "roads" weren't roads at all, but trails the squad car barely fit down. Branches and leaves brushed the sides of the car, some scraping loudly as they passed.

"Awfully bumpy drive," Chris said from the passenger seat.

"That sounded like you want me to slow down," Leah said. "I ain't slowin' down. Besides this vest is diggin' into my side."

Both of them had put on bulletproof vests before leaving the station. This wasn't something they normally did, but they didn't normally know ahead of time that their assailant was armed. And she was armed with a .22-caliber gun, not one that was very powerful. The vests could easily save their lives.

The car bounced into a hole in the trail and out again. Chris's head nearly hit the roof of the car, despite his seatbelt. "Jesus! Can you slow down just a bit?"

"She's had that woman six days, Chris. Her pattern is to kill on the sixth or seventh day. I'm not slowing down."

"Great. We'll all be dead." With one hand he gripped the seat, with the other he braced himself against the dashboard.

They turned left onto a logging road, which was wider and in much better condition than the trail they just cleared a swath through to get here. "Thank God," Chris said.

"Thank me," Leah said. "I'm the one gettin' us there."

According to the directions Mayor Robertson had given to Leah, they had just passed the halfway point of the journey. Leah wondered how Detective Truitt was making out. She knew with little doubt that if Dan showed up before them he would just go in by himself. Guys like him consider themselves above the law, almost vigilantes. Leah didn't want that to happen. She needed to beat him there. That was one of the reasons she was driving so fast, but she kept that to herself.

Then everything went bad. Luckily Chris spotted it before Leah did, or she'd have run right into it. "Watch out!" he yelled. "Tree!" Straight ahead of them, a tree had fallen across the road.

Leah hit the brakes just as she made out that it was there. They stopped with only feet to spare.

"I'll get out and move it," Chris said, but Leah had her doubts that he could. It was a pretty big tree. Looked like a Douglas fir from where she sat.

Chris exited the vehicle and tried dragging the tree by one of its branches. No go. Then he tried pushing on it. Still nothing. It didn't even budge. He came back to the car completely winded. "I have no idea what we're going to do. That thing won't move."

Frustrated, Leah bit her lower lip. She hadn't come this far to give up now. She wondered if any of the trails they'd passed in the last ten minutes on this logging road looped around and came back to it on the other side of that trunk? It wasn't worth the gamble. They could wind up driving in circles. There was no way to get their bearings out here.

"What have we got in the trunk?" she asked.

"What?"

"In the trunk of the car. What do we have?"

".12-gauge, CSI kit, camera, usual stuff."

"What 'bout ramps?"

"What do you mean?"

"The ramps we use when checking the underside of our vehicles. We got them in the back still? I know they were there for a while. I'd left them there, forgetting to bring them back into the station."

"I can check. I still don't see—"

"Please," Leah said, "just check."

He checked. Came back carrying two orange car ramps. "What do you wanna do with 'em?"

"Set 'em up on this side of the stump. Make sure they line up with my wheels."

"What are you gonna do?"

"Jump the log."

"You're crazy. Who do you think you are? The Fonz? You'll destroy the car's suspension."

"Chris, just set them up. We have little choice."

Chris set them up. He got Leah to pull close so he knew they were lined up exactly with her wheels. "I'm stayin' outside of the car while you do this. Hope you don't mind."

"Not at all," she said. "I was hopin' for that, actually."

She backed up about fifty feet to get a good run at the ramps, threw the squad car in DRIVE and floored it. The car lurched when it hit the ramps and she thought the ramp was going to turn sideways. But then she felt the front of the car go airborne and she was still headed straight. The front came down as the back followed through the air. The car hit the ground with a large thump and the suspension slammed against the ground, sounding out a huge complaint.

But she'd done it. They were on the right side of the tree.

Chris came over to the driver's side window. "I can't believe you just did that. Does the car still run?"

"I don't know. Put the ramps back in the trunk and let's find out."

Chris did as Leah asked and the cruiser did still run. If there was any damage at all, it wasn't outwardly displaying it.

By comparison, the rest of the trip to the cabin went smoothly. They found it exactly where the mayor had said they would. Leah made sure to park the car a quarter mile down the road from it so as not to alert Luanne of their presence.

Before they could even get out of the car, another police cruiser pulled up behind them.

Chris looked at Leah expectantly.

"Detective Dan Truitt," she explained. "He brought in the Faith Abilene case. I've been workin' with him ever since. I decided to call him and tell him that we'd found our suspect and he insisted on comin'. Looks like he made it just in time to join the party."

Truitt came walking over.

"Dan Truitt," he said to Chris.

"Chris Jackson," Chris said. "Nice to meet you, Detective Truitt."

"Just call me Dan, or Danny Boy, or—"

"Just call him Dan," Leah said, cutting off Truitt. Now wasn't the time for his ridiculous repartee.

"So, I assume the cabin is a little ways up and we're back here so we won't tip our hand too fast?" Dan asked.

"Yeah."

"You're both wearin' vests. I feel left out."

"Should've brought one. We know she's armed."

"With a .22. It's a girl's gun."

"Still could kill you."

"True. I could say the same thing about some women I dated. So what's the plan?"

"According to the mayor—I did mention this was his cabin, right?—there is no back door. But there's a side door leading to what right now is an unfinished annex in the process of being built. Currently it's just an open room with two walls missing. Basically, it's got a dirt floor that's covered in sawdust. I'm assumin' that's where Scarlett Graham is. I think one of us should hit that area, one should stand point, and one should kick in the front door."

"I'll take the room with only two walls," Dan said.

"Okay. Chris, why don't you stand point at the corner between the front door and the annex? I'll boot in the front. If things go bad, Chris, you come to help."

"Which way?"

"Whichever way you hear things going bad. If I'm screamin' from the kitchen, come my way. If Dan's hollerin' from the annex, go his way. I don't think Luanne has any partners. She's workin' all this alone."

"All right," Dan said. "Everyone ready?"

Leah and Chris nodded.

"Let's move."

CHAPTER 61

They sneaked up, guns lowered to their sides and pointing to the ground. Leah made a wide arc for the front door, being careful to stay out of the way of the cabin's window that looked out on the forest. Dan and Chris broke away as everyone separated. Leah saw Dan making an opposite arc to the one she did, and Chris disappeared into the trees to take point at the corner of the cabin between the finished part and the unfinished part. From there, he'd be able to see into the annex where Leah assumed Luanne was keeping Scarlett Graham.

Making it to the front door, Leah didn't even hesitate before kicking the door in. It only took one kick to do it. Quickly, she swept the room with her gun. It was like a small living room. She saw the closed door that led outside to the annex in the process of being built. The living room was clear.

She shouted, "Police!" and moved farther on, finding the kitchen. Another small room. A quick glance around with her gun in hand, she discerned it empty as well.

Then she heard a voice call out: "I hope there's more than one of you, cuz if there ain't, you're dead, little girl." It came from one of the bedrooms down the hall. Leah quickly moved to a position beside the hall where she was safe from any gunfire. She still had her weapon close by her side and pointed down.

"Suspect is in the house!" Leah yelled. "I repeat: Suspect is in the house!"

Chris came running in through the front door.

"Take the other side of the hallway," Leah told him. "Luanne!" she called back. "You're way outnumbered. Give up now and it will be easier on you."

"Easier on me?" she laughed. "Don't tell me 'bout the law bein' easier on anyone. What do I get for murder one in this state? Seven years? I doubt it can be much more than that when my sister's killer only got five years. You *do* realize my sister was murdered and the killer only got five?"

"I know what happened to your sister," Leah said. "I know it seems like the drunk driver got off too easy, but this is no way to handle it."

Leah looked at Chris. "How's Scarlett?" she whispered.

"Alive. Spooked out of her mind, but alive."

"And her eyes? They look like the picture?"

He nodded. "Let me tell you, the picture doesn't do it justice. Her wrists and ankles are bound and she's lyin' on that cold concrete floor of the annex. Dan's takin' care of her."

"At least she's safe," Leah said, realizing she'd said it loud enough for Luanne to hear.

"Safe's a funny word to use," Luanne hollered. "I would not be usin' the word *safe* if I was in your shoes right now. You've seen what I've done to those other women!"

"Luanne! I'm comin' down the hallway now. I expect you to give yourself up!" Leah yelled.

"What you expect," Luanne screamed back, "and what you get ain't always the same things. I expected justice when it came to my sister's killer. What I got was something completely different." To Leah, she sounded on the verge of hysteria.

Luanne shrieked the passage from Song of Solomon. Leah suspected she knew the words by rote:

2:1 "I am the rose of Sharon, and the lily of the valleys."

2:2 "As the lily among thorns, so is my love among the daughters."

2:3 "As the apple tree among the trees of the wood, so is my beloved among the sons. I sat down under his shadow with great delight, and his fruit was sweet to my taste."

2:4 "He brought me to the banqueting house, and his banner over me was love."

2:5 "Stay me with flagons, comfort me with apples: for I am sick of love."

There were three doors along the hall. One was probably a washroom, the other two likely bedrooms. Leah had no idea which one Luanne was in. "Cover me," she whispered to Chris. He nodded and started creeping up behind her. Then, to Luanne, Leah said, "Why did you do it, Luanne? Those folk you killed were innocent."

"My sister was innocent!" she screamed back.

"And why the eyes?" Leah asked. "Why did you stitch up the eyes?"

"Did you not read the report on my sister? She was blinded in the crash. It's only fair game that my victims are blinded before they are killed."

"I'm going for door number one," Leah whispered to Chris. Once again he nodded and crept up behind.

"I can hear you, my little police friend," Luanne said. Leah still couldn't figure out which room she was in.

"I'm not trying to hide, Luanne," Leah said. "I want you to come out so that this doesn't end in another tragedy. Can you do that for me?"

Laughter filled the house, just short of sounding psychotic. "Another tragedy. This has been one tragedy after another. You think me coming out will end that? I ain't dumb."

"What were the crosses for? The ones you put in the victims' pockets?"

"I put them there in hopes that they would find justice when they finally met the Lord, because God knows there ain't no justice down here on earth."

The first two doors down the hall were both open. Probably the bedrooms. Problem was, both doors were in line with each other. Leah couldn't check out one without putting herself in harm's way of the other. She nodded to the one on the left. "You take that one," she whispered to Chris. "I'll take this one. On three. One, two . . . three."

They both stepped into the openings of the doors and raised their weapons, sweeping the rooms. First going for the corners, then for the furniture, and lastly for the bed. Anywhere someone could be hiding.

Leah let go of a breath she hadn't realized she'd been holding. "She ain't in this room. She must be—" She crouched into a firing position just as the air was filled with the sound of a gunshot. Everything went black as Leah felt herself being thrown back into Chris.

"That's one down," Luanne said. "How many more to go? I know I've heard at least two of you. How many cops does it take to catch a killer? So far at least two."

Chris quickly dragged Leah's body into the bedroom he was covering and pulled her around the corner. Luckily, the bullet was only a .22 and hit her in the upper chest, lodging itself into her vest. She'd have a pretty hefty bruise by tomorrow, but she'd live.

"Come out with your hands up, or so help me God I'll shoot you dead," Chris said to Luanne.

"Big words," Luanne said back. "I wonder if you have the firepower to back them up? I think I've proven that I do."

Chris stepped into the hall, keeping his weapon at the ready. Luanne's .22-caliber Beretta was no match for his 9 mm. He allowed the doorway to cut the angle of vision into the room as he slowly moved, looking for any sight of where Luanne was hiding.

Then he saw her. She was behind the bed. He took a shot. She shot at the exact same time and ducked back down. Both rounds must've passed one another midair. Neither hit its target.

"Eeny meeny miny moe, catch a black cop by the toe," Luanne

said, and quickly popped up and squeezed off a round. This one barely missed hitting Chris in the left arm. It was close. Too close.

Chris's heart raced as he tried to think of how to end this standoff. He decided the direct way was the best way. She'd obviously crawled to the edge of the bed; the door being slightly ajar had hidden her clean out of sight.

With a deep breath, Chris used his foot to kick the door all the way open and sure enough, she was standing there with her weapon pointed straight at the doorway. Just like before, the house filled with the sound of gunfire and the smell of cordite.

Only this time, it wasn't Chris who was hit. It was Luanne.

Chris glanced behind him to see Leah on her knees, her gun pointed shakily straight out in front of her. She'd fired off a round before either Chris or Luanne could do so. Leah got Luanne right in the shooting arm (her left arm), knocking her weapon clear out of her hand.

Running into the room, Chris grabbed Luanne, throwing her down onto the bed and cuffing her. As Chris read her rights to her, Dan came inside and told them that, other than the stitches on her eyes, Scarlett Graham seemed no worse for wear. He'd taken the tape off her mouth and undid her arms and legs.

Still a little shaken, Leah set off to the annex to see what she could do for the girl until they got her to the hospital. She knew there was no point in calling for an ambulance way out here—they'd never make it. They'd have to wait until they got into Alvin city limits.

Leah held the girl for what seemed like an eternity but was probably closer to ten minutes or so. "It's goin' to be okay," she kept saying. "She can't hurt you now. We've got her." She had no idea if her words were bringing Miss Scarlett any comfort, but they certainly couldn't hurt.

Turned out that Dan knew a much easier way back to Alvin than the route the mayor had given them to get here. Dan told them to follow him. Leah asked Chris to drive so she could stay in the backseat with Scarlett. Leah thought Chris probably loved this idea, as he considered her a somewhat reckless driver.

Luanne screamed something awful when they loaded her into Dan Truitt's car and Leah didn't envy him one bit. She had an idea that the woman would probably scream the entire eighty-mile trip back to Alvin.

In comparison to the ride up, the ride back was actually pleasant. They'd put an end to a serial killer's career and the day had turned out to be very nice. The sun had just begun to fall in the west, and streaks of orange and gold were starting to form overhead.

It was a good day to be a cop in Alvin, Alabama.

CHAPTER 62

Ethan sat in his big, squeaky chair behind his desk. Hockey was playing on the television mounted in the corner near the ceiling, but the volume was muted. Leah had no idea who was playing. She wasn't into sports at all, but every so often Ethan would glance up and his attention would drift away from their conversation and to the game.

Leah was sitting on one seat and Chris on another. All three of them had freshly poured cups of coffee. It was still morning. The previous night had seen its share of excitement, so there really was no start time this morning. Leah drifted in around ten. Her chest still hurt and had a huge purple bruise on it from where her vest took the .22 round. She guessed she'd have that for a while.

Ethan was the only one up early. He was already here watching the game when Leah showed up. Chris had come in about twenty minutes after Leah.

Ethan called a meeting in his office.

"I'm gettin' my coffee first," Leah said. She was on her third cup.

"Sounds like a plan," Chris said, and waited behind her for his second cup.

Outside, the January day was cold and bright. Green plants grew in front of the window, their big leaves reaching for the sun.

Two cardinals ducked in and out of leaves before taking off, following each other in flight. Looking closer, Leah even saw a pink butterfly sitting on a lush green leaf before leaving for places unknown.

"So let me see if I got this straight," Ethan said, looking at Leah.

"Got what straight?" Leah asked.

"You solved a series of serial killer cold case files brought to you by a psychic?" Ethan asked, finishing the statement he'd started before taking a big gulp of coffee.

"It would appear so," Leah said. "Although the clues she gave me were vague at best."

"Even still, I don't believe it."

"There's nothing to believe," Chris said. "Everything she told Leah happened three months ago in Birmingham. All she had to do was read the *Birmingham Times.*"

"Why would she care?" Ethan asked, taking a sip of his coffee.

"If you'd have asked me that a month ago," Leah said, "I'd have told you she wouldn't and that the whole thing was ridiculous."

"So, should we put this woman on the payroll? Make her part of the department?"

Leah laughed. "No, I don't think she's that helpful."

"What you're sayin' then is that you did most of the work."

Leah thought this over. "Yeah, I guess that's what I'm sayin'. She just gave me the kick in the pants I needed to go investigate a crime from two and a half months ago that had been all but forgotten."

"Maybe you should be investigatin' more of these cold case files?" Ethan said. "You seem pretty good at them."

Leah sighed. "I dunno 'bout that. This one damn near killed me." She touched her chest where that .22 slug had hit her, and winced.

"You know, if you'd have told me you were on a case based on information from a psychic, I'd have pulled you off it," Ethan said.

"I know. That's why I never told you."

"So you lied to your superior officer."

"No, I neglected to tell some elements of the case to my superior officer."

"Holding back information is . . . Wait, haven't we been down this road before? It doesn't go in a very interestin' direction."

"How 'bout we say this?" Leah said. "Every time I was round you, I forgot 'bout the psychic part entirely. Besides, I had enough information to continue my investigation after the first day when we found the body in Willet Park. Everythin' was sort of taken out of my hand at that point."

"I can't stop thinking that, if the psychic knew to tell you 'bout the other body, she somehow knew this new body would show up two days later," Chris said.

"Madame Crystalle, you mean?" Leah asked. "The psychic?"

"Yes."

"Hmm. I hadn't given it that much thought," Leah said. "Maybe this is somethin' we should consider."

"I think it is," Ethan said. "I simply can't believe she has psychic abilities. What did she tell you?"

"That the number seventy-eight was important (the first body was found in Graysville on Highway Seventy-eight). She gave me a partial on a Welcome to Graysville sign. She told me about the eyes being stitched up, although in not so many words. And she told me 'bout the writing on the bodies."

"Wait a minute," Chris said. "The writing was held back."

"Jeez, you're right."

"Did she mention the crosses? Did *we* ever figure out the crosses?"

"She did *not* mention the crosses. I simply wrote them off as Luanne's callin' card, so she'd have somethin' on the body to prove it was her. She left the crosses knowin' we'd hold that piece of evidence back.

"Madame Crystalle also said I'd find a body in darkness, which completely explains the Graysville murder far better than the Alvin one."

"I'm having trouble with her having prior knowledge to the words written on the bodies," Ethan said.

"Me too now," Leah said. "I think it's time to pay a little visit to Madame Crystalle. I'll go to her house after hours and try to catch her at home."

"Before you do that, please tell me our mayor is clean in all this?"

"Basically, Luanne was reenacting the murder her sister went through. She sewed up the victims' eyes so they'd be blinded the way her sister was. She kept them drugged and drunk so it would be similar to being on life support in a coma. For the same reason, she kept them bound. She only kept them for a smaller time frame. One week would go by and then she'd pull the plug—or in her case, shoot them in the side of the head with her daddy's old gun."

"And she only picked up women who looked like the woman who killed her sister," Chris said matter-of-factly.

"That's right," Leah said. "Twenty-somethings with thick blond hair. She'd pluck them from the Six-Gun Saloon because it was an easy place to find single girls. She didn't care if they were alcoholics or hookers. In fact, she probably preferred it."

"And the mayor had no idea this was going on, even though she was using his cabin as a hideout?" Ethan asked.

"None," Leah said.

From the other room, the phone on Leah's desk rang. She was sitting farthest from it. "We gonna get that?" Chris asked.

"May as well," Ethan said.

Chris walked out of his office and answered Leah's desk phone. "One minute," he said. "Leah, it's for you."

Leah's eyebrows came down, puzzled. She got up, walked out to her desk, and picked up the receiver. "Hello. Detective Teal here."

"Detective Teal! Dan Truitt here, how the hell are you?"

"Better."

He laughed. "That's kind of why I'm callin'. I was wonderin' if you would allow me the pleasure of takin' you out again."

"Last time you took me out, I got shot."

"That wasn't a date, and you invited me."

"Whatever."

"Would you like to go for another steak? It's all on me."

"That rightly depends," Leah said. "Will you let me order my own food this time?"

There was a pause while Leah guessed he was considering this.

During the silence, Leah realized something about Detective Truitt had hit a chord with her. "When were you thinkin' of us goin'?" she asked.

"Well, that depends on you. I can work round your schedule."

"How 'bout you give me a call Thursday and I'll see how I feel for the weekend?"

"That sounds great. I'll call you then."

Leah slowly put her receiver back in its cradle. A smile crept across her face. She felt like a little kid again. Somebody liked her.

"Who was that?" Chris asked as she returned to Ethan's office.

"Dan Truitt. That detective from Birmingham."

"Did he want some more information 'bout the case you just solved? He was there. You'd think he had everything he needs," Chris asked.

"Turns out he needs a little bit more," Leah said, dreamily.

Madame Crystalle's real name turned out to be Amira Caspari and she lived up in Blackberry Springs in a highly wooded area. Mostly full of oak and birch, but the area was also home to the occasional willow and cypress, which dotted the landscape, mainly squeezing themselves into the riverbank, their gnarled roots trying to drink up all the water they could.

Her house was a light blue rancher spread over a small area with a circular driveway and a detached garage. Although they weren't in bloom now, it looked as though, in the summer, the area around her house was full of flowers. She also had fruit trees and two walnut trees planted in her yard.

It was seven o'clock, so Leah hoped Amira would be home. Funny, in her head, she kept having to remind herself that the woman was *not* Madame Crystalle and did *not* have special powers. Part of Leah regretted finding this out.

After walking up to the porch, Leah rang the bell.

A minute later, Amira Caspari answered the door looking only vaguely like Madame Crystalle. There were no ribbons in her hair. Her clothes didn't shine and twinkle. She had a track suit on. She looked more like someone's mother.

"Amira Caspari," Leah said. "I'm—"

"Detective Teal," she said, cutting Leah off. "I have expected you." Her Persian accent was thicker than ever.

"You have?"

"Yes, you want to know where I get those clues. But first, did you manage to solve case?"

"Yes, we did."

"That is good news."

"It was. It turned out to be the mayor's sister-in-law. She's in custody."

"Even better news. Please, come in." Amira opened the door wide and allowed Leah entrance. "Don't take off your boots. Come into kitchen and have a seat and I explain everything. Would you like coffee or tea? I can make you hot or cold. Or special Persian coffee. Good for stomach."

"No, thank you very much. I am fine."

Leah was certainly taken aback by the fact that Amira seemed to know she was coming. She wondered again if maybe she was a little psychic after all.

"I shall return shortly," Amira said. "I must acquire something from my bedroom."

Leah hesitated. "May I escort you?" she asked, worried Amira may be going to look for a firearm of some sort.

"If you feel you must, I don't mind. I promise is nothing bad. Is simply a scrapbook."

Leah decided to go with her gut. "Go ahead by yourself," she said.

"Thank you."

The kitchen sparkled. Everything had a place. The lights reflected off the silver toaster and microwave, the granite countertops gleamed in the sunlight coming in through the window, which was covered with open shutters. Her bright white fridge hummed along, beside the stove of the same color. The floor was patterned with dark green and white diamonds. It was one of the nicest kitchens Leah had ever sat in.

Amira returned a few minutes later with a large scrapbook.

"First off, let me tell you little secret."

Uh-oh.

"I do not come from Persia. I come from Romania."

"Why do you tell everyone you're Persian?"

"Good for business. People associate Romanians with gypsies and everyone afraid of gypsies."

She laid the scrapbook in front of Leah and flipped it open. The first page was a newspaper clipping glued front and center of a man having hanged himself in an apple tree. "What the hell is this?" Leah asked, once more thinking this woman had an evil streak she just couldn't pick up on.

"I collect weird crimes. Anything strange. Especially if it happens close by. It helps with my work knowing about strange tragedies since many people come to psychics after deaths of loved ones or friends, especially when the death is not right somehow.

"If I read about car crash where three cars have head-on collision and the next day one of the wives of one of the drivers who died in crash comes to me for reading, I can give her much more accurate account of what happened. It doesn't just help me, it helps them too. I am very intuitive. I can take fact and mold it so that the woman of dead driver ends up with some, how you say? Closure. And I end up with good reputation."

"I see," said Leah, who couldn't believe the woman just admitted to being a fraud.

"I subscribe to most newspapers from towns all around Alvin strictly for this reason."

"I see," Leah repeated.

"When I saw article for first killing in the *Birmingham Times* with eyes sewn up, I knew it had to be saved. I also know, from the experience I've had reading these types of things, that such a crime is never a 'one shot.' It would become a serial crime. I tried calling the Birmingham police station, but they didn't want to talk to me or they thought I was crazy—I don't know which.

"I think it was because my English not so good then and all they saw was a gypsy woman telling them about serial killer. They thought I was explaining a vision I saw. They wouldn't take me seriously.

"So when you came to shop, I decided to try and use you to finally get someone to investigate. Sorry if I took advantage. That the next killing happened within days of our meeting was just coincidence."

"Well, it worked. That's the main thing. I have a question, though?"

"What's that?"

"The writing across the chest. How did you know 'bout it? We held back that evidence. So did Birmingham."

She turned to the front page of the *Birmingham Times* with the picture of Faith Abilene. "Look at picture. They did not do a good job hiding the writing."

Leah realized she was right. You could see, at the bottom of the picture, the top of the letters where the waterproof black Magic Marker ended. You couldn't make out what it said, but you could certainly see that there was some phrase written there. And, of course, Madame Crystalle had never *told* her what it said.

"You brought her to justice for all this?" Amira asked.

"Yes," Leah said, still stunned at the woman's openness.

"This is good for everyone. Be proud of yourself."

"So . . . tell me . . . you aren't psychic at all?"

"Depends on how you mean. Being psychic means being intuitive. As I said, I am very intuitive. I feel people's vibrations. Most of the time what I tell people turns out to be true."

"Well, that's interestin'."

"For instance, I am sensing you have choice to make regarding man. And I believe you can't decide whether your choice results in you being unfaithful to someone who has been out of your life more than five, maybe ten years. My advice? Take chances. It is time to move on."

Nervously, Leah turned the page of the scrapbook. "And where is that in here?"

"It is not. All that's up here." And Amira tapped the side of her head.

CHAPTER 63

Me, Dewey, Carry, and Jonathon returned to Madame Crystalle's so Jonathon could get his fortune read by someone other than Dewey.

"Welcome back," Madame Crystalle said in her Persian accent. "And how are all of you?" she asked.

"I dunno," Dewey said, narrowing his eyes. "How 'bout you tell us?"

I elbowed him in the arm.

"Abe!" he said. "Quit doin' that!"

"Then quit sayin' stupid stuff."

"How was that stupid?" Dewey asked. "It was a fair question."

"I'm guessing you all fine," said Madame Crystalle.

"There ya go," I said to Dewey. "Happy?"

"I guess. 'Fine' is not very precise, though."

Carry cleared her throat. "Will you two shut up?" Then to Madame Crystalle, she said, "We'd like you to read the future of my boyfriend, here, Jonathon."

I could tell she was still getting used to calling him her boyfriend and seemed to use every opportunity she could find to do it.

Jonathon took a seat at the table across from Madame Crystalle.

Madame Crystalle took his left hand and stared down at his palm. "Ah!" she said. "I see wedding bells!"

"Not soon, I hope," Jonathon said.

"No, not too soon."

"Wait!" Carry interjected. "You never told me *I* was gonna get married."

"You'll probably just end up with a dog," I said.

Madame Crystalle told Jonathon a bunch more stuff, like that he'd live a long, happy life and learn to appreciate his mother (whatever that meant). Then she read his cards and he found out he was going to start his own business after college.

When they were finally done, Dewey started talking again.

"You know," he said to Madame Crystalle, "I'm psychic, too. I've made thirteen dollars so far tellin' folk their future!"

I rolled my eyes, but Madame Crystalle stared at him very seriously. "Really?" she asked. "Sit down."

"I can't," Dewey said, "on account of I ain't got no money. I left my thirteen dollars at home."

"I no charge for other psychics."

Dewey quickly sat in the same chair Jonathon had been in moments before.

"I do a quick reading," she said, taking both his hands in hers and staring straight into his eyes.

"Yes! I do feel psychic energy coming from you!" she said.

Dewey beamed. I think he almost peed himself.

Madame Crystalle looked to me. "Think number between one and fifty."

I did. *Thirty-two.* "Okay," I said.

"What number is he thinking?" she asked Dewey.

Dewey concentrated a long while until finally blurting out, "Thirty-two."

"Well?" Madame Crystalle asked me. "Is he right or wrong?"

There was no way I was going to let Dewey think he was psychic because of one lucky guess. "Wrong," I said. "I was thinking of eleven."

Madame Crystalle glared at me.

"What?" I asked.

"You lie."

"What do you expect? I can't just let him think he read my mind. I'd never hear the end of it."

"But he did read your mind."

"Wait a minute," Dewey said. "Abe was thinking of thirty-two?"

I looked down at the gold shag floor. "Yeah, I was."

Dewey's eyes went wide. "I really *am* psychic."

"More like psych*o*," Carry said.

"Why does everyone keep sayin' that?" Dewey asked.

"No," Madame Crystalle said, defending Dewey's position. "More like psychic in training."

"But I'm already professional," Dewey told her. "I made thirteen dollars with my psychic stand."

"Psychic stand?" Madame Crystalle asked. "What 'psychic stand'?"

"It's like a lemonade stand, only I give tarot card readings to folk instead of makin' 'em drink lemonade. I charge a dollar a readin'. I'm pretty good at it, too. I get better all the time."

"You're my competition!" Madame Crystalle said.

Dewey blushed and looked down at the gold cloth covering the table. "Sorry."

"I kid you," Madame Crystalle said. "I don't think I have worries yet. But keep practicing and your skills will grow. You do have innate powers. They only need developing."

I figured Dewey had no clue what "innate" meant. I didn't either. Nobody asked, though.

"Hear that, Abe?" Dewey asked me excitedly. "I have *powers!* Like *real* powers! Not like when we play D and D!"

"Yeah," I said, "but playing D and D is more fun, though."

"I won't have any more time to play on account of I need to develop my *real* psychic powers."

Okay, this one hurt a bit. I'd actually miss Dewey if me and him stopped playing, and how psychic could he be, really? He still believed in Santa Claus.

"Don't worry," Madame Crystalle said. "You keep playing.

Your psychic powers have long way to go and need to develop themselves for a while. So don't put Dungeons and Dragons away yet, Dewey."

"How did you know *I* was talking about Dungeons and Dragons?" he asked.

She stared at him a second. "How do you think?"

Walking into the bright winter sun that day from the cramped basement of Madame Crystalle's, Dewey looked like he felt more important than he ever had in his whole entire life.

Finding out you were special was a wonderful thing, and the best part? I felt really great for him. It was like a Christmas miracle.

For maybe just a second or two it made me wonder if Dewey was right.

Maybe there really was a Santa Claus after all.

A Thorn Among the Lilies

Michael Hiebert

ABOUT THIS GUIDE

The suggested questions are included to enhance
your group's reading of Michael Hiebert's
A Thorn Among the Lilies.

Discussion Questions

1. What are the main themes running through this book? Hint: There are two.

2. How do these themes manifest themselves?

3. Do you think Anna Marsh's punishment fit her crime?

4. Do you believe in psychics? By the end of the novel, how accurate did Madame Crystalle's reading of Carry really turn out to be?

5. Do you think Leah should have really started an investigation based on what a psychic told her?

6. Do you think Leah would have stayed on such an investigation if a body hadn't washed up in Willet Park right away, prompting her investigation?

7. Do you agree with Carry trying to hide her relationship from her mother despite Madame Crystalle telling her that Carry's mother would be okay with it?

8. Do you agree with Leah telling Abe what a serial killer is, despite how he took it?

9. Do you agree with Leah keeping a low profile on the case, especially the fact that she's using facts that came from Madame Crystalle? Do you think she should have let Chief Ethan Montgomery know where her original ideas came from?

10. Do you agree with Police Chief Ethan Montgomery trying to keep the FBI from becoming involved in the case so he didn't have to worry about dealing with "the feds?"

11. What are your opinions about Leah questioning people at church?

12. Do you think being the son of a police detective has made Abe more careless around dangerous situations than he should be? Is he more willing to jump into action where he should probably be more prudent?